Please feel free to send me an
publisher filters these emails.

Nique Joaquin - <u>nique_joaqui</u>

CW00642368

Sign up for my blog for updates and freebies!
<u>nique-joaquin.awesomeauthors.org</u>

## Copyright © 2016 by Nique Joaquin

All Rights reserved under International and Pan-American Copyright Conventions. By payment of required fees you have been granted the non-exclusive, non-transferable right to access and read the text of this book. No part of this text may be reproduced, transmitted, downloaded, decompiled, reverse-engineered or stored in or introduced into any information storage and retrieval system, in any form or by any means, whether electronic or mechanical, now known, hereinafter invented, without express written permission of BLVNP Inc. For more information contact BLVNP Inc. The publisher does not have any control over and does not assume any responsibility for author or third-party websites or their content. This book is a work of fiction. The characters, incidents and dialogue are drawn from the author's imagination and are not to be construed as real. While reference might be made to actual historical events or existing locations, the names, characters, places and incidents are either products of the author's imagination or are used fictitiously, and any resemblance to actual persons living or dead, business establishments, events or locales is entirely coincidental.

## About the Publisher

**BLVNP Incorporated**, A Nevada Corporation, 340 S. Lemon #6200, Walnut CA 91789, info@blvnp.com / legal@blvnp.com

## DISCLAIMER

This book is a work of FICTION. It is fiction and not to be confused with reality. Neither the author nor the publisher or its associates assume any responsibility for any loss, injury, death or legal consequences resulting from acting on the contents in this book. The author's opinions are not to be construed as the opinions of the publisher. The material in this book is for entertainment purposes ONLY. Enjoy.

# Praise for Break Me, Mate

"I LOVE this book. I found it on Wattpad and couldn't get enough of it. She is one of my favorite writers because she loves what she does and gives it her all. I couldn't be prouder! She has a great future in writing and this book will be a top seller!!!"

– Keshawna, *Goodreads*

"I was reading her book on Wattpad so I am following her to this she is so very good writing she should go very far as an author I love her style of writing she keeps you right the edge of your seat and wishes she could get more chapters to understand this stuff she is such a good writer I am very glad for her getting published great job that's all I can say"

– Tallie55, *Goodreads*

"I love this book!!! Read *Break Me, Mate* on Wattpad, and I absolutely adored it! I would recommend this book to anyone who likes werewolf books with a strong female character who has no problems standing up for herself.I absolutely love the book, and I think it's a great book for anyone to read!"

- Alexandra Lorentzatos, *Amazon*

# Break Me, Mate

By: Nique Joaquin

BLVNP

ISBN: 978-1-68030-819-8
© Nique Joaquin 2016

# Table of contents

*Dedication*

*For my mom and dad who are both the strongest people I know and love, for my best friend Christina who supported me both as a writer and a person, and for my readers who have stuck with me through thick and thin, the good and the bad, this book is for you.*

# FREE DOWNLOAD

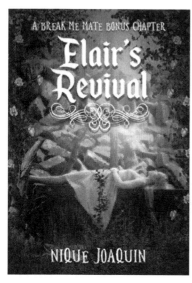
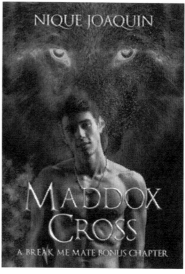

Get these freebies and MORE when you
sign up for the author's mailing list!

nique-joaquin.awesomeauthors.org

# Chapter One

I took a deep breath. The earthy smell of the forest made my body relax as I came into position. Both my hands were clasping the gun in front of me. The gun was at the ready, and my right pointer finger pulled the trigger. The gunshot rang loudly, yet no one stirred. It was a brief noise that echoed for miles. Of course, people heard it, yet the forest was still as isolated and cold as it was since the banquet began.

*Another target hit.* I sighed to myself.

Training at twelve midnight during our pack's annual Full Moon Banquet was pretty damn uneventful, but I hated crowds, and I hated meeting new people. I already knew the people I needed to know for my father's pack to be safe. Besides, I was only here until tomorrow, and then I would be going back to my squadron.

I pulled the trigger once more in a careless effort. The gun kicked back in my grip ever so slightly.

It was a headshot… and yet I knew that it was a clumsy shot.

I was using plain bullets for training. After all, who needed fancy silver wolfsbane bullets at the range? I checked the magazine of my weapon. It was almost empty. I slid the magazine back in and looked up just as the moonlight began to hide behind the clouds, inevitably making it darker while midnight fast approached. I decided then that I might as well walk the perimeter just to make sure the area was safe.

Werewolves could never be too careful. The entirety of the Blood Moon Pack was far too busy celebrating the night of the full moon, and despite alpha orders, our security was slightly weaker tonight.

*I'll be doing a few rounds.* I mind linked my father, Alpha Stephen.

*Alright. Stay safe. Tell me if anything happens,* he responded calmly.

I pulled my wavy blonde hair into a high ponytail and reloaded my guns with wolfsbane bullets. With a firearm secured on each hip, I began my first round. The Full Moon Banquet took place over by the waterfalls in my father's territory, and I knew that at least a few teens would take the chance to screw around in the *shady* areas. After all, most wolves liked to take advantage of the oh-so-romanticized full moon.

I wore a military green turtleneck tank that hugged my chest and a pair of comfy black jeans that I paired with some heavy-duty boots. I personally thought that I looked fairly badass for someone who was turning twenty-two in three days. My twin brother, Ender, wanted to have our birthday celebrated tonight. He had finally met his mate, Brianne, a couple days ago when we met up with a few other wolves for a council meeting on border security.

Apparently, the infamous Macabre Pack was on the prowl, and just last week, they were spotted near the borders of Red Raven— an ally of ours who lived close by. Stories about them varied from area to area. However, what I did know was that when I was traveling around, I stumbled across the aftermath of one of their attacks, and the sight wasn't pretty.

The smell of death was left in every nook and cranny of the place, so the name Macabre suited their pack pretty damn well. I remembered the sight of everything— the bodies that were left scattered around, and the burning mess right in front of the pack house which still stank of gasoline as it burned to the ground. The Macabre Pack left everything broken, bloody, and in absolute shambles. The other packs had a right to be fearful of them.

*Everything alright?* my twin, Ender, asked through the mind link.

*Fine and dandy. Just keep having fun, brother,* I responded. Ender was younger than me by two minutes and was going to become alpha mainly due to a few unexpected events, but it wasn't like I cared.

Let's just say I was not exactly the friendly material. Ender was at least on the more human and reasonable side of things. I tried to stay focused as I took my walk. Just as I was about to get bored enough to start shooting trees, I heard the familiar voice of a teenage pup giggling. I took a quick whiff of the air.

*Damn it.* I cursed in my mind. I sprinted for the river and mentally groaned when I spotted my younger sister, Celine, in the river with a guy I knew as Chad.

"Fun time's over, 'lil sis," I announced as I walked out of the trees close to the edge of the river. I leaned casually against a nearby tree and watched as Celine's eyes widened and almost threatened to fall out of their sockets.

"Elair!" she screamed, and it was only then that I realized that my blonde-haired sibling was butt naked.

"You know, you better get your ass back in that banquet before I tell father," I said before looking over at Chad who was pouting with all his might. "And you better get your ass back in that banquet, too. Your father may be beta, but you aren't, and just so you know, just because the two of you are mated, doesn't mean you guys can screw like rabbits. It's a full moon. Neither one of you is even halfway through senior year."

"But—"

"No buts, Celine. Get Out!" I hissed. I was thankful that Chad was a nice guy. He was not too arrogant, just playful, which was why they were out here screwing around in the first place.

Celine sighed and looked over at Chad.

*Sorry sis,* she mind linked me.

*Yeah, yeah. Leave the water—*

I heard a snarling sound from behind the trees.

"Celine, get the hell out of there!" I shouted, then I pulled out my guns and pointed them straight at the source of the sound.

*Chad, take care of her and run,* I mind linked. Chad and Celine immediately shifted and made a run for it as the growls got louder. From what I could hear, there were at least three of the damned trespassers.

*Got a bit of trouble here. Southern border, along the river. Counted three trespassers,* I mind linked all the patrols in my reach.

"Hey, I love playing hide and seek and all, but I really hate it when trespassers play it," I said loudly. I heard another growl and sighed. "Okay, sweeties, mommy's getting a little tired," I said as I cocked the gun.

Three wolves emerged from the forest, and I groaned.

"Ugh, out of everything, I really hate it when I'm right," I announced. "Three wolves. I got this," I said, giving myself a pep talk.

The wolves barked and made some sort of a snorting noise. One of them, a brown one, looked like a rabid hyena ready to bite my head off. She got ready to do so, and I smiled as she began to make a run towards me.

"Yeah, yeah. I'm one cocky motherfucker. I know, which is why when I do something like," I paused and shot the wolf in the shoulder making it whimper loudly in pain, "that... people get pissed."

The two other wolves began to growl, and I watched the one I had hit turn human. Guess today's bullets had stronger wolfsbane than usual. *I'll have to note that later*, I thought to myself. The two wolves growled at me with a mix of snarls.

"Please, I didn't kill her," I explained as I twirled a loose hair with my finger. "If I did, I wouldn't leave any witnesses," I added as I pointed both guns in the wolves' direction.

I waited silently for the two wolves to make their move.

*Three... two...*

One of them made a run for my arm, and without any hesitation, I shot him. With the sound of just one small whimper, he was down. The other one sprinted just fast enough to bite my arm, which sucked for him as I dropped the guns and shifted quickly into my beloved silver wolf. I was taller than him, an advantage I could make use of. I growled at the trespasser and pounced.

I bit into his right front leg and tasted the iron-flavored-blood in my mouth. He whimpered but tried to bite me in a futile attempt to defend himself. Instead, I used my sheer force to push him down, so that I had him on the ground, his neck wide open for me.

*Permission to terminate a trespasser that just tried to kill me?* I asked with the mind link.

*Is the situation desperate?* my father responded—probably too calmly. I couldn't help but roll my eyes.

I appreciated that he thought I was strong enough to handle the situation, but a little concern wouldn't have hurt. I growled as the trespasser tried to free himself from me. I snarled, and a feral noise escaped my wolf, making me proud of the fear that immediately filled the wolf underneath me. Before I could communicate back with my father, another growl sounded from the forest, and I looked up, only to find a black mass of fur hurling my way. I suddenly found myself pinned to the ground by a large black wolf, and I growled as he peered into my eyes in utter silence.

Ten seconds passed.

It has been way too long. I was pretty sure attacking me meant 'I'm gonna fucking kill you right now' in werewolf culture unless I missed a memo.

*What the hell?* I wondered. This wasn't how things went. He was supposed to try to kill me. Not to mention that unmistakable aura... His body was already screaming alpha with all the power he was trying to exert over me. My death would have been *such* a spectacle.

Talk about disappointment.

I squirmed underneath him, but he didn't even budge, which wasn't surprising considering how heavy this motherfucker was. I mean, had he probably thrown himself at me any harder, my bones would have been crushed, and I would have had to go all desperate and try to make a run for it.

Well, until my bones healed, that is. But right now, my concerns laid on the fact that this guy was heavy, and he knew what he was doing.

*Almost there,* my younger brother Vaughn said through the mind link.

*Hurry up,* I replied calmly.

Meanwhile, the alpha kept staring at me. When I broke eye contact, he growled. I looked at him again, confused. What the hell was his problem?

I growled back in response and snarled, but he, instead, chose to sniff my face rather than attack me. Someone else growled from behind him, and I watched as Alpha black-fur snarled in response. The wolf behind him barked ferociously, and the Alpha growled at him before looking at me. Then, he did the absolute weirdest most disgusting thing ever.

He sniffed around me, licked my face, and then got off me.

And it didn't stop there.

He grabbed a piece of cloth from my shirt, the same military green one that I had torn from struggling, with his teeth and sprinted off without another sound into the darkness of the woods.

*What In The Actual Fuck?*

# Chapter Two

"Where are the wolves from last night?" I asked Reed, the head of security for the dungeons.

"Down in the caverns. You sure you wanna be the one to handle them?" he asked me. Reed was a tall, dark-skinned guy with a beautiful mate who just so happened to be the pack doctor, Donna.

"Yeah, I'll be fine. Thanks, Reed," I told him as I patted his shoulder.

"You can go grab your son and have your promised ice cream date," I added, and he chuckled in response.

"You remember that? I thought you were too busy reading the reports to even pay attention," he said with a laugh.

"Ha ha. Of course, I do. Soft spot for kids, remember?" I nudged him with my elbow. "Now, go," I said as I shooed him off.

He left me, jogging down the path leading to the housing area, and I made my way towards the dungeons, which was quite a long way from the pack house. I was already standing at the prison's entrance when my father decided to mind link me.

*Elair, my office, now,* he said. Well, more like commanded, causing me to groan mentally. I needed information out of those damned trespassers, preferably before I left. Not to mention walking all the way here took me forever.

*Alright, heading there now,* I responded, knowing not to step on my father's toes when he gave an order.

"Guess I'll have my fun with you guys later," I mumbled under my breath as I shoved my hands into my olive drab jacket.

I had no idea why I loved that shade of green.

Anyways, I made my way to the pack house which, I really needed to stress, was located pretty damn far away from the dungeons considering no one would want most of my eleven younger siblings to figure out that we imprisoned and, at times, tortured trespassers. We ran a tight security ship around here. Well, I liked to think I did.

Since I tore up my outfit yesterday, I had to pull on a new pair of heavy-duty combat boots. My wavy blonde hair was down, and I would actually put on some dark blue smoky makeup for a bit of a more intimidating effect.

Ha, I was a stylish jailer. I was so cool.

Kidding. I was just so weird today.

When I made it to the pack house, a large modernist black and white mansion, I headed right up to my father's office. It had an over the top waterfall effect on the walls and was located on the third floor. Without hesitation or even any thoughts as to why I was called here in the first place, I twisted the knob to enter. The office itself was designed in a simple fashion. Glossy black marble covered the floor, and a modernist black and white chandelier hung from the ceiling, illuminating the room with the slightest hue of white. The rest of the light came from two tall rectangular windows positioned adjacently that allowed the sunlight to come through. The only other things in the room were sleek black shelves aesthetically filled with books, a wall with a large portrait of the family, a sleek black desk, and a large black office chair right behind it.

To be honest, I was completely surprised to see that my dad had company. It was not every day that I am not made aware of visitors. I could usually tell. There were four other guys in father's office I didn't recognize. My father was fairly young, only in his early forties. I guess that was the result of meeting your mate at seventeen, deciding to marry at eighteen, and have your first child soon after. Well, first children, I guess, since my mother gave birth to fraternal twins. Both of my parents are blonde-haired and blue-eyed. Naturally, and as genetics would dictate, the Richelieu children were born with their signature blond hair and blue eyes.

"Did the party not finish last night?" I asked in a playful tone as I walked in, but I immediately froze up at the smell of a particular Alpha. The scent immediately made my teeth grit, and I put my hand on one of the guns on my hip. It was the same smell from last night. "Okay, father, what the hell is trespasser-leader over here doing in your office?" I asked, pissed.

"Calm down, Elair," My father said patronizingly, and I arched a brow. "We've been *negotiating* for a while now, actually," he added.

"What? Why are we negotiating? We have members of their pack locked away in the dungeons." I pointed out as I made my way towards them.

"Elair, please. This is Alpha Cross of the Ma—"

"Macabre Pack," the yet to be introduced alpha said, interrupting my father's talk.

My father turned silent, and that was when I realized that this guy probably had influence. Silencing another Alpha and interrupting them could only happen if one recognized the other's superiority.

"Uh-huh. The infamous big bad wolf pack of doom. Coolio," I said dismissively before turning on my heel and marching towards my father. I decided to take a seat on my father's desk whilst getting a good look at the four wolves.

They were tall and probably scary looking to most wolves. But hey, I was not judging, after all, I've worked with the worst. Hence why I liked working in the dungeons when I visited Blood Moon.

"They've promised that our territory will remain safe from them," Father said, and I arched a brow.

"And why on Earth would they promise that?" I commented as I pulled a leg up to my face and set a foot down on the desk. My leather leggings made the action feel all weird, but I did it so screw it.

I watched as Alpha what's-his-face trailed his eyes over my legs and eventually lingered on my bare neck. This guy was so weird, but I guess he could be eye candy material. It was at least appealing to look at and... well, most Alphas are model material. I guess it made it easier to deal with them. Alpha Blackie over here has got a strong body that looked like it was threatening to rip through his figure-hugging gray V-neck tee. I observed him before my gaze landed on his face, only to find a smug smile on his lips. Fuck was up with this dude?

"This little negotiation sounds way too good to be true coming from the Macabre Pack. What's the deal?" I asked, removing my gaze from the Alpha as I swung my legs, which wasn't an action I could often do— tall girl problems.

"A trade," Alpha Blackie answered, and that certainly grabbed my attention.

"What kind of trade?" I asked. It would have to be pricey. I mean, this was the Macabre Pack.

"A trade for safety, of course. Macabre swears to leave this pack and its territory alone, as long as my two captured companions, my beta's newfound mate, as well as my own little mate comes with us," Alpha said loud and clear.

"Huh, sounds good to me. So tell me, who are the two lucky lovebirds? I might as well go round them up since I'm supposed to leave today," I asked with a hint of sarcasm, and the Alpha arched his brow at first but then chuckled in amusement. A dark look immediately loomed over his face.

If anyone wanted to know why I was not scared of his presence or the fact that he had guys threatening to kill us, it was probably because the squadron I worked for has dealt with the craziest of the crazy. Fear was a tool, and that was what packs like Macabre were known to utilize.

"My beta knows his mate. He'll fetch her after this. The other *lovebird* as you call is..." he said as he walked towards me, and I raised an eyebrow. When he got to a point where our distance was reduced to about half a meter, I hopped from the desk and stood up.

"Whoa there, cowboy," I said as I held my hands up. My jaw dropped when I realized what he was trying to say. "Hold on. Are you saying I'm your mate? Because... well, how do I put this simply? I don't feel you, bro," I said as I dodged him and his disgustingly creepy approach towards me.

"Also, just a side note, I'm supposed to head back to my squadron for—" I added, but my father interrupted.

"Elair, please," my father said sternly, and I gave him a pissed-off look, but I soon noticed that the other wolves have reached a point of high tension and were threatening to shift within seconds. The atmosphere in the room had gotten far too hostile.

"Did we mention we took someone as a hostage?" the Alpha told me, a cocky grin gracing his face.

"What?" I snapped.

"A little blond-haired boy." My breath hitched, and I mentally cursed. He got me at the blond-haired part. "He said his name is Wesley, 7 years old... still living and breathing as we speak," the Alpha continued. I glanced at my father and realized that underneath his calm demeanor was a steadily rising anger. He was struggling to keep his composure.

"Okay, fine. Who's the other one mated to your Beta's ass?" I asked coldly. He smirked triumphantly.

"A girl named Winter." I mentally sighed in relief. Sure, she was a pack member, but she wasn't another sibling.

Besides, she was someone who was capable of protecting herself.

She was under my training yesterday, a volunteer at that, but she was only seventeen from what I'd read about her. I liked reading my volunteer trainee's files beforehand— in case I break an arm or two.

"If I may be so bold, *mate*," I began to say, stressing the dreadful word, "how old is your beta?"

"He's twenty-four."

"Oh, wow. Okay, I'm sure she can deal with that. I've got a few questions, though." The Alpha nodded, telling me that it was okay to ask, so I spoke up. "So if we go with you guys, does my brother come back or does he rot in a cell? Also, where's the beta? I don't sense him in here at all. Thirdly, I can't leave right away. I have... certain things to prepare," I said motioning to the air. Alpha fuckface smiled at me, making me feel *slightly* queasy.

"Your brother, of course, returns. My beta is currently with his mate. They are already discussing their relationship if you must know. We leave in twelve hours. I will return your brother within the hour if I have your word," he told me. I observe him and shook my head. God did I hate blackmail when it was used on me.

"I don't think you understand. I have a different head to answer to, and I can't just leave in twelve hours," I answered coldly. "You have my word that I'll be leaving with you. But I can't just up and leave today."

"I'll speak to her for you," my father answered from behind me, and I whirled around to see him already dialing up a number on his phone.

"I am *not* leaving today," I hissed "It's not... You know what? I'm not even gonna bother explaining," I said before turning on my heel to face the Alpha.

"You seem to think that you have a choice," the Alpha said to me with a smirk, and I rolled my eyes.

"And you seem to think I give a shit about you *apparently* being my mate. Well, newsflash, fuckboy, I don't. So you listen very carefully. I'm not formally recognized as a part of this pack anymore, which may come as a surprise to you, but I have things to deal with before I leave. Otherwise, this place is going to be a mess. So do yourself a goddamn favor and listen, okay?" I snapped before I turned to my father.

"I'll go meet with my squadron. I'll see how fast I can sort things out." I paused, looking over at the Alpha whose name I had already forgotten. "I'll deal with you... personally."

The three other Macabre members were staring me down, and I felt a little nerve pop as I walked over towards them past their Alpha. One of them was angrier than the other two. I noticed his tightly held fists were trembling with anger, and he looked at me like I was a pile of shit. I smirked at the realization that dawned on me. I faced off three wolves last night... and one was a girl, the brown one I had shot. Hmph, it looks like someone else had a mate issue, too.

"Okay, I get it. This one over here is angry because I shot his mate down. Well, just so you know, she tried to get me first, and if you look at me like that again..." I paused as I brought out my gun and cocked it right between his eyes. He flinched, and at the last moment, I moved my aim an inch and fired. The sound of one of my bullets hitting the bulletproof wall resonated inside my father's office. "I will fucking end you," I said before putting the gun back into its holster.

"Now if you excuse me, I have business to take care of," I said matter-of-factly as I walked out of the room, slamming the door behind me.

# Chapter Three

You know what?

Alphas really did suck.

Figuratively speaking, of course.

And I was not just saying that because of Alpha what's-his-face over here.

Actually, no.

Scratch that.

It *was* because of Alpha what's-his-face. I was on the phone talking to my squadron when all of a sudden he decided to hang ominously around me. Which wasn't only creepy, but was also really fucking annoying. How did one get rid of an alpha that liked to stalk you?

*Someone, please tell me.*

Alpha talks aside, I did manage to talk to my squadron earlier about leaving. If anyone wants to know, the squadron I was talking about wasn't a part of my pack. We were technically a member of all the packs in the surrounding territory serving as the main line of defense in case of emergencies. Think of it like the Avengers. From what I gathered from my baby brothers we were pretty much like that, the defense line.

Anyways...

The squadron had no specific name, really. We were all selected by our packs to represent an organized defense of the best 'warriors.' I lead one of them since my aunt was one of the head trainers, and unfortunately, thanks to Alpha what's-his-face, I had to give that title away. I was still irked by the fact that he thought he was my mate, but I knew better than to think that he was lying or at least lying without a purpose. Alphas like him didn't mess about. At least I hoped he was not. Besides, he should have killed me on the spot last night.

Or even better...

rejected me.

But no. Instead, he chose to be creepy and stalk me.

I walked through the woods, knowing full well that he was right behind me. Not that he even cared to hide. I stopped at a clearing and spun on my heel.

"Okay, Mr. Alpha, what is your problem?" I snapped, and he shamelessly stepped forward.

"You," he answered, and I sighed.

"Ha, ha funny, Alpha," I said as I folded my arms over my chest. "No, really, please, enlighten me on the whole mate thing since my wolf clearly didn't get the memo."

"That's convenient. Considering I never wanted a clingy mate in the first place," he said as he casually leaned on a tree. "And you can call me Maddox, Maddox Cross." I arched a brow.

"And I'm Elair. Nice to meet you," I said in a sarcastic tone.

"Have you finished sorting things out with your little squadron?" Maddox asked me, and I shrugged.

"I don't know, Cross, have I? You've been stalking me the whole time, so why don't you tell me," I snapped, but he simply smirked in response.

"Then we'll leave sooner than I thought we would," he simply answered, but before he walked off, I heard someone storming my way with a fierce growl.

I rolled my eyes at the source. It was the guy I pointed a gun at earlier.

"Move, Cross," the guy said, anger dripping in his tone. Maddox growled at him.

"Leave," Maddox seethed, and the guy snarled.

"She shot Jillian! She deserves a thorough beating," he responded.

"And you took a seven-year-old boy from his pack. Granted, you all say he isn't hurt, but that could always change. I know how this game is played. So until my brother is back in my family's arms, Jillian stays in that dungeon, and she could rot there for all I care," I said with a nonchalant shrug. "Now, I'm gonna go pack up my things. I want my brother back before I leave. Then I'll release your little mate along with your other friend," I stated as I pushed past them.

As it turned out, Maddox made good on his promises.

"When will you come back?" Wesley asked me as he swung his legs on my bed.

My room was a little guest room on the ground floor of the pack house. It was small and compact with a plain white bed and enough space for my daily dose of yoga. Yes, I did yoga. How else was I supposed to calm the fuck down?

"I'm not sure, Little Lee, but I'll try to visit," I said just as I shoved my last article of clothing into my carry-on. I turned to face him and ruffled his hair.

He ran in here as soon as he was returned. That was what Wesley told me, at least, and he had a huge lollipop with him that was almost the size of his face.

"Do you want to bring this lollipop?" he asked. I shook my head as I knelt in front of him so that we were somewhat of the same height.

"I'm good, Lee. Listen, did Alpha Maddox do anything to you when you were taken?" I asked, and Wesley shook his head.

"He was real nice. Last night, he told me if I went with him, I could have as many sweets as I wanted!" *Tricky bastard,* I thought in my head. "He says you're his mate and that mates were supposed to be together. Are you going to be together?" Wesley asked. *Shit.*

"Maybe, Lee. You know me, there's nothing I love more than family," I said as I smiled at Wesley. I pinched his cheeks, and he giggled.

"We love you, too!" he said, and I smiled, but it faltered when I smelled Maddox's scent nearby.

"Give me a big bear hug before I go?" I asked, and Wesley nodded his head before hopping off of the bed and wrapping his arms around my neck.

The door to my room swung open, and I sighed. I breathed in the scent of Wesley's favorite shampoo and the detergent my mother was obsessed with. I lifted Wesley up and saw Maddox leaning on the doorframe with a weird look in his eyes.

"Time for me to go, Lee," I said as I put Wesley down and kissed his forehead. "Be good, okay?" Wesley nodded his head and waved to Maddox before I made it to the doorframe.

"Safe and sound," Maddox muttered.

"So are your friends," I replied before walking off, but just as I thought I was far enough, Maddox grabbed me with the strength of a goddamned god, and I froze in place.

"We'll walk together," he said. I think it's important to point out that he didn't ask a fucking question.

"Yeah, yeah. Sure," I mumbled before using my own strength to pull him by me. I swung my carry-on at him, and he used his free hand to grab it. "Hold it for me, will you, mate?" I teased in a high-pitched voice while batting my eyelashes at him before huffing and continuing to walk.

"Are you always so difficult?" Maddox asked, and I shrugged.

"I don't know, am I?" I snapped just as we made it to the foyer.

My father and siblings were there, except for Ender. I watched as my mother emerges carrying the latest addition to the family, and hopefully the last considering there were twelve of us already. My mother was a very slim woman, but man could she bust a move. Looks could be very deceiving. She was only about three inches shorter than my father, and she had wavy golden blonde hair. Her eyes were a very dark shade of blue, and she was currently wearing a beautiful white dress that made her look like a goddess. My father literally worshiped the ground she walked on.

If you wanted to see a queen in real life, come see my mother. I have yet to meet anyone with so much kindness and grace. She came over to me, and I noticed that the other members of Maddox's pack, including pissy-pants, was gawking at my mother. It was understandable because she was only in her early forties and she looked like she could be my older sister. She smiled at me before handing my baby brother, Roland, over to my father. He took him without a word into his arms, and she came to me, hugging me tight.

"Visit us, Elair, as often as you can," she said in her soft voice. I nodded my head and buried it into the crook of her neck, savoring the smell of her favorite perfume before we pulled back.

"Of course," I said, feeling her fingers begin to tremble as she patted my head and ran a hand through my hair.

*And I thought we just had you back*, she told me through the mind link. I saw the tears well up in her eyes, and I gently wiped them away before hugging her again.

*I'll be back before you know it*, I replied, and she hugged me even harder. I breathed in my mother's favorite rose perfume one last time before we let go of each other.

"Take care," my father said. It was hard to find any emotion on his face, and I knew it was because Maddox was here and he was afraid to show too much vulnerability.

*Alphas and their pride, I guess,* I thought. I nodded my head as he hugged me with one hand while he held Roland in the other. I kissed Roland's forehead and gave my other siblings a huge group hug. These were the only people in the world that mattered to me. I sighed when I realized that Ender probably wasn't coming... which might be a good thing, considering he would go crazy if he found out my mate was the Alpha of the Macabre Pack. After I had said my farewells, I turned and found that Maddox was on his phone. I clicked my tongue to get his attention. He looked up and nodded then motioned to the door.

I made my way out and saw three large black Bentley SUVs. I watched as Maddox loads my little carry-on into the back of the one in the middle. Opening the door to the backseat for myself, I sighed in relief when I noticed that two seats were separated from each other although not by much. It was really only separated by a leather bump, but it was good enough for me. I was about to hop in when I heard the distinct voice of my twin brother yelling. I sighed. And here I thought I was gonna leave in peace.

"You can't just take her away from us, you bastard!" Ender yelled, and I heard him snarling already.

The wolves that were with Maddox were growling in response, but Maddox himself remained calm. He simply glanced at me before he turned to look at my brother. Ender was dressed in a black shirt covered up with a brown leather jacket. He and I looked alike because of our blonde hair and blue eyes. He was tall, but I did not lack in that department either. Also, he was well-built, but he wasn't like Maddox whose veins looked like they were ready to pop anytime. *Bleh.*

"I'm not taking her away. I'm taking what is rightfully mine," Maddox replied with a smug look on his face. I mentally rolled my eyes. I didn't want this to be any trouble, honestly.

"As if I'd let you take her away. You'd probably just tear her to pieces once you have her!" Ender yelled, surprising me. Ender was angry, and his body was shaking with anger. From the look of Maddox's tense muscles, he could barely handle his temper, too.

"She is my mate. She deserves to stay with me," Maddox replied.

"Bullshit! You've killed so many that you don't deserve a mate. You don't deserve to have anyone love you, you piece of shit!" Ender shouted as he started to walk towards us. The other wolves began growling, trying to force Ender to back down, but of course, Ender's guts willed him to move straight past them. Like brother, like sister.

When he was about a meter away, Maddox began to growl as well. I sighed to myself. I popped off the ledge I was hanging out in and immediately made my way to Maddox's side.

"Ender, stop," I said as I hesitantly moved the tiniest inch closer to Maddox until I could practically feel the heat from his body radiate off him.

"Elair, you can't just let him trample all over you and force you to—"

"Ender, I said stop," I said calmly. I offered my brother the best smile I could muster before doing something that absolutely repulsed me. I intertwined my fingers in Maddox's, and I watched as Maddox visibly relaxed... and also had the fucking nerve to squeeze my hand in return. *Ugh.* I fought the urge to cringe.

"But—"

"I'll be fine, Ender. He's my mate. I trust him," I lied through my teeth. Man was I glad I was a good liar.

"Elair—" I held a hand up to stop him before I looked over at Maddox.

"I need to talk to him. It'll only be a minute," I said, and Maddox nodded. His eyes were still a dark shade of dangerous intentions, but he let go of my hand.

I made my way over to Ender and gave him a big hug.

*I need him, Ender,* I lied through the mind link. I just knew Maddox was loving this. I was sure alphas wanted nothing more than a doting mate despite his whole I-don't-want-a-clingy-mate speech. I pulled away just as Ender mind linked me.

*Elair, you can't be with him. He's a murderer.*

"Ender," I said coldly. Ender stiffened as I sent him a cold look.

"But—" he continued. I sighed loudly.

"Goddamn it, Ender. I need to go with him. How would you feel if Brianne couldn't come with you?" I said in an exasperated voice. *You would never want your mate away from you, right?* I asked him, and Ender gave me a sad look before pulling me into a tight hug again.

"You better get your ass to visit us here," Ender said, making me chuckle.

"Of course, who do you think I am?" I asked rhetorically. We pulled apart, and Ender rolled his eyes before reaching into the pocket of his leather jacket, taking out a little black box. I arched a brow, and Ender tossed it over to me.

*Pre-happy birthday, twin*, Ender mind linked. I looked at it. It fit perfectly in the palm of my hands. I nodded before placing it into my pocket.

"I don't have something to give back," I said with a shrug.

"Don't have to. Just visit," he said, and I rolled my eyes.

"You, my dear twin, are a walking cheeseball," I said just as Maddox's wolves started heading into their respective vehicles. I felt Maddox's presence behind me and sighed. "Gotta go." Ender nodded his head. He still glared at Maddox, but it was lighter thanks to my little lies.

I turned, and Maddox immediately headed into the SUV. The driver up front started the car. I sat right beside him before closing the door and watched as the sight of my pack house and my territory fade away.

*Take care of yourself*, Ender mind linked

*You too. I'm expecting little nephews and nieces by next year*, I joked. I knew Ender was laughing.

"A visit might not be good anytime soon," Maddox said from beside me. I rolled my eyes.

"Do you think I don't know that? They all know I won't visit soon. It's just something we say to comfort each other," I said as I laid back on the chair. I reclined the damned thing and pulled out my phone.

"The mating ceremony will be held on the next full moon," Maddox said without looking my way.

"Sure thing, cowboy," I said as I skimmed through the photos I took for the past days I had stayed. I only had about twenty, and they were all taken with my little siblings and Ender.

"Thank you," Maddox said, clearing his throat.

"For what?" I asked.

"For calming me down."

"I did it for Ender, mostly," I honestly replied. "I'm going to sleep through this trip. Do your Alpha stuff or something," I said as I rolled over to my side. Maddox didn't say anything, but I knew he was a bit pissed off at my tone. Nevertheless, he stayed quiet, and I thought he brought out a laptop since I heard the sound of typing.

Thank     God     he     was     the     quiet     type.

# Chapter Four

Several hours and a plane ride later, I found myself somewhere in the middle of a largely forested area. It was not surprising considering wolves liked forests, but damn was it cold. I have never been gladder to be a werewolf in my life. We were near the mountains, and I could practically smell the fresh wind that came down from them.

You know what?

I actually liked Maddox's territory, and I thought he caught onto it because I have been standing in front of this huge ass lake for about an hour. It was really tranquil, but that might be because it was two in the morning and we've just arrived. Judging by the fact that it was cold, and we were by the mountain ranges, I guessed I was in Oregon or Washington. It was somewhere north because the time difference was way too huge of a gap for it to be in the same time zone.

"Like what you see?" Maddox asked. I sighed just as a cold puff of air blew in front of me.

"Definitely," I said as I turned around to face him, only to find him wearing a fairly tight muscle tee. His ripped chest was on full display. I arched a brow, but I didn't dare to entertain him by asking why.

"Our room is ready. I had someone prepare a few things for you, so clothes shouldn't be a problem." Maddox informed me, and I nodded, not really wanting to start any type of conversation. When he started walking away, I followed him and savored the rich smell of the forest.

There was nothing I loved more than nature and family. There was something about trees and the wind in the early morning that invigorated me and calmed me down. I followed Maddox and soon found that the pack house was a mere ten to fifteen-minute walk away from the lake. As I walked with him, I observed how strangely quiet it was. Then I reminded myself that it was two in the morning and that probably the only people awake were the night guards that seemed to follow a strict patrol. Still, as a precaution, I grabbed Maddox's arm, causing him to stop. He paused to look at me. Not really wanting to ask him the question I've been meaning to ask, I hesitated before opening my mouth.

"There's no welcome party, is there?" I decided to ask, trying not to sound too concerned. He shook his head.

"None," he said, and I immediately sighed in relief. "I'll introduce you later. It's too early," Maddox simply explained, and I nodded. Somehow, he managed to make my hand fall into his and squeezed it. His hand was warm, and it surprised me as the rest of my body was only just getting used to the cold climate.

The pack house was a huge log cabin with several floors. It was built on a clearing situated on a hill. There were three levels, and each one was currently in the dark since everyone must have been fast asleep. We walked right up to it and entered, immediately finding ourselves in the living room. I spotted a crystal chandelier in the center area that was surrounded with large glass window sections, and boy was I a sucker for large windows. I could probably sit there all day. The living area was spacious with a bar right by the entrance. The whole log cabin theme was obvious in the interior design of the place. Maddox lead me in, and I relaxed as I felt the warmth of the home fill me.

Maddox quietly led me up to a room on the third floor and opened the door with a key card. The house was all woodsy and, surprisingly, filled with warmth. Its modern style was beautifully contrasted by a few antiques. The rustic fireplace in the living room and the old framed paintings were stunning, and I was absolutely fascinated despite it being so dark. However, I arched a brow as Maddox unlocked the room and led me in.

There was a faint smell of a few other wolves having been here, but I remembered Maddox saying that there were people arranging the room beforehand.

The room itself was pretty damn huge.

Of course, Maddox was the Alpha, so I shouldn't have been too surprised. The bed was king-sized and had a brown leather bed frame. There was not much decoration to it, just plain white bed sheets, a duvet, and two large white pillows.

The space was large, and there were split sections to the room. It was almost like a bachelor pad, to be honest. There seemed to be an office on the other side of a partitioned wall, and the bathroom itself had its own mini hallway that probably led to a walk-in closet. In front of the bed, fairly distanced, was a big TV placed against a large panoramic window that made me almost crack a smile in relief.

I could see the entire area from the room, and I loved it.

Not that I was ever telling Maddox.

I folded my arms over my chest and walked over to the windows.

"I'll be working, so make yourself comfortable. Your bag is already in the closet," Maddox said, and I nodded my head, not bothering to look at him as I heard him walk towards the other partition on my right. After a while, I heard him pause.

"Was there anything else?" I asked and walked over to him. I caught the weird look in his eyes again. I couldn't read them well in the dim lights, but he was thinking about something. Instead, he shook his head and continued on to the office.

It was only when he flicked a light switch that I realized that the office was covered in shelves filled with books. I felt the inner bookworm in me celebrate. His office was also styled in a mix of modern and antique. His modern table had a glass, a laptop, and a few utensils neatly arranged on it. The chair was a reclining brown leather one, and there was another reclining leather chair with a footrest that faced the windows. A glass coffee table with a tiny potted plant that seemed to be lavender sat right by it.

*Guess where my new favorite spot was?*

*Uh-huh. Just wait until Maddox leaves me alone.*

When Maddox took his seat, he was in full-on alpha mode. So I turned away from the windows and headed over to the wall of closets that separated the office from the bedroom. I slid one open and rolled my eyes upon finding that there were already hangers and clothes arranged in it... and this was only one of these large things. I grabbed my bag and dragged it out from the bottom, unzipping it quickly to find something to wear to bed.

I groaned when I came up with nothing. I zipped up my bag and shoved it back. I was only supposed to stay at Blood Moon for three days, so the only sleepwear I had was a large shirt... and I left it in the laundry with our maid, Amelia, back in Blood Moon. I skimmed the drawers. I didn't think I even wanted to know who arranged this closet because every single piece of underwear had some sort of lace, and almost every 'pajama' I came across consisted of a pair of bootie shorts and a nightie that looked more like fancy lingerie.

Not having much of a choice in terms of comfort and absolutely hating wearing pants or leggings to bed, I grabbed the most decent little nightie and went into the bathroom. The bathroom had a wooden theme, but it was coupled with marble floors and clean cut white tiles. I slipped into the garment which was an all black lace fringed mini-dress that almost cut too short below my ass. But hey, if I was the alpha's mate, he deserved a tease, right? Despite my discomfort at the cringe-worthy satin bootie shorts, I still pulled them on. I was not going to let him see me in my underwear even if the goddamned nightie hugged my chest and I wanted to rip it off.

I was relieved when I saw that whoever prepped the room had given me some girly things to play with like a makeup remover and a couple of spa stuff that my sisters had back home. So I quickly took off my makeup and washed my face. Just before heading back to the room, I picked up my clothes and heard a rattling noise, so I checked the pockets of my pants. I remembered that Ender had given me a present, and I immediately took the little black box out.

I shook it and heard it rattle. I couldn't help smiling as I lifted the cover. Inside the box was a small square shaped bottle of wolfsbane, just enough for me to load a bullet or two with. I smiled at Ender's little gift before taking it in my hand and leaving the bathroom. I placed the box on the nightstand before slipping into the bed. With a sigh of relief, I completely crashed.

Several hours later, I was officially awake, and Maddox was still in his office. The sun was out already, and I've been on my phone playing some game that my little brothers put in there. Ever played Smashy Road? I have literally been playing it for an hour. I had zero regrets.

Well, maybe a few.

When I was sick of sitting in my nightie and chilling all by myself. I walked over to the closet and grabbed a black silk robe that fell just above my knees and had a lace back.

*Seriously.*

Did the person who prepped my new closet expect me to screw Maddox like a rabbit? You should see the last section of the cabinet. It was unbelievable how those things could still be called clothes. And yes, before I spent my hour on Smashy Road, I explored the closet. What else was I supposed to do?

After I had pulled on the robe that literally covered nothing, I walked over to Maddox's office. He didn't even bother looking up as I made my way towards his bookshelf.

I read through the titles and grabbed a familiar-looking one, 'The Scientific History of Lycanthropy.' It was something I used to read back in the squadron. I took it and plopped my ass down on the reclining chair and lifted my legs onto the footrest. I was about to read when I caught a pair of eyes staring at me in the forest. I put the book down and stood up.

My eyes zeroed in on what looked to be a woman staring at me. She was sizing me up from a distance, looking a bit like a creep with her black robe.

"Is something…" Maddox's voice began from behind me but then I heard him stand up and walk over to me. I felt his arm wound around my waist, and I looked behind me to find him breathing in my scent.

"What do you think you're doing?" I snapped.

"You can't walk around like that. Not near the windows." He admonished, and I rolled my eyes.

"Not my fault whoever prepped my closet shoved lingerie in there. This is seriously the most decent one," I said as I ripped his arm from me. I decided to ignore the creepy looking bitch outside and grabbed the book as I sat back down on the chair.

"My shirts are in the inner closet. You can wear them," he said.

"Should've probably said that earlier," I said with a shrug and looked up at him. His amber eyes were dark again, and the minx inside me wanted to tease him.

I couldn't help it. Alphas were easy to control with a little skin, if you know what I mean.

"When are we eating?" I asked as I sat cross-legged on the chair. I knew I was wearing bootie shorts, but Maddox was so tense, it was funny.

"We can eat after you change," he said.

"Cool, and if I don't?" I asked with a smirk.

I watched as he froze and swallowed a dry lump in his throat. He was trying to control his temper and the dark signs of lust that was showing through his amber eyes. After a few seconds of awkward silence, I laughed before getting up and tracing my finger across his collarbone, enjoying the goosebumps that trailed his skin.

"I'm just teasing you, Cross. I'll shower and change into something appropriate. Oh, and I'm planning on training today, be it by myself or to kick someone's ass," I said as I walked past him and straight into the bathroom.

I was still laughing to myself when I hopped into the shower which did that awesome rain thing. What? As if anyone really remembered what these types of showers were called. I was no interior designer. It felt like soft rain was falling from the high ceiling, and I tried not to spend too long in there. I stepped out, wrapped myself in a fluffy white robe, and pulled my hair into a towel turban before heading out to grab a few clothes.

Maddox was on the phone with his back turned to me so I moved quickly and grabbed clothes from the closet.

I slipped into some lace underwear, a pair of black cargo pants, a tight fitted cream turtleneck sweater that revealed a bit of my midriff, and a pair of combat boots. Training was easier with cargo pants since they were less restraining than jeans, and something about turtlenecks flattered my figure. Celine put me up to it the first time, and it stuck as a favorite. My hair was still wet, so I quickly pulled it in a loose low bun and put on some dark makeup with a quick swab of lip tint just to help add some sort of creativity to my day.

Once I was done, I found Maddox quietly saying things to his phone.

"Breakfast?" I asked, and Maddox looked over at me. He nodded, and I watched as his eyes skim over to my exposed stomach. "I'm not changing." He just nodded again and walked over to me. He tucked one of my loose hairs behind my ear and looked into my eyes, studying me.

"I've called a friend to check on your... wolf."

"Why?" I asked, arching a brow.

"You told me that you didn't feel the mate bond," he responded.

"And I still don't," I added, and something changed about his demeanor. He got even more tensed.

This was exactly why I hated meeting new people. It was just so awkward. After a few more awkward seconds, I decided to speak up.

"Whatever floats your boat, Alpha," I said with a shrug. "Now, can we please have breakfast?"

Maddox's lips somewhat turned up and what I thought were his dimples threatened to show. But, of course, the whole egotistical alpha thing kicked in, and he just nodded his head as he turned to leave.

Minutes later, I found myself on the ground floor in an empty kitchen. Maddox knowingly moved around, and I watched as he quickly diced a few onions and some cheese. The kitchen was huge, and I caught myself admiring the place once again. I should really get used to this place ASAP. I wouldn't want Maddox catching me admiring the tiny carvings on the walls. That would be embarrassing.

"Toast?" Maddox asked, and I nodded.

"Sure, need any help?" I asked, and he shrugged. I mentally groaned at the stupidity of my question. He was making omelets, so I doubt that needed much help. However, I stepped up behind him anyways and took the knife from his hand. "I'll handle the rest for the omelets. Go cook bacon or something," I said. Although I didn't mean to, it came out like an order.

Maddox's eyes were full of the you-should-stop-offending-your-alpha look, but he obeyed. He made his way over to one of the double door fridges. Yes, there was more than one, and they were huge. He pulled out a roll of bacon to cook. I worked around what Maddox cooked and set myself to frying the omelet. The glorious smell of breakfast blessed my nose, and I sighed in relief.

Just then, I felt my phone in my back pocket vibrate. Plating the omelet, I slid my finger across my screen and answered.

"Morning," I greeted.

"Morning!" Wesley's gleeful voice greeted back.

"Hey there, Lee. Shouldn't you be at school?" I asked as I put my phone on loudspeaker and set it down.

Maddox placed bacon on our plates along with two pieces of toast on each. Then he put glasses of orange juice down on the table. I took my seat at the central counter which made the perfect breakfast bar.

"Holiday!" Wesley yelled, and I took a bite of my toast. "Is Alpha Cross there?" Wesley asked.

I rolled my eyes.

"He is," I said as I slid the phone in between Maddox and myself. I mouthed the words 'say hi' to Maddox. He swallowed a large lump of food down and cleared his throat before speaking.

"Hey," he greeted simply. I rolled my eyes. *Great greeting, Alpha,* I thought. I honestly wished I could mind-link him.

Then again, that would require the mating process, and although I had nothing against having a mark on me, I had everything against what that process implies.

Mainly, the whole mating thing. No, thanks.

"I still have the other sweets you gave me yesterday! I gave some to all my brothers and sisters!" Wesley said proudly, and a teeny tiny smile graced Maddox's face.

"Good," Maddox said. I sighed before picking up my phone. Could he not speak in one-word sentences?

"Hey, Lee, I gotta go eat now so I'll call you later, okay?"

"Pinky promise?" Wesley asked.

"Pinky promise," I repeated, knowing Wesley would forget. I heard him giggle before saying bye. I hung up and drank my juice before I noticed Maddox staring at me. I arched a brow.

"Is there a problem?" I asked, and Maddox shook his head.

"Training's in ten minutes," he said.

"Great," I said as I nodded my head.

Awkward                                        much?

# Chapter Five

I watched as Maddox ominously hangs around a group of fifty wolves that were set on sparring. They all looked very well disciplined. Maddox informed me earlier that these were his best men and women. So here I am, observing a field of wolves training in man-to-man combat with Maddox interrupting every once in a while to step up the difficulty. He didn't introduce me, and I couldn't be any happier. Honestly, I didn't want to go through the whole intro process, anyways.

One of the male wolves looked over at me, and the other wolf he was sparring with laughed. Maddox's eyes immediately zoned in on the guy, and I rolled my eyes. *Alphas and their overly protective and possessive natures,* I thought to myself. I watched as Maddox stalked his way towards the pair of wolves, and I found myself moving with him. I got close enough, and I pressed a hand on the center of his chest.

"Chill," I said before I heard one of the wolves snicker. I looked at the source and found that it was the one that has been staring at me.

"Maddox, seems like you've got yourself whipped. Let me know when you get sick of her, might wanna try her myself," he said.

"You seem like you deserve an ass whipping," I snapped before looking at Maddox. "I'm going to go do that, so give me permission, Alpha," I said in a demanding tone. Maddox was still sensitive to my defiant attitude, so he hesitated to give me approval. However, he still gave it to me with a silent nod, and I smirked before patting his shoulder.

"Move over, bitch," I said as I effortlessly pushed his friend aside. He was stunned but stood back, probably due to the evil face Maddox was pulling at him.

I watched as the guy who spoke earlier crack his knuckles. Ugh, I hated that sound. It irked the absolute hell out of me. I twisted my hair into a tight bun atop of my head, and I stretched my arms.

"Well, my name is Trevor, sweetheart, and I'd like to have the name of the beautiful young lady that challenged me," he said as he ran a hand through his disgustingly sweaty brown hair.

"The name's Elair. Remember that when I have your ass handed to you on a silver platter," I said, glaring at him.

"Oh, plea—" he began, but I quickly moved. I slowed my movements down for predictability, and when he blocked one of my moves, he smirked.

"I don't like cheaters, babe," he said with a flirtatious tone.

"There's no such thing as cheaters in a free fight, kid," I respond, and I heard a bunch of voices go *ohhh*. It was only then that I realized that there was an actual crowd around us. No other group was sparring anymore, and Maddox wasn't stopping it from happening.

"Feisty," Trevor said back, and I rolled my eyes as he made a move to punch my side and kick me on the other.

I jumped away from him and quickly retaliated by ducking and getting behind him. Once I was there, I didn't hesitate to plant a rough kick on his back that sent him flying forward.

"I'm over here, kiddo." I teased, and he turned to face me with an angry look in his eyes. "Oh wow, I'm *so* scared," I said sarcastically. When he made a run for me, I observed his eyes.

I knew he was planning a good move, so instead of defending myself, I sprinted forward and slid below his arms, kicking his leg. I hooked my arm onto his planted foot and used the momentum of my movements to trip him over. I jumped to a standing position and smirked as he began to push himself off the ground. I immediately shoved my foot in the middle of his back, and he fell smack down.

"You must be the gamma... in training, of course. Wonderful to meet you," I said as I finally recognized the reason behind the cockiness. He was not that built yet, and although his movements were good, they aren't refined, and he was way too easily pissed off.

I spotted Maddox in the crowd with a proud look in his eyes, and I removed my foot from Trevor's piteous back. The crowd was cheering, laughing, and teasing Trevor. Maddox made his way over to me and placed a hand around my waist. The warmth of his hand touching the bare skin on my hip made me relax, reminding me that it was way too cold out here.

"This is Elair, daughter of Alpha Stephen of Blood Moon," Maddox roared, and the crowd went silent as they bowed their heads in respect. "She is my mate and your future luna."

*Oh God, why?*

All of them bowed their heads in my direction, and I was surprised by Maddox's discipline. None of them defied him. Even Trevor got up to bow his head in respect. I smirked at Trevor and held a hand out.

"No hard feelings," I said, and he chuckled before shaking it.

"Damn it, Cross. Your mate's insane," Trevor said. Maddox glared at him, causing Trevor to back away into the crowd. Maddox paused for a second, he must've got a mind link going on, so I watched as he sighed before speaking up.

"Continue training. I have business to attend to," Maddox ordered, and they all nodded as they went back to their positions. Maddox glanced at me, and I stared at him questioningly before he gave me a look that said 'follow me.' I obediently followed him back to the pack house.

"What's the deal?" I asked as we entered through the glass doors.

"My friend's here to check on you," he simply replied, and I nodded my head absentmindedly. Maddox motioned to the large and neatly arranged couches, and I sat down, watching as he stood there with his arms folded over his chest.

A deep crease formed in between his brows and his jaw tensed up, eyes lost in thought. Just as it seemed like he got something he wanted to talk about, a set of three people walk in. Two of them were tall men dressed in suits. One of them wore one in all black and the other in all white, and to be honest, they both looked like stark opposites. In between the two men was a girl much shorter than them. She couldn't be taller than five foot two, but that didn't make her look any less intimidating than the men.

She was stunning, and I meant that in the most profound way possible. Her hair was left loose, showing off the long and black locks that held a soft natural wave to them. Her eyes were odd. One was a pale blue, and the other was a striking green color that helped add to the aura of power that surrounded her body. She was dressed in a casual outfit, though. Her top was a plain white shirt, and she was pulling off a pair of denim jeans with some sneakers. She looked like a high school student, but there was something about her that didn't really read like she was from high school.

"Elair, right?" she asked as she walked in front of me. I nodded my head and watched as her eyes observe me. "My name is Helari. Simply put, I'm a witch," she said, and I grinned.

"Do you take enchanted bullet orders?" I asked, and she giggled.

"It's not something I normally do, but it sounds interesting. What do you do with them?" Helari asked with a smirk. "Call me, Ari. Helari is such a mouthful, and nowadays, people prefer shorter names," she said. I felt the wisdom from her. This girl was a hell of a lot more than she looks.

"I use them for defense. It's a lot easier to shoot than to shift and bite someone. It buys me time." I explained. Maddox made a slight nod with his head.

Speaking of guns, though. It was so weird not having my holster around me. Then again, I didn't think I needed it, and I didn't. Not when Maddox was a little puppy guard and wouldn't let me out of his sight.

"So... let's get straight to the point here," Ari said as she sat beside me. "Maddox told me you don't feel the mate bond," she said, and I nodded.

"I won't deny it at all. I don't feel it," I said as I wrapped my arms around myself.

"Okay then. Do you mind if I do a bit of the weird stuff with you? Spells and all that," Ari said.

"Sure," I said with a shrug.

I was not really going to defy something like a check-up. Despite what I might seem, I was pretty sensitive, okay? I just didn't like showing it. It would suck for anyone to not have their mate.

Besides, Ender was right about one thing. If Maddox wasn't my mate, he would've torn me to bits... or at least that was what I've heard. What I found completely weird, though, was that Maddox didn't show a single sign of being the rabid werewolf that people talked about. He didn't reek of death, and from what I've seen so far, his people were well trained. Well, most of them.

Ari took my right hand and smiled at me as her eyes began to glow. A warm sensation emanated from her hands, and I watched as the veins in my arm begin to glow with a white light.

The light continued to surge into my body, causing a sensation so alien like a probing device of strings. I felt it tug on some intangible part of me, and I could feel my wolf clawing at me. A piercing throb of pain stroke the back of my neck, and I did my best to handle it. I clenched my jaw as the pain spread throughout my being, like a piece of my body was being ripped apart. I closed my eyes tightly and balled my free hand into a fist. The warmth traveled up to my throat, into my face, and all the way to my brain. My arms and legs were numb and filled with the sensation of tingles like that of pins and needles.

I moaned in pain, and my body writhed involuntarily. I suddenly felt as if a thousand knives were being simultaneously shoved into my body, cutting and splitting me apart. I screamed in agony, but I heard nothing. My eyes have been closed for the longest time now, and I couldn't see. Then I got a glimpse of a distant memory.

I was six years old, sitting on a familiar tree stump with another little girl my age. She looked just like me, except her eyes were deep brown, and she had short blonde ringlets instead of my wavy pair. A woman came up to us, a woman I recognized. She was my trainer, my aunt Eleanor. Her blue eyes gave her daughter, the girl beside me, a disapproving look. Her eyes landed on me, with a strange tinge of a dark emotion... a twisted look... a look I have learned to get used to.

I felt a sharp stab in my heart as another memory plunged me deep into the recesses of my mind. It was dark and cold. There was no light other than the tiny window in the cellar. I was dressed in our squadron's training gear, a pair of black pants and a blood-red jacket over a black shirt. In walked my aunt. There was a young wolf strapped tightly to a chair. He was beaten and bloodied, but my aunt paced towards him with grace. She beckoned me to follow, and I made my way over to stand in front of the poor man. My aunt handed me a gun and whispered a few words into my ear. I picked up the weapon and without hesitation, shoot him straight in between the eyes.

That moment, although I couldn't hear a thing… I swore I could remember Aunt Eleanor and the exact way she told me the words.

"Very good, darling."

Another stabbing pain hit me from both arms, and I screamed in pain. I opened my eyes and found that I was in another memory. Except this one was different. I was lying down on a black marble slab. My arms had long slit lines of bloodied, almost unintelligible etchings down from my elbows to my wrists, and I watched my blood pool out and fall onto the slab and into little grooves that lined the stone. I remembered this moment. The smell of my blood consumed my being as my aunt proceeded to cleanse me.

"Elair… in an hour, you will finally shift, and you will hold full control of your body and soul. Make us proud, darling," Eleanor whispered into my ear before she disappeared into the shadows. My eyes drooped down, and I fell into sweet oblivion… numb from all feeling and sensation.

# Chapter Six

*I groaned as I slowly woke up. I opened my eyes and almost jumped out of my skin. Just a few centimeters away from my face was Maddox. He was asleep, and I was dressed in nothing but a plain white shirt that reeked of his scent. I looked down at myself, and my eyes widened. I was wearing nothing but his shirt. I tried to push him away, but as soon as my fingertips made contact with his skin, an electric shock made me pull them away. The shock exhilarated me. I stared confused at my fingertips before I spotted Maddox's now open eyes. He was watching me with those amber eyes, and it was the type of intense stare you didn't want to look into. But defiant little Elair just decided to go ahead and stare him straight through, and another electrifying and exhilarating shock filled my body.*

*I thought he noticed this because his hand reached up and grabbed my own. My breath involuntarily hitched, and before I could protest, Maddox was on top of me, his legs on either side of my thighs as he dips his head down and kisses my neck right at the spot where my mark would be. I moaned against my will, but my body didn't fight him.*

*Just as his hands gripped my shoulders, I felt a sharp pain in my neck, and I gasped. Warmth seeped from my neck, blood began to soak through my hair, and Maddox's mop of black hair did nothing to hide the fact that he was marking me without my consent. I was about to scream when he covered my mouth and continued to work. I felt the anger surge within me, and just as I was about to push him away, the sound of a vibrating phone grabbed my attention.*

My eyes opened wide, and I lifted my body off the bed. My breath was shaky, and my blood felt like it was boiling. Instinctively, I touched my neck to find it clean and bare. I sighed in relief. I was in Maddox's room, and I was relieved when I saw that Maddox's spot on the bed was empty. A vibrating sound caught my attention, and I grabbed the phone on the bedside table and saw that there was a call from an unknown number. I slid my thumb across the screen and answered it.

"Elair." I greeted.

"Soon," a voice hissed before it hung up. I arched a brow. The hell?

I looked at my phone. It was four in the morning. *Stupid prank calls.* I rolled my eyes before putting it back in the nightstand.

That was when I realized that my dream was right about one thing. I was wearing Maddox's shirt... only his shirt with nothing beneath it, and I reek of alpha. And no, I didn't reek of alpha everywhere. I did not imply that he screwed me unconscious. *Yuck.* Just so we're clear. Not that I didn't already smell like alpha. I mean... given my blood. Anyways, I got out of the bed and walked over to the closet. I grabbed some red underwear and opted to dress down a bit and not to show off my mid-section. I hopped into the shower for a quick wash before dressing up quickly in a fancy black long-sleeved top with sheer sleeves, a deep plum colored pair of high-waisted shorts, some similarly colored chunky heels, and some jewelry, particularly rings because those were always fun and they hurt people like a bitch when you punch them

I felt hunger gnaw at me before I finished straightening my hair. I had fairly little makeup other than a bit of shadow, eyeliner, and mascara. I walked out of the room and decided to grab some breakfast.

So I made my way to the kitchen... which surprisingly, actually had people cooking stuff in it. They all bowed their heads respectfully in my direction, and I decided not to respond as I opened one fridge to grab a tiny tub of yogurt. I opened it up and grabbed a spoon to eat it with before cutting up a couple of fruits and putting it into a cup. With my fruits and yogurt, I sat at the breakfast bar as some girls and boys hustled around to get some food cooking.

"Do you guys always cook for the pack?" I asked and watched as one of them froze and looked at me. It was a young boy no older than fourteen.

"Yeah, we take turns, though," he said with a smile. He had long brown tousled hair and freckles on his face.

"Mind if I help out?" I asked, and he looked around in surprise.

"If Alpha Cross doesn't mind," he said.

"He won't. Not if I can help it," I said with a shrug before chucking my trash into the garbage. "You guys cooking pancakes?" I asked with a grin and everyone, about five people, turned to face me. Some of them were way too tense, and none of them were any older than my younger sister Celine, the almost eighteen-year-old minx who decided to go skinny dipping back home. I never did properly reprimand her for that now did I?

"Yeah..." one of the girls, a dirty blonde haired, brown eyed, and petite one said, calling my attention back to the present. I folded my arms over my chest.

"You guys need to relax. I'm helping out, not scolding you. Besides, it's morning, and you guys are old enough to know what you're doing. It's your kitchen, not mine." I pointed out, and they all grinned back at me.

"Can you help us with the blueberry ones? Mason always burns them," a girl beside me who had brown hair asked, and I smirked as the guy that spoke to me earlier frowned.

"It's your fault, you always raise the temperature too high!" Mason somewhat shouted, and I laughed as I walked over to Mason's side and quickly worked around what I got.

After I've cooked, I watched as the other members of the pack piled in and greeted me with respectful bows. Mason, the two girls, the blonde who I've learned was Jill, and a brunette named Gwen walked over to me.

"Thanks for helping us out," Jill said with a smile, and I grinned.

"You're welcome. I've got nothing to do anyways," I said with a shrug.

"You're Cross' mate, right?" one of the pack members asked as he shoved a mouthful of pancakes in his mouth.

"Uh-huh." I nodded. *According to him, at least,* I thought to myself.

"You guys doing the whole mating thing on the full moon?" another asked.

"That's what he told me," I said casually.

Seeing them here... it was hard to imagine them as cold-blooded killers. Then again, who was I to judge?

"Oh, if you're wondering where Alpha Cross is, he's in the dungeons. We held a couple of try-hard trespassers last night. It was pretty weird," someone said, bringing me out of my thoughts before he was interrupted by another girl.

"Yeah, since it's hard to even cross our borders. They got in at about the same time that girl came," she said.

"Which girl?" I asked, arching an eyebrow.

"Helari. She came here on some business. I guess whoever she visited was important." The girl explained, and I nodded my head.

"Would you guys tell me where the dungeons are?" I asked, and they all looked at each other in silence. I rolled my eyes. "I'm not an idiot, and I'm not a weak little pup. I can handle the sound of screaming agony, for crying out loud," I said as I folded my arms over my chest.

"It's not that we don't want you there. It's that Alpha Cross is never in a good mood, and walking in there is suicide," one of them said.

"Not for me. I need to know what's going on." Especially since Helari's visit was apparently for me.

"It's on the other side of the lake," Ari's voice said, slicing through the air and silencing everyone in the room. Her aura was different, and she was emanating with power.

Her long black hair was down, and her clothes have been changed into a plain black yet formal t-shirt dress. It emphasized her porcelain white skin.

"Thanks," I said indifferently as I walked past her. I heard her follow behind me as I exited the kitchen and head out.

"Do you feel any different?" Ari asked me as we walked to where the dungeons supposedly were.

"Nope," I honestly said as I brushed past trees and went around the lake. Ari stopped walking, and I heard her sigh, causing me to stop. "What?" I snapped on accident. I didn't know why, but I felt very irritated.

"It's still healing," Ari said.

"What is?" I asked, taking deep breaths in an attempt at calming down.

"Your bond," Ari replied. I heard a sound from behind me and smelled Maddox's vague scent. I turned around, and there he was. He looked angry, but I watched as his face soften as he met my eyes.

"I wanna talk to them," I said.

"I can't let you do that," he responded. I walked up to him and stared him down.

"I said I want to talk to them. I didn't ask for your permission," I snapped.

"And I said no." He pointed out, and I turned away from him, surprised Helari wasn't there. I ran a frustrated hand through my hair and sighed.

"I'm going to talk to them," I said as I faced him once more, and he gave me a hard look.

"No, you're not," he shouted, and I fought the urge to groan in frustration.

"Listen, Cross. This is my business too, and if you really want me to be part of your pack, you're not gonna leave me out of this," I angrily said.

"They are none of your concern," he said through gritted teeth, his amber eyes blazing.

"Oh, fuck you," I hissed as I pushed past him. He grabbed me, and I dodged it, staring him down.

"Don't you dare go against my order," Maddox growled, and I arched a brow.

"Really? Because I've been obeying your orders since I got here. So if you think I'm just gonna sit and wait for you to protect me, I'm not. I can fight for myself, Cross."

"I didn't say you couldn't fight, I said you can't go in there."

"And why the hell not?" He let out an exasperated sigh.

"You want to see them so much? Fine," he said, changing his mood all of a sudden. I smiled triumphantly as he walked past me towards the dungeons.

The Macabre dungeons were guarded heavily. There were two guards outside and four others patrol in circles around the area. It was disguised as a tiny metal shed that actually led down to a set of stone steps. It was cold and dark in here, and it looked like a medieval torture house with a couple of modern security measures. My shoes clicked on the stone floor, and we walked past large high-security metal doors. There were no sounds coming from any of them, meaning they were completely sound proof. The cameras placed along the halls were apparently on 24/7 with more of them in complete hiding.

Each hall of cells had a large locked door with a key and a passcode. From what I saw in the beginning, there were three underground floors— well, technically four. The fourth was maximum security. The only way to get there was for the prisoner himself to be lowered whilst fully wrapped in wolfsbane covered metal cages into a hole twenty feet deep. It was a death sentence and a painful way to die in isolation.

We stopped at the end of a hall, and I watched as Maddox unlocked it. There were two other wolves behind me, for my security apparently. We walked into a cell. It was spacious and dark, with the only light coming from a spotlight in the center of the room. It was shining down onto two young men bound by rope and thick metal clasps to their chairs. I couldn't help arching a brow. One of them was beaten and bloodied. The only thing I could tell about that guy was his military cut hair and strong build. The one across him was the same, but his cold hard stare could pierce through ice. There were tools on the far side of the room and a container of a wolfsbane infused solution.

"Look who came to join us!" the one that was awake said with a creepy smile. Maddox tensed up, and I sighed as I walked forward into the light.

"Looking for me?" I asked.

"Always, little pup," he said. His teeth have been sharpened which added to the whole eerie vibe.

"Why were you looking for me?"

"We're all looking for you, little Elair... poor little pup, forced to be broken... never to be fixed," he said in a creepy sing-song voice. I smirked at him before looking at his unconscious friend. "Oh, don't worry about him. He'll wake up soon, too. He's been dying to meet you," he said with a loud maniacal laugh.

I nodded and looked at Maddox before walking over to the tools and picked up a set of knives. I grabbed the container of wolfsbane and made my way back to crazy-pants. There was a stool in front of him, and I sat on it, pulling it closer to him.

"How do you know me?"

"Long long ago. Poor little pup. Forced to be broken. Never to be fixed," he replied with a wide-eyed look. "My, how pretty you've become. Good, good. Broken pup, happy pup."

"Why do you keep saying that?" I asked, and he smiled, showing off his teeth.

"Because you're the pup, always have been... always will be," he said.

"Who called me this morning?" I asked, and Maddox suddenly moved right behind me.

"A friend of a friend, the owner of the pup. Yes yes... the broken little pup," he said in a sing-song tune. I grabbed one of the silver knives and dipped its blade into the wolfsbane.

"Sing that to me again. Whole, if you can," I said, and he grinned.

"Of course. Poor little pup, broken little pup, forced to be broken, never to be fixed. Her owner loves her so. Her owner leaves her so... broken little pup sad and all alone. Forced to be broken... always all alone... till her owner comes to take her good as gold and good at games... happy, happy pup. Broken yet owned," he sang, and I watched as he stared into my eyes, searching for fear. "Well trained pup!" he added with a laugh.

I took the knife and held it so that it was easy for me to stab him. In one swift movement, I planted one straight through his left thigh. He screamed in agony, the wolfsbane burning into his flesh before he looked at me and laughs.

"Like owner, like pup!" he shouted at me, his splattering spit revolting. I tilted my head, and he followed suit.

"Sing," I said, and he smiled.

"Poor little—" I pulled the knife out of him. "PUP!" he screamed, and I dipped the knife back into wolfsbane.

"Keep going," I said with a grin. He smiled and laughs at me.

"Good pup. Well-trained. Look look, friend! Wakey wakey!" he said, looking behind me. I watched his eyes. They shifted between wolf and human, and I saw his teeth elongate.

"I told you to keep going, didn't I?" I asked as I took the newly soaked knife and stabbed him in another spot. He screamed again and laughed.

"Broken... pup," he said in a low growling voice, and I smirked.

"Poor little pup, broken little pup, right?" I said. "Don't miss a single word. A single wrong word, and I'll stab you, okay?" I threatened and watched as his eyes turned into a mixture of deranged joy and anger.

"Forced to be broken. Never to be fixed," he hissed at me with a smile.

"Good," I said as I stood up to grab another two knives with both hands. I dipped them in wolfsbane and stood in front of him.

"Her owner loves her so... Her owner leaves her so..." he sang, and I nodded my head as I walked around him. Maddox and the two wolves were watching me, observing the way I act.

"Broken little pup... sad and all alone..." he continued.

"Who's the broken little pup?" I asked with a smile

"You are," he answered, and I stabbed one knife straight into his shoulder. He screamed, and I watched his eyes grow wide as his head turned to look at me behind him.

"Let me try," I said with a grin. "Forced to be broken," I hissed as I stabbed his other shoulder.

"Always all alone," I repeated in his ear as I twisted the knife deeper into his shoulder. His scream tore into the air, and I watched as he writhed in his chair. "So tell me, who is my owner?" I asked.

"You already know! She knows! She hides! Poor pup! Broken pup!" he shouted. Maddox angrily stalked his way towards me, so I held a hand up.

"I want you to give me a name," I whispered into his ear before walking around to face him again.

"No, no, no... You already know," he said with a smile, and he tilted his head. "Poor pup. Wait for him," he said with a booming laugh. I walked over to his unconscious friend.

"Hi, your friend is a bit deranged, and I'm sorry you're unconscious," I said loudly at the crazy asshole. I set my hands on either side of his friend's head, and with one quick move, I snapped his neck. He screamed in agony and pain, his eyes flashing pitch black as his fangs elongate.

"You killed him! Brother! Sleeping brother! Killed in his sleep!" he screamed, and I walked over to him and extended my claws.

"Tell me... who is he?" I asked. I felt something surge inside me, and the man in front of me had his eyes full of fear.

"No, you know. You *know*!" he screamed.

"I want you to tell me," I said. He began to sweat and tried to move his head away from me. I was about to strike him with my hand when it was held back, and I heard a large crack. Behind my prey was Ari who has snapped crazy-pants' neck himself.

I growled at her and then snarled at Maddox.

"How dare you," I hissed. Maddox's eyes analyzed me before looking at Ari, never letting go of my hand. She nodded and held a hand up. A surge of pain filled my chest, and I felt faint, but Maddox held me up.

"Elair, your eyes..." Ari's voice said, and I growled.

"You killed my prey," I hissed, but Maddox held me tighter, threatening to break my bones.

"I had to. Your aura changed," she said. I widened my eyes.

"What?" I asked, feeling the pain disappear and Maddox's grip loosen.

"Maddox," Ari called, and he looked at her with a clenched and tense jaw. "Take her back to the pack house. I'll perform a cleansing. Heighten security. Kill all trespassers for all I care," Ari said. Maddox nodded as he gripped my hand tightly once more and dragged me out.

# Chapter Seven

"What the hell do you think you're doing?" I hissed as Maddox pulled me away. He was already dragging me all the way up the pack house and into his room.

The only reason I couldn't kick his ass was the fact that his grip was like iron.

"Sit down." He coldly demanded, and I rolled my eyes.

"No way. I just did you a favor, and Ari killed him! Not to mention you dragged me out like a madman!" I argued, and Maddox's face turned absolutely rigid and covered in anger.

"You were out of control," Maddox answered in a cold hard-lined voice.

"I was not out of control. I was getting answers!"

"Your eyes turned red!" Maddox boomed.

"What?" I narrowed my eyes at him.

"You heard what I said. Your irises turned red. You didn't even look the slightest bit human," he said as if making an observation. "So sit down and let me check—"

"No, I'm not having you check on me again. I have gone through so much crap within the last twenty-four hours, and I don't even know why." I snapped.

"Elair, sit," Maddox commanded.

"Stop ordering me around!" I growled.

"Then just sit down," Maddox said in a restrained voice, his anger displayed in his blazing eyes. I balled my hands into fists.

"No," I defiantly said, and Maddox released a heavy breath.

"Sit!" he yelled, but I didn't flinch. I folded my arms over my chest.

"I said sit!" Maddox roared at me. I arched a brow and sighed.

"And I said, no. Then again, who's gonna listen to poor little Elair?" I retorted as I pulled my blonde hair into a ponytail. "Listen, Cross, I get it. You're the alpha, the leader, the killer, but I'm not yours to push around. Your whiney little alpha voice is killing me," I said sarcastically. In one swift movement, Cross decided to try to push me against the wall, but I caught him just fast enough to twist his arm around his back.

I used my sharp heel to kick him down, and I smirked as he squirmed underneath me.

"And that, my dear friends, is how you make the Alpha heel," I said as I released him. "Too bad I don't have an audience," I added as I walked to his office and grabbed one random book off the shelf to read.

"Why can't you just let me do something?" he asked. I rolled my eyes as I took a seat on the reclining chair.

"Because you can't, and I don't have a major issue. Fix me, sure. Give me a mate bond since it looks like it's been missing, but don't you ever think that you have control over me, Cross," I hissed, but just as he walked over to me, a flicker of black caught my eye. Maddox saw it too because we both looked out the window and found a single person standing in the trees.

Maddox growled. He was probably mind linking someone. I looked at the figure and felt a burning pain climb up my body. I spotted four wolves coming for him from the pack house, and I looked away, deciding that reading was not the best thing. I put the book on the chair, got up, and went to pick up my guns.

"You guys have a shooting range?" I asked, and Maddox looked over at me as I pulled out my two guns and strapped my holster on.

"I'll take you there," he simply said. He was back to his cold and overly well-controlled self.

"Great. Don't you have any alpha duties?" I asked.

"I can handle them with the mind link. Do you have any idea who that was?" Maddox asked, referring to the person outside.

"If I did, I wouldn't have kept silent," I said as I loaded my guns and filled my holster with the bullets that I needed.

We made it to the shooting range, which was located in the basement area of the pack house. It was a useful little room considering how much shooting calmed me down. It was almost as effective as yoga. Maddox decided to watch over me and sit down right behind me as I shot the targets across the room.

"Can I ask a question?" I asked as I shot the head of one of the targets. I didn't look at Maddox, but I heard him grunt in response. "What's with the whole 'big bad wolf' rep you guys get? You guys seem fine to me," I commented as I shoot the arm of another dummy.

"It's because we kill until no one is left. It assures we don't have enemies left. Survivors turn to vengeance. Killing everything and everyone removes future risks," Maddox explained. I nodded my head as I shoot again.

"Is Ari a big leader somewhere?" I asked. "She seems... on a higher level of supernatural beings," I muttered.

"She has her own organization. It's independent of the infamous Council... if you were wondering," he said. I nodded my head in response.

"And you're part of it? Ari's organization?" I asked as I reloaded.

"I'm sworn under oath to follow her commands," he responded. That piqued my interest enough to turn my head.

"So, in plain terms, she owns you the same way someone might own me?" I asked, putting the guns down. "So there are others like her," I added.

"She doesn't own me at all. Anyways, the Council can't control everyone. There are other organizations. Some are like Ari's who eliminate threats and vouch for peace so long as no territory of hers is taken, no conflict takes place. She's independent of the Council, but there are others that want to create an uprising. More than anything, Ari fears that the person who claims ownership over you is waiting for the right time to strike." Maddox explained.

"Got it. So you somewhat understood everything that crazy-pants said back there." I commented, and I noticed that Maddox hesitated before nodding his head in response. "You knew I pushed a bit too far, and you let me do it?"

"I wanted him to experience pain," Maddox said with a shrug.

"Huh," I mumbled before shooting one last bullet straight to the heart of the target. "Who knew we were so alike?" I mumbled. I heard what may have sounded like a soft chuckle, but alphas like to be straight-faced, so he stopped himself.

I felt his presence come closer until I felt him right behind me, causing me to turn around. He offered something to me in his right hand, and I looked at it. In it was a dagger that was made of silver and yet had an eye-catching white crystal at its hilt. It looked like a ceremonial blade. The inlaid turquoise gems surrounding the larger crystal only added to its elegance. He handed it to me. I looked at him in confusion.

"It's your birthday," he said, and I blinked at him.

"Right," I said as I looked down at the gift once more and took it from his hands. Maddox cleared his throat. "Thanks," I awkwardly said before Maddox nodded his head and sat back down, watching me as I placed the weird dagger down in front of me and proceeded to shoot down targets.

Maddox was serious about not letting me out of his sight. He was always with me, and when he had a meeting, he dragged me along. I was left just about completely lost. It has been three days since the torture day. Which meant there were about twenty more days left until the mating ceremony. Which, by the way, I have figured out, meant that we had to do the hoo-ha. Which to me, was disgusting. But hey, werewolf culture. Go screw and then bite the bleeding hell out of each other.

Ew, I cringed just thinking about it.

I was sitting in on a meeting between Maddox and his mini council consisting of his beta, gamma, delta, and the heads of other warrior units.

"This is a part of their territory that's weakly guarded." Maddox's beta, who I've learned was named Jasper, explained.

Jasper was tall. He had a shaven head and had caramel colored skin. He was nice enough, and he told me about how Winter, his mate from my pack, has been doing. Apparently, Jasper was a charmer because he had already marked her. Amazing, right? Which explained why I haven't been able to mind link a soul out here. I haven't shifted in days, and man has it been killing me.

I needed a damned run.

Jasper looked over at me and nodded, signaling me to come over. He and I have talked a few times, and I found him easier to talk to than Mr. straight-faced Alpha who I was stuck with 24/7. I walked over, and Maddox placed a hand on my hip as per usual. I didn't even say anything about it anymore.

"We're thinking of placing you in charge of training your own squadron here," Maddox said, pointing to an area on the right side of the lake. "We know you're capable," he added. I smirked at Trevor who was behind the current gamma, a forty-year-old man named Carson.

"Sounds great," I said. "It also sounded like a battle strategy has been formed."

Maddox nodded and looked at me.

"There's a pack that's been plotting to get to us. We've caught them spying around the borders for a bit. They're getting close, but they couldn't pinpoint exactly where our location is. Ari's been here, so she has masked us pretty well, but they're too close for comfort." Jasper explained.

"We're planning to attack them next week. We heard they were having a meeting with someone. Ari's been digging up some dirt, and it's one of *them*," Maddox said. I knew that by *them* he meant one of the organizations we talked about before.

"And so, my biggest question comes forward," I said as I looked at Maddox straight in the eyes. "Am I coming with you?" I asked and saw him swallow a lump in his throat.

"Everyone, leave," Maddox said with finality.

The little council immediately left with a respectful bow while Jasper gave me a reassuring look.

Have I ever talked about how weirdly organized Maddox was? There weren't any angry commands or weird arguments between them. If they did, it was low and emotionless. They only throw in real facts and come to a real solution. There was absolutely no wasting of time here. Talk about absolute dedication and discipline.

"You're not coming." Maddox asserted once his council was gone.

"Of course, I am." I countered.

"I'm not letting you go because I want you to manage the pack here," Maddox sighed.

"Yeah, right," I said, giving him a weird look. "I call bullshit."

"You are not going."

"Um, yes, I am going." I countered. Maddox groaned.

"You can't—" Before he could talk any further, I put one of my fingers to his lips, causing his breath to hitch.

"I'm going," I said with finality. He held my hand and pulled it away from his lips and sighed.

"No, you're not," he said. I groaned as he turned to put the map away.

Maddox was wearing a plain gray v-neck that hugged his muscles. He paired it off with a pair of black jeans. Although I've only been here a couple of days, I already knew that most of the girls swoon over him, but I've yet to come across anyone who has actually slept with him. Someone seemed faithful. I groaned at the thought of intimacy. I hated touching people— aside from kicking their asses and touching my own family members. But damn, if I wanna go fight, I gotta go... whatever it takes.

"Fine." I snapped as I walked away from him and slammed the door shut, knowing full well that he would follow me.

I made my way out into a forest clearing and walked behind a tree before throwing off my shoes and carelessly stripping down. I already knew Maddox was modest enough to turn away from me, so when I shifted, I was not surprised to hear him do so. I left my clothes where they were and made a run around the area, letting my wolf take over my senses.

I made a run for the hills and dodged roots, shrubs, and trees before I finally came to a stop to admire the view. Maddox was right on my trail, and his black figure soon emerged behind me. I looked at the view. The lake was there, and I could barely make out the soft brown hue of the pack house. I closed my eyes for a second before I sat down.

I just wanted to listen for once, so I did.

I listened to the soft sound of birds chirping in the trees, the sound of tiny scratches from little squirrels, and the howling wind that made the leaves rustle. I opened my eyes, only to roll them when I found that Maddox had decided to sit in front of me. His black wolf was staring right at my silver one. I barked at him to move, but he didn't. Instead, he playfully pounced on me, causing my wolf to stumble over. I fell on my back and barked at him angrily. *Dick.*

I pushed him with my legs and pounced on him too until I was on top. I then barked triumphantly before Maddox spun us over again. This wrestling match continued to the point that Maddox pushed us downhill, and we had to dodge the trees and shrubs while wrestling each other... a feat easier said than done. Maddox barked and nuzzled my neck when he landed on top of me in a clearing. I barked back before he paused and looked up, his ears twitching. He was mind linking someone, and I knew running time was over.

I got up off the ground and shook my fur before I made a run for the pack house. Maddox was fast on my trail until I heard him growl. I stopped immediately and looked at him. He looked back at me and barked as if trying to tell me to go ahead.

Deciding that I might as well go ahead since Maddox can handle it himself and I had plans to make him bring me to the attack, I ran for the pack house without so much as another bark.

Having Maddox hang around me for days and then finding him busy doing his stuff was kind of like having a fun toy taken away from you. Yes, I admit. He was okay to hang around. He was at least not the overbearing alpha I was expecting. He was quiet, and he let me do whatever I wanted as long as I didn't cross any of his rules.

I guess he should've counted himself lucky. I was used to being stuck in an area of nothing but forest, so when I had nothing to do, I did something like yoga or read books. The squadron back home was my whole life, so I never really headed out into any big cities or towns unless it was called for. Besides...

I hated people.

I took a look at my reflection in the bathroom. It was already eight in the evening, and I was able to cook dinner, read one of my favorite chapters on Lycanthropy, and do my yoga. I sounded like a human being for once. Except for, you know... the whole reading about the chapter on Lycanthropy that explained the effects of wolfsbane on the senses. Maybe I should've tried reading one of those human books... *Nah.*

I put on some lingerie that I knew would keep Maddox on his toes. He was so uptight that these types of things always put him off. As sadistic as it may sound, I did love it when I made him nervous. It was just so funny.

I needed some other form of entertainment that involves human interaction.

I should probably talk to Winter more often since she was from my pack and all. I twirled my hair around my finger and found myself smiling. The lingerie set was basically a cute black lace bra with matching underwear. The underwear was practically see-through other than the crotch area. I had to say, despite my ass being on display, this thing was comfy as fuck, and I admired its softness. I put on one of Maddox's tank tops, which showed off my chest area and was just short enough to end right above the bottom of my ass.

I grinned at the sight of me. Despite looking like I was going to the beach, I actually thought I looked like I could twirl an alpha around my little finger. I ran a hand through my hair. I had no makeup on other than a tinted lip balm that tasted like fresh mint. After hearing the door to our room open and close, I smirked.

*Game on*, I thought to myself. I walked out the bathroom and found that Maddox was sitting on the bed, shirtless and deep in thought.

I walked over to him and sat by his side. His eyes immediately locked onto mine, and even in the dim light of the room, I could see the worried look on his face.

"Something happened?" I asked.

"Another two trespassers, same type. No useful responses. Just the same creepy sing-song chant over and over," Maddox replied. I nodded my head, but before I could speak. Maddox tensed up. "What are you wearing?" Maddox asked me

"Thought you said I could wear your clothes?" I said with a shrug.

"I said—"

I put a finger to his lips again and sighed.

"No one can see me, at least... not when you're right in front of me," I said, pointing out at the fact that he blocked any view of me from the open windows of the room. Maddox swallowed a lump in his throat.

He got up and walked over to the nightstand, pressed a button, and I watched as a dim black screen fall over the windows. I raised an eyebrow. When the hell was that there?

"Bed," he said, and I mentally groaned. Damn it, I had to be the one to push this guy.

I stood up and sashayed my best over to him, placing my hands on his shoulders and softly massaging his stiff back.

"With me," I whispered in his ear. I could feel the goosebumps that my fingertips left behind, and I heard him take a deep breath to try to relax.

"I have wo—"

Before he could respond, I turned him around and pushed him onto the bed.

"Later," I said, straddling him. I lowered my head to his neck and left soft pecks across his collarbone and downward. Maddox was staring at my movements, and I let my hands trail all around his body.

"Maddox," I said, knowing full well he would recognize the fact that it was the first time I've called him by his first name.

"Let me come with you," I said in a whisper as I trailed my lips up from his chest to his neck, to the spot where his mark would be, and up his jaw.

"No," he said, but he didn't fight what I was doing.

"Please," I said as I kissed his chin and worked my way around.

"You're not... coming with me..." he said, and I fought the urge to smack him. Instead, I teased him by kissing the edge of his lips and grinding myself on his groin. "Ela—"

"Maddox," I said, and I watched his eyes think about it.

"Only if this little stunt isn't just for tonight," Maddox said, a mischievous look gracing his amber eyes. It was my turn to swallow a lump in my throat. I placed my hands on his chest and lowered myself back down onto him so that we're only apart by a few centimeters.

"If that means you're bringing me along everywhere, then sure," I said with ease, and Maddox stared into my eyes, his amber pair burning into my sapphires.

"Fuck it." He cursed before reaching up to my hair and pulling me down, crashing his lips onto mine.

*Oh,*                                                    *crap.*

# Chapter Eight

*I am so boned*, I thought to myself. I really had nothing much to think about.

Since Maddox was, admittedly, one of the best kissers in this world. He flipped us over, and I was at the point where every kiss left me absolutely breathless. Every time he kissed me, something inside me pulled at my skin. With every one he left on my lips, my neck, and my chest, which was still covered up despite Maddox tearing off his own tank top off me earlier, left my stomach filled with butterflies. His amber eyes were ablaze with lust as he looked at me. This meant so much more to him than me. Supposing he was my mate, of course.

Everything he felt was so much stronger than mine. Sure, I was feeling pretty good right now, but it would never compare to how my touch would make *him* feel. Although I was not one for sappy love tingles, I was also not one to fuck with people's feelings.

This was dangerous.

This was risky.

I didn't know what's coming over me, but it was scaring me. It was making me nervous and makes me want to scream in frustration. It reminded me of my dream, except that this was real. I could feel the heat surge from within me with every move he made. Part of me wanted to stop and the other, more risk-taking Elair, wanted to see where this was going.

But I didn't get to find out because after Maddox had nipped at my skin, he stopped and kissed my forehead.

"Sleep," he said as he abruptly got up and left me alone to go to the bathroom.

I swallowed a lump in my throat and sighed. Running a hand through my hair, I tried to process what just happened.

God, I haven't even kissed anyone since like what? Since I was five, and this weird kid got all up in my face?

Yes, welcome to the world of Elair Richelieu, pro-squadron leader, kick-ass trainer, and self-titled noob kisser.

"Ari will come back tomorrow to check on you again," Maddox said as he came out of the bathroom, and I nodded my head as I pulled the sheets over me. Maddox opened one of the closets before coming over to his side of the bed.

"Here," Maddox said as he handed me a gray shirt. I looked at it and nodded as I pulled it over my head to put it on. It definitely covered more of myself. "Good night, Elair," he said, and he turned off the lights.

I thought I've gone into shock.

That was it.

I was in shock.

On the bright side, I was going to the whole invasion thing.

Yay.

I turned and found Maddox sleeping peacefully with a content look on his face. *Yeah, good for you*, I thought to myself. He was probably real happy that he turned the situation around so that it was good for me and even better for him. In my stupidity, I actually said yes.

I bit my bottom lip and mentally groaned. I couldn't do anything about it now, so I might as well just sleep my ass off.

I got up the next day to an empty side of the bed that was still warm. The sound of the shower told me that Maddox was bathing, and I stretched my arms out only to gawk at the marks on my skin.

"Oh, God…" I groaned. That bastard. He totally planned to take away my joys of wearing crop tops, and now I had to wear some sort of high-necked top. I pulled the shirt off me and found that I now have little marks down my skin from the top of my chest all the way down to my abdomen. I ran a frustrated hand through my hair, internally screaming when I found another mark on both crooks of my neck.

Instead of putting the shirt back on, I decided to tease him once he was out. So like any pissed off twenty-two-year-old, I made my way to the closet. When I heard Maddox open the door, I bent over to grab my luggage bag. So when I heard something fall to the floor, I smirked to myself and grabbed my favorite leggings before reaching for a hugging sleeveless turtleneck that I had. I turned around and smirked at him before sashaying past him and into the bathroom.

I showered quickly and pulled on my black leather leggings and my deep blue turtleneck. I put on a bit of mascara and a tinted lip balm before walking out to find Maddox looking at me. Maddox made his way over to me and ran a hand through my damp hair, the sexual tension immediately rising as he tilted my head upwards. Our eyes searched each other, amber stones against sapphires, before he abruptly broke the little trance we had and removed his touch from mine.

He nodded his head in approval. I rolled my eyes as I walked to the closet, pulled on some black leather combat boots and walked out. Maddox followed me as I made my way into the kitchen and the whole area became quiet. It was fairly late, and the teenage pups in the dining area were surprised that Maddox followed me again and that I was probably putting on a resting bitch face.

Seeing as breakfast was already prepared, I grabbed two waffles and poured some melted butter on it along with some whipped cream, blueberries, and a drizzle of maple syrup. I sat at the breakfast bar and waited until Maddox sat down with me, a single cup of coffee in hand. I arched my brow and sighed as I picked at my breakfast until Maddox's arm snaked its way around my waist.

The other members started mumbling amongst each other. They've all began to talk rather than mind link each other. I watched as Maddox's mouth twitched, showing signs of a smirk, as he sipped on his coffee using his free hand while the other was still wrapped around my waist.

"What are your plans for the day?" Maddox awkwardly asked.

"Training. Care to join?" I asked. I would love to kick his ass for leaving all that marks on my body.

"We can do that after you meet with Ari," Maddox said.

"When is she coming?" I asked with a sigh.

"In about twenty minutes. It won't take long."

"Alpha Cross, could I ask a question?" One of the young ones, Mason, asked. Maddox nodded, and Mason swallowed a lump in his throat.

"The girls were asking if Luna Elair would like to come with them to the mall today," Mason said shyly, and I spotted Jill and Gwen giggling. Maddox looked over at me, and I gave him a smile.

"I'm technically not luna yet, but yeah, I'd love to. But he'll be coming…" I said, motioning to Maddox whose grip was still on my hip. "You sure you guys are okay with that?" I asked. Mason nodded his head excitedly.

"Winter can come with you," another voice said. I spotted Jasper sweating from what looked like a good sparring session since there was way too much dirt on his tank top. "She looks like she needs to get out more," Jasper said.

"Me or her?" I asked, and Jasper chuckled.

"Both of you."

"Cool," I said with a shrug.

"We'll go at eleven," Maddox said with finality. "I'll have the guards run the perimeter all the way to the nearest town. I don't want any trouble while we're out." Jasper nodded in response.

"Sounds good to me. We'll have Trevor handle training for your sect. I've got Carson handling the deeper sections. Some of our older wolves were getting pissed off by how loud the younger sects got the other day. Something about wrecking one of the pagodas." Jasper reported, and Maddox raised an eyebrow. "And just so you know, that includes your old man," Jasper said with a snort. Maddox sighed before looking at me. I arched a brow as well before he dragged me closer.

"I'll have him meet her soon," Maddox said, and Jasper grinned.

"Sounds like a great idea. He'll love her," Jasper said. "Be warned, he's a real bear-hugger. He's the one that created the whole massacre legacy... the kill or be killed strat that's made everyone think of us as bloodthirsty hunters. Not true. A lot of the times, it's other packs looking for a fight since we stand on one of Ari's ancient territories," Jasper said, piquing my interest.

"Well, that's certainly interesting," I said, looking at Maddox. I was still curious about Helari herself, but that could wait.

"The reputation is so that no one attacks our territory. It's easier to scare off the others. No matter how cruel it is, keeping survivors means risking the safety of both our pack and Helari," Maddox added. Just as I was about to tell him that he had already told me that, someone cleared her throat behind me.

I turned around and found that Ari there.

"Ready for a little check-up?" Ari asked, and I nodded my head.

Ari's hair was pulled into an intricately braided bun, and she wore a modest long-sleeved maroon dress that ended just above her knees. I followed her into the living room and sat down on the couch.

"The last time I did this, you shifted involuntarily," Ari informed me. I arched a brow. That would explain the whole waking up in Maddox's shirt ordeal. "Whoever bound you doesn't want me to undo it."

"Can you find out who it is?" I asked.

"Supposing whoever bound you left some sort of trace behind, I might be able to locate your supposed owner," Ari said, and I sensed a feeling of warmth on my back. It was Maddox standing behind me. "Maddox will restrain you in case I trigger your wolf." I nodded my head in understanding before Ari lifted her left hand.

She closed her eyes for a split second before opening them. They were glowing once more, and I felt a warm sensation spread throughout my stomach. A tingling feeling ran down my spine, and I felt the hairs on my back and arms stand to attention. I held one of my hands up and stared as my usually stable hand began to quiver. My fingers trembled, and I felt a strong urge to push away whoever was causing me trouble.

I heard a growl, but it wasn't Maddox's.

It was my own.

I felt two hands grip my shoulders, and I snarled at the touch. I felt my canines elongate involuntarily before I heard them...

voices whispering in my head.

*Soon... soon... soon...* one of them said. A sharp pain hit the back of my head, and I gasped.

*Poor broken little pup...* a distinct voice said in my mind. *I will return for you soon,* the voice repeated.

My chest tightened, and a scream escaped my mouth.

*Stubborn as always,* the voice in my head said. The whispers continued as others were singing that stupid miserable song.

*... Forced to be broken, never to be fixed...*

The song droned on and on.

# Chapter Nine

There was nothing but darkness and silence.

I knew my eyes were open, but there was nothing for me to see. There was just darkness.

That was until I felt a warmth surge from my chest and a pull so strong that it almost forced me back.

I gasped.

I broke into a coughing fit and opened my eyes to find myself in the living room. Ari stared down at me, and I realized that I was bent over on the floor.

"Shit," Jasper blurted out as my eyes snapped to his figure in the corner. "Elair, your eyes... they're blood red."

"What?" I said, and I caught my reflection in a small mirror hanging on the wall.

They *were* red. I turned my heel to leave, but I crashed into someone. Maddox stood in front of me and held me in my place. I sighed loudly.

"Follow me," Maddox said as he took my hand and led me off, leaving Ari and Jasper behind in the pack house.

Maddox brought me to a clearing in the forest before letting my hand go. He faced me before getting into a fighting position. I arched my brow.

"The hell are you doing?" I asked.

"Let it out," Maddox said.

"I have nothing to let out, Cross," I said. He shook his head before swinging one of his arms at me. I dodged it quickly. He was going all out.

"Elair," Maddox firmly said. I groaned as I got into my own fighting stance.

Maddox launched a punch headed straight to my face, and I dodged it by going down low and jumping behind him. I swiftly lifted my right foot for a high kick, but Maddox blocked it with his left arm. I ducked when I saw his right arm swing back for another hit. His right foot also went up for a kick, and I quickly dodged to the left. I got behind him and released a heavy breath, watching the mist form in front of my face.

Maddox turned quickly and faced me with a calm demeanor. With one quick move, Maddox used his arms to grab my shoulders, and I knew he was about to knee me in the stomach. I used my arms to hold on to Maddox before swinging my legs up and kicking him off me. The sound of his back hitting the trees echoed around us, and I groaned as I landed with one knee on the ground. He wasn't using full force now, and I watched as he got back into position.

Maddox began to make a run towards me, and I immediately prepared myself for the hit. He got close, and I jumped from my position, swinging my legs so that they wrap around the top of his head. I used the force of my weight to shift his balance, but he resisted, and I ended up swinging to get off him. My legs were in the air as I landed arm first from a backward jump.

He immediately turned, grabbed my arm, and hurled me towards him. I crashed into his chest and stopped moving as I felt the warmth of our bodies clash with each other's.

"Better?" he asked me.

"I was fine." I groaned as I pushed him away.

"You say the opposite of what you mean," he retorted before taking my hand. I was about to pull my hand from his when I heard the sound of footsteps.

"Alpha Cross," someone called out. We turned to face the source, but Maddox's arms were still around me, trapping me in his embrace.

I watched as Winter, Mason, Jill, and Gwen made their way over to me along with three other teenagers I didn't recognize.

"Hey, Luna!" Jill and Gwen greeted happily. I rolled my eyes before turning in Maddox's arms. His hands were now at my hip instead of my back. I would probably never get used to being called luna.

"We were wondering if you two are ready to go," Gwen said. I looked at Maddox, who gave me a look that said I had his permission.

"Yeah, we're good," I said with a shrug, and Maddox further snaked his right arm around my waist.

"Oh yeah, these guys are Dennis, Carter, and Roger. Dennis is my brother," Jill said as a brown-haired teen walked up to me with a smile. "Dennis is mute," Jill explained casually. I arched a brow and looked at Maddox. I then sighed as I mustered up a smile.

"You good, Winter?" I asked, and she grinned widely at me.

Winter had pixie-cut hair that was dyed completely white. Her eyes were brown, and she had a kind smile... and killer moves. I remembered training her in hand-to-hand combat. This girl could handle herself. She was pretty good for a seventeen-year-old.

"Yup, it's pretty weird still, but I'm good," she said with a smile. The mark on her neck was on full display with the white crop top she wore.

Ugh, I was jealous. *Damn it.* I wanted to wear crop tops, too. Stupid Maddox and his marking tendencies. Winter blushed, and I realized it was because I've been staring at her mark.

"Is it weird that we went straight on?" she asked.

"It's really up to you. As long as you're happy, then so am I," I said with a smile.

"Thanks, Luna," she said, a grin plastered on her face.

"You can just call me, Elair. You're the Beta's mate, after all." I said. Winter nodded her head then looked to Maddox for permission, and he nodded in response as well.

"Well, shall we go?" Winter asked, and I smiled.

"Sure."

One hour and twenty minutes later, I found myself in Portland, Bridgeport Village. Did it ever occur to anyone that

we could just go shopping at the local depot? I watched the
teens run around with Winter since she was technically still a
teen while Maddox and I walked together.

"Want anything?" I asked him, and he shook his head
silently. "Okay then," I muttered. I spotted a coffee stand and
immediately walked over to it, Maddox followed me as I
ordered two cups of coffee. He paid for it, and I handed him the
other cup.

We sat on a nearby bench when I smelled something
out of the ordinary.

"What's wrong?" Maddox asked.

"Wait a second," I told him before I stood up and
sniffed the air.

Yep, weird was definitely right.

"The hell," I muttered. I closed my eyes and listened
closely.

I singled out a voice I recognized and growled.

"Elair," Maddox called, but I felt my anger boil
through my veins. I put the cup down and looked around.

A mop of familiar blond hair caught my eyes, and I
stalked over to it. Sure enough, there stood my brother,
Vaughn. I saw his eyes widen in surprise, and his mouth
opened to begin some sort of explanation. He was with two
other members of the pack. I pulled my fist back and, as
quickly as I could, punched him straight in the face. The event
took place so fast that no one noticed as he stumbled backward,
caressing his face with his hands. My fist stung a bit from the
impact, but it was nothing near unbearable. Not when I was
angry.

"Ow!" Vaughn complained.

"What the hell are you doing here?" I hissed. "Actually, what the hell are all of you doing here?" I asked, demanding an immediate answer. I felt Maddox's presence behind me.

"Well, we were sort of looking for you," one of the wolves said.

"Are you all idiots? What if you crossed territories? You barely know how to stay in line back in Blood Moon." I scolded the two wolves as Vaughn regained a steady balance.

"Is it so bad to visit?" Vaughn asked.

"Vaughn," I said as I rolled my eyes, and he raised his eyebrows. "Shut up before I knock you out. I'm not stupid. Visits to any territory are supposed to be announced." I snapped.

"Sorry... We just wanted to know if you were doing okay," he said and nodded his head obediently.

"Phones, Vaughn. They exist now. Call me," I said, and he bit his lip.

"But Ender said—"

"What has Ender got to do with this?" I asked before smacking my own forehead. "Give me your phone," I told Vaughn.

"O-okay," Vaughn muttered before reaching into his pocket and giving it to me. I unlocked it with ease before dialing Ender's number.

"Hey, Vaughn, have you found her?" Ender's voice greeted, and I growled lowly into the phone. I heard him choke on his breath.

"Ender, the next time you want to know how I am, be a normal brother and call me. Don't send a goddamn search party, especially not a group of three teenage wolves," I hissed and felt Maddox's arm snake around my waist, allowing me to focus on something other than my rising anger at my two foolish brothers.

"Sorry about that... But can you really blame me?" Ender said through the phone, and I fought the urge to crush it in my hands.

"Ender, if you were in front of me, I would knee your balls so hard you're going to go straight to hell and back." I threatened.

"Then it's a good thing I'm—" Before he could finish his sentence, I sniffed the air and walked towards Vaughn. I took a whiff of his scent before growling.

"Jesus Christ, Ender, I swear to God if you are anywhere near Oregon I will snap your neck and bleed you out," I hissed, and Ender let out a weak laugh.

"On a scale of one to ten, how angry will you get if I was totally in Oregon."

"One hundred." I snapped, but before I could act or say anything else, Maddox took the phone from me and handed it to Vaughn.

"They can stay at the pack house until they choose to leave," Maddox told me, and I sighed before looking at Vaughn.

"I swear to God, Vaughn. I will murder both you and Ender if you guys try something this reckless again," I said, and I watched as Vaughn's gaze landed on Maddox's arm that was around me.

*Didn't think you really were mates. Sorry,* Vaughn said through the mind link. I rolled my eyes.

*Well, we are,* I responded. Well... It was not like I could really tell them the complicated things about my mate bond.

My family would freak out, and Ender would probably end up bringing an army— or a search party, whichever one locates the crazy fuck-head that *owns* me fastest.

"Do you think we could go ahead?" I asked Maddox. I was beginning to get bored out of my mind, anyways. Maddox was about to respond when I heard Winter call out to me.

"Elair!" I turned to look at her and found that she has two shopping bags in her hands.

"Yeah?" I responded, and Winter grinned.

"Do you mind if you come with me to buy a few things? I need your help," Winter said with a soft blush, and I looked at Maddox and Vaughn. Winter noticed my brother and her eyes widened.

"Vaughn? What the hell are you doing here?" she asked, and Vaughn rolled his eyes. "Okay, never mind I asked. I'm sure I can find out later," Winter said before linking our arms together. She had a mischievous look in her eyes before she took me away from Maddox and walked off.

"Must be fun having such protective brothers to watch over you," Winter chuckled.

"Kill me," I muttered before walking off with her.

"I'm not trying something like that on. Even if it is over my clothes," I said.

"Come on, it'll be fun!" Winter said excitedly, and I rolled my eyes.

She has been trying to get me to buy lingerie for the past hour. I have already got a million pieces of lingerie in my closet. I didn't need more. It was not like Maddox and I were mated yet, and I had no intentions of

"You know, one way or another you're gonna run out of stuff to wear," Winter said.

"Please don't tell me you and Jasper screw like bunnies because that paints an image I did not need to see," I said, and Winter laughed.

"I'm just saying, won't it be fun to tease your mate?"

"It's not like I don't already," I muttered. I mean, I've been teasing him since my little shenanigan in the blue nightie... and last night was pretty intense enough.

"Fine. But at least buy something for yourself if not for him," Winter said, and I sighed as I looked around. I moved away from the lingeries and grinned when I finally found something that I could wear. "Oh, well, that works too," Winter commented with a sly grin on her face.

"Uh-huh," I said with a smile.

Oh, payback for all those hickeys was going to be so much                                                              fun.

# Chapter Ten

"Are Vaughn and the others okay?" I asked Maddox as we head out to training. Last night went pretty fine, considering Vaughn and his friends listened to me and I left Vaughn with a black eye.

"They're settled. You can visit them if you want. They said they would join training," Maddox said, and I shrugged.

"Nah, my brother can handle himself. Did you figure out if Ender was here or not?" I asked.

"He's not," Maddox said, and I sighed in relief.

"Good," I responded as we made our way through the forest, and I watched as Maddox sighed to himself.

"The attack... it's taking place a week from now," Maddox said in a seemingly nonchalant tone.

"And?"

"I want you to promise me you'll follow my orders from here on out," Maddox told me as he turned around and tucked a loose strand of my hair behind my ear.

"I'm not stupid, Maddox. I'll follow your orders, no questions asked unless they take away my human rights," I said. Maddox almost smirked at the fact that I used his name, again.

"Good," he simply said as he stepped forward. He pressed a soft kiss on my forehead quickly before turning again to move on to where the training grounds were.

I followed him there. Maddox walked into the plain training ground, and I spotted two groups running in separate lines around the large open area. They were all dressed in black sports clothes just like Maddox was clad in a black shirt and a pair of black jogging pants, which was why I was glad that I wore a full black turtleneck sweater and a pair of black leather pants. The usual combat boots were on, and I brought one of my guns with me, tucked into the single holster I had for it. My hair was tied into a ponytail, and I wore nothing but eyeliner and mascara on my face.

Maddox stopped, and I watched the group run around. I spotted the guy I met back in Blood Moon who was pissed off at me shooting his girlfriend. He glanced at me and then at Maddox. There was no display of emotion on his face, but the grunt that Maddox gave told me that he has been mind-linked. Maddox held a hand up, and the two groups ran over to us in lines of four. There were sixteen in each group.

"Elair, take the left," Maddox said, and I nodded as I walked towards the group. Maddox strode to the right, and we split the training ground in half.

The wolves quietly began their training. I ended up with the guy I shot, and I watched as he stalked his way over to me. I arched a brow and sighed.

"Luna. My name is Iain," he greeted with a quick bow of his head. "I'm sorry for the way I acted before."

"I can't blame you. I did shoot her. It could've gotten worse if you guys didn't get to my father the way you did." I admitted, and Iain nodded his head. "How is she?" I asked, and he looked at me with a quick flash of surprise in his eyes.

"Jillian is fine. So is Rain, the other wolf that was shot. Are you a gunman?" Iain asked.

"Mostly. I have anger issues when I'm in a fight for life and death." I explained. *Well, that was what Eleanor told me*, I added in my head.

"How bad does it get?" Iain asked.

"It's been years. I can't get into a fight that threatens my life. Last time I did... I just found my opponent dead," I honestly said. I also found several others around me dead. That was a time I could never forget and not something I wanted to remember. Ironic, considering even I couldn't remember what had happened that led to my opponents' deaths.

"I used to have problems with my anger as well. Alpha Cross makes sure I keep in line. I'm sure he'll do the same with you as his luna," he said.

"I sure hope so," I said with a smile. "Go spar with that guy. I think he's waiting for y—"

"Sis!!!" Vaughn's voice yelled, and I groaned as I spotted him running towards me.

I looked at Maddox, who smirked before looking back at his group. I took one look at my brother and sighed as well just as Iain arched a brow at them.

"Spar with me?" Vaughn asked before I grabbed Vaughn's arm and twisted it around so he got his back to me and used my right leg to kick his shoulder down. He fell to his knees with a groan, and with one quick kick, I had him secured to the ground.

"Try to get out," I told Vaughn.

"That's... impossible," Vaughn said with a huff. I rolled my eyes.

"In battle, Vaughn, you're not going to have time to say that. I would have blown your head to bits," I said, and Vaughn groaned.

I looked up and spotted everyone in my group stop to stare at me.

"Everyone, meet my brother, Vaughn," I quickly said.

"Thanks, sis," he said with a dry laugh. I rolled my eyes as I let go of his arm, letting him land on the ground. I reached for my gun, took a cartridge of dummies, and loaded it.

"What do you do if you get trapped like this?" I asked, and Vaughn groaned as he scrambled to get up into a fighting position.

"Ready to dodge," he said with a smirk.

"Dummies," I simply said, and I knew Vaughn understands. I aimed at his legs and purposely missed as he jumped off. Normally, dummies don't do much damage, especially with wolves.

However, I've gotten a few customized. It hurt like crap, but it was basically like a BB gun with enhancements.

The bullets were blunt and didn't contain anything harmful. If I broke something, a normal werewolf would heal from it in seconds.

"This is going to hurt," Vaughn said, a worried look in his eyes.

"Good you know." I smirked as the group formed a circle around us. "If a bullet hurls your way... do your best to dodge it, though I doubt I'll miss by much," I told them, and they all nodded their heads. Their eyes watched as I made a move towards Vaughn who he dodged past me.

His movements were a bit slow, allowing me to get a foot in and trip him. Vaughn popped up immediately but too close, and I elbowed him in the side. He was knocked off-balance as he ran away, and I lifted my gun, shooting immediately. I shoot once, hitting him in his side. He cursed under his breath as I intensified my focus.

"Faster, Vaughn. You'll die at this rate," I said.

"Shut up," he said, and I sighed as he charged my way. I was not stupid, so I didn't shoot him. I only had about two rounds of bullets, and there was no way I was wasting those.

Vaughn got as close as possible, and his arrogance made him smirk to my face. I stared into his eyes, quickly tossed the gun in my other hand, and aimed at his stomach. I pressed the trigger twice, and I watched as he groaned and fell to the ground, hands on his stomach.

"Holy shit!" he practically screamed.

"Displaying arrogance in a fight is unacceptable, Vaughn. You can be arrogant, just don't push it too hard that I see it," I said, and Vaughn whimpered as he pulled himself up. Iain came over and pulled him to his feet.

"Thanks," Vaughn said, and Iain nodded his head and looked at me.

"Mind if I try?" Iain asked, and I shrugged.

I pulled the round out and checked on my dummies. *Huh, looks like I'm placing an order,* I thought to myself. Iain got into position as the group pulled Vaughn to the side.

I loaded my gun again.

"Ready," I said, and Iain nodded as he got into position. He quickly charged towards me and lifted his leg for a kick. I dodged, but he pulled down and kicked where I was going.

I smirk as, despite having a gun in hand, I managed to utilize my two hands to land on the ground and lift off of his legs. I landed quickly, pointed the gun in Iain's direction, and shoot. He dodged it and ran towards me. *Charging at your opponent, huh*? I thought to myself. He got within two feet and began to punch, aiming at my face. I dodged carefully before slamming my gunned arm down on one of his extended arms. He glanced as his balance was offset and his arm bent, allowing me to make my move.

I found an opening and kneed him hard in the stomach. He didn't budge, however. Instead, he moved to the side, huffed, and got right back to charging at me. I aimed straight at his head, and he dodged to the right. He tried to get a high kick on me, and I stopped it with my right arm. I flipped my right arm so that it was on the other side of his leg, gun in hand, and I aimed at his chest and shoot once. Iain was smart, though. He immediately ducked when he found me in position. My shot hit the ground, and I grinned.

Iain's face was devoid of emotion, and I watched as he calculated his next move.

Iain and I laid on the ground in tired breaths.

"Good... fight..." Iain breathlessly said, and I wheezed out a laugh.

Maddox walked over and offered his hand to me. I grabbed it, and he lifted me off the ground. It was already sunset, and I have absolutely sweat my ass off.

"Settled things?" Maddox asked Iain, who replied with a nod as he got up.

"I'm out of dummies," I whined, and Iain chuckled in response. My group ended up sparring on their own as Iain and I continued. Eventually, someone figured out that we were never going to quit.

"Iain's my best fighter. He heads the front," Maddox told me.

"Explains the quick and quiet moves," I said, and Iain grinned.

"Thanks," Iain said, and I watched as he smiled and turned around. In the background was a girl, who I was supposing was Jillian. Iain nodded at both Cross and I before he sprinted off towards her.

"Had fun?" Maddox asked.

"Most fun I've had in days," I replied as Maddox and I made our way back to the pack house.

Maddox was sweating as well, his wet shirt clinging to every crevice of his body. Once we got to the pack house, the sweet smell of mac and cheese hit my nose, and I watched as the place got packed with hungry wolves. Maddox beckoned me over to the stairs and into our room. I mentally groaned but followed him up there, nonetheless.

Inside, there was a table set by the windows with food. I smirked before taking off my sweater, revealing the soaked military green tank top I had on. Maddox eyed me and sighed before walking over to the table. I did the same, and we ate in silence. Maddox sighed just as he downed a glass of water.

"Your brother, can he make it home by tomorrow morning?" Maddox asked.

"He'll be out of your sight by then. I don't want him here when we go off to fight," I said, and Maddox nodded.

"I want you to bring the dagger with you," Maddox said, and I arched a brow.

"Why?" I asked.

"It's important. It will help with whatever's going on. I have a bad feeling about where we're going," he explained.

"Okay. Not sure how it'll help, but it's your orders," I said with a shrug, and Maddox eyed me. I arched a brow and stared back at him.

"I'll go shower out in the hall. You can show—"

"I have a better idea," I blurted out, and Maddox raised an eyebrow. "Lake. Swimming. Ten minutes," I said, and Maddox showed a hint of a smirk before letting out a small huff.

"Sure," Maddox said.

I opened my closet, grabbed last night's purchase, and made a quick run to the bathroom.

Wearing Maddox's shirt over a pair of mini shorts was one of the easiest ways to tease him. He trailed right behind me as we walked in the dark of the woods. I had gotten used to the cold by now, so the weather was fine. As soon as we reached the little dock on the farther side of the lake, I pulled the shirt off and stepped out of the shorts, and I heard Maddox growl behind me. I ignored him as I jumped in, the water sending wonderfully cold shivers down my spine. Eventually, my wolf genes kicked in, and I warmed up fast, but Maddox had a dark and dangerous look in his eyes.

"What are you wearing?" Maddox asked in a low voice as he stepped towards the edge of the dock.

"A swimsuit?" Maddox growled before taking his clothes off until he was left with just his plain black boxers. He jumped in and immediately wrapped his arms around me, growling lowly as he studied me.

I mean, the swimsuit was pretty awesome. It was an all black bikini that really... only covered the main parts. The top was somewhat like a halter, but sheer panels connected and held the black cloth that kept my breasts in place. The bottom was high waisted and only covered the mid-sections of my front and back, the rest being sheer fabrics as well.

"Anyone could rip that thing apart and—" Maddox began, but I silenced him with my finger.

"I don't find hickeys very attractive, Alpha," I whispered into his ear as I wrapped my legs around him under the water, his jaw stiffened as I lift myself up so that my head hovered above him.

I trailed my lips down his nose and onto his own. Maddox, glad to even have me so close, molded his lips to mine but with as little effort as possible. He let me do as I pleased and I smirked as I trailed my lips down to his neck. The spot where his mate mark would be was where I made my handiwork, doing my best not to break the skin as I decided to leave my own marks on his body.

A soft gasp escaped his mouth as I pressed against him. Maddox groaned as I continued marking his skin the same way he did to mine. Once I was done, I lifted myself up again and smirked as Maddox reached for the back of my head to bring me down for a kiss.

I followed his lead, and we shared a soft kiss that Maddox immediately began to deepen, but I pulled away and splashed him with water, laughing at him.

Maddox glared at me, and I stuck my tongue out.

"Not tonight, Alpha."

# Chapter Eleven

"You sure you'll be fine?" I asked Vaughn for the nth time. Vaughn rolled his eyes at me. He was just about to leave for the airport, and Maddox had made sure that they were escorted out.

I didn't want any funny business.

"I'll be fine, Sis. Don't worry," Vaughn told me, and I sighed.

"I can't help it. You may be stupid sometimes, but you're my brother," I said, ruffling his hair. Vaughn groaned before smiling at me.

"Bye, Sis," he said as we gave each other a big hug. Maddox, all of a sudden, appeared right by my side and Vaughn's eyes widened for a split second before he smirked at me.

*Nice mark, sis. Didn't know you had it in you.* I raised an eyebrow before looking over at Maddox and gawking. What the hell?

Hours after Vaughn left, I found myself still staring blankly at Maddox as he ate his breakfast. We were in the dining area with the rest of the pack, and everyone had been staring at Maddox's low cut shirt that showed off part of the trail of hickeys I left him last night. Maddox sure knew how to get on a girl's nerves. We ate across each other, and I watched as the other pack members whispered on and on about the hickeys. I sighed loudly.

"Really, Maddox?" I asked him, and Maddox smirked at me, knowing full well that my little revenge backfired.

"It's not every day my mate decides to mark me temporarily," Maddox said with a wide grin. "I'm quite proud of your fine handiwork."

"Uh-huh," I said with a roll of my eyes. My phone buzzed in my back pocket, and I immediately fished it out. Maddox raised an eyebrow, and I sighed before showing him the screen.

He nodded his head, and I stood up, heading straight out into the sunlit patio to answer the phone.

"Morning, Mother," I greeted.

"Morning, how are you there?" Mother asked.

"Pretty good, surprisingly," I said, and she laughed.

"Good, and has the Alpha been treating you... *well*?" Mother asked, hinting something shameless with her tone, and I felt a heat rush to my cheeks. Thank God Maddox wasn't in front of me.

"Mother," I said in warning, and she laughed even harder.

"Well, you can't blame me for asking. I only want you to enjoy each other... and to live to see the next generation," Mother said with amusement, and I rolled my eyes.

"I don't even want to know what that's supposed to mean," I told her, and she chuckled.

"You know, it isn't bad to surrender to him. He *is* your mate, Elair. Nothing wrong with staking your claim on what's rightfully yours," she told me, and I leaned on the intricately made railing of the patio.

"Mother, did Father tell you?" I asked, and she sighed.

"Elair, I heard that you didn't feel the bond. It's not something I want to discuss out loud especially with Ender being such a hothead. You're lucky he's out training," Mother said. "But, Elair, I know you. If you didn't already have feelings for this boy, you would've left." It was my turn to laugh.

"Mother, you know the circumstances. I can't just—"

"Elair," my mother said sternly, and I felt the seriousness in her voice. "If you plan on torturing this boy by not returning his feelings or by not even trying, I suggest you reject him and leave. Save everyone the trouble of your selfish behavior," she told me, and I sighed.

"It's not that I don't return his feelings, Mother. I just can't... I know it won't be on par," I told her, and she sighed as well.

"It can be. If human mates can learn to love our kind, so can you," Mother said in her calming voice.

"I am trying," I told her.

"I know, darling, but if you put up a false lover's facade, then you'll never reach him."

"Mother, he can barely reach me." *I'm the problem in this little mate equation*, I added in my mind.

"Nonsense. Put down your walls and let him reach you. There's only so much he can do on his part. The rest would be all on you. If love does not come, then for once, the Goddess may have made a mistake that you can undo. But if you are willing to undo it, do so before the mating process. Goddess knows how mentally and physically damaging it can be if you let it go so far," Mother told me, and I sighed.

"Yes, Mother. By the way, have you heard from Aunt Eleanor?" I asked.

"Why?" She asked. I sensed the hesitation in her voice.

"I'm experiencing... strange things," I told her and just as I was about to add more, a pair of warm, strong hands wound their way around my waist. Maddox inhaled my scent as I continued speaking. "I need to know what happened. Everything is such a blur," I told her, as Maddox squeezed me supportively.

"Well... I don't think I can tell you over the phone. If I may, I'd like to talk to Alpha Maddox about this," Mother replied, and I handed Maddox the phone. He took it and put my phone to his ear.

"You have my approval," he told her, and I could hear my mother's laugh.

"Very well then. I'll see what I can do. Look forward to your father's message, Elair. I think we'll arrive just after Wes' recital."

"Is he performing the violin?" I asked, and my mother giggled.

"Yes, he's been practicing on video. I'll bring the tapes with me. He says they're for you." I smile at that before Maddox handed me the phone.

"Alright, bye, Mother," I said.

"I'll see you soon," she told me before she hung up.

Maddox's arms around me stay where they were.

"When did you start listening in?" I asked.

"Aunt Eleanor," he said, shrugging off my question, "should I know her?"

"You'd be better off not... but she trained me," I informed him, and he nodded his head.

"I have to go deal with a few things. Care to join me?" Maddox asked, and I shook my head.

"I'm not in the mood to listen in," I said as I untangled his grip from my waist. "Tell me what you talk about later," I said, and Maddox nodded, but just before he turned to leave, he grabbed my hand and dragged me towards him.

He placed a firm kiss on my lips, causing my eyes to widen. His lips moved against mine, and I felt my eyes close just as he parted away. With a soft hint of a smirk and a mischievous glint in his eyes, he left me feeling just a tad bit colder than before.

I looked up at the sky and let out a huge sigh.

"It seems you have a problem," a male's voice said from behind me. I turned and spotted one of Helari's usual bodyguards. This one was the platinum blond-haired one that wore an all-white suit.

He smiled kindly at me. This man simply exuded eighteenth-century gentleman.

"I have a myriad of problems," I said, and he chuckled.

"Of course. My mistress is quite intrigued by you, little wolf," he said, to which I arched a brow. "My name is Mikhail."

"Elair," I said with a shrug. "Has Ari found out anything new?" I asked.

"I'm afraid not. She is willing to try something. However, she is unsure that Alpha Cross will allow it."

"And what is it?"

Mikhail smiled at me in an eerie manner, but I shrugged the feeling off. His eyes were so pale blue that you wondered if they could pierce through you like shards of ice.

"An *unlock*, if you will. It involves a bit of blood and a lot of pain... especially for you," Mikhail told me.

"Did Helari ask you to tell me this?" I asked, and Mikhail smirked mischievously.

"Of course, not. Despite me being the white servant, I'm the more mischievous of our group. Scar is a bit too uptight to play the games I do," he said.

"Where's Helari?" I asked, nodding.

"She should be arriving soon. Helari has been watching over this territory in case the said owner appears," Mikhail said.

"And the problem continues," I muttered. "I'll inform Helari of my decision, thanks for informing me," I told Mikhail, who nodded his head and smiled.

"Of course," he said before leaving me alone with my thoughts.

I walked straight back into the pack house and fixed myself a cup of coffee. Just as I was about to head up, I heard the sound of a loud slam followed by shouting coming from the office.

Coffee cup in hand, I walked to the office and opened the door that was muffling the sound of a certain angry Alpha. Jasper, Trevor, Iain, and the other leaders including three females I hadn't seen before, stood still and all of them looked at me. Each one of them was looking down at the floor while Maddox's grip almost snapped the wooden conference table in half. Maddox's head was down, and his entire body was trembling with anger.

I sighed, sipped my coffee, and walked towards him, setting my cup down just beside his hands. Then I reached for his face and made him look at me.

"Hey, get back here," I said softly, and Maddox's blazing and almost glowing amber eyes blinked several times. A low growl escaped the back of his throat.

*Well, there goes the soft and soothing route.* I rolled my eyes before I let my wolf out and snarled threateningly at him. The sound ricocheted all around the office, and Maddox stared at me, his eyes challenging me to back down. His wolf was in control, and it was probably because of something really bad. So, I did what any female would do to an out-of-control male. I flicked my wrist back and slapped him so hard across the face that everyone in the room let out a gasp.

"Could everyone leave us for a moment?" I asked loudly in a cold voice. There were no words spoken as everyone left the room and the door clicked shut.

"What the hell happened?" I snapped, and Maddox, still in shock from the slap, turned his head and faced me.

"Children. This place we're attacking. Those women you saw were surveying the area when they spotted three children that were shot clear through the head," Maddox said, and I swallowed a lump in my throat as Maddox turned over three sheets of paper. They were printed out photos of the bodies.

On their arms were blood etchings, and I found myself trying to recall a memory that was hazy and blurred.

"Elair," Maddox called out, and I turned to look at him. His hands touched my face, and he breathed a sigh of relief. "Sorry," he said.

"For what?" I asked.

"Losing myself there," he said.

"This isn't exactly something we can be calm about. Where were the children from?" I asked, and Maddox sighed.

"They're humans, Elair. I'm guessing Helari has sent a few of her people to prepare a decent funeral for them."

"Humans? Why would there—"

*Sacrifices,* my mind answered for me.

Maddox sighed and ran a hand through his hair before sighing once more.

"I'm not going to regret killing the lot of them," Maddox told me, and I nodded.

"What happens... by the way... to the children you come across?" I asked, and Maddox looked down for a second.

"Helari handles the children. They aren't killed, but... think about it as a memory wipe. It's customary, and although some don't agree with it, memory wipes are necessary if we don't want to leave traumatized or vengeful children."

"So... they're wiped clean and stay with her?" I asked, and Maddox nodded.

"Helari runs a good school and organization. She takes in abandoned wolves, humans, witches, and the list goes on. Anyone needing her help, she takes care of. In return, they swear total loyalty to her... denying her requests are an absolute death sentence," Maddox said to me.

"Are you sworn to her?" I asked.

"Yes, but not in the way that they are. My family has served her for generations," Maddox chuckled as he faced me and ran his fingers down my face, tracing it softly.

Before either of us could say any more, a knock at the door had Maddox putting on a straight face again.

"Come in," he announced, and I watched as the doorknob was twisted, and Helari walked in.

"The children were etched with markings from the Sentinels. It's been a while since they've pulled such a bold move," she said. At the sound of the word 'Sentinels,' I felt a surge of pain hit my eyes.

Maddox immediately gripped my hand and stared into my eyes.

"Helari," he called, and Ari was immediately in front of my face as well. Her eyes widened before she sighed.

"Shit."

# Chapter Twelve

Ari took a deep breath before chanting something barely audible. An involuntary snarl was ripped from my mouth, and my eyes widened at the sound.

"Maddox, the Sentinels' markings... they're on her," Ari said, and Maddox's eyes widened as he looked down at my body. I followed his gaze to my arms.

On them were etchings, similar to the ones on the children, but they were glowing underneath my skin. There was line after line of them. Maddox reached out for me, and I flinched as a low growl escaped my lips.

"Elair, calm down," Ari told me, and I felt a rush of energy course through me. A female voice in my head suddenly spoke out.

"Elair, sit still!" it said. I put my hands to my ears and closed my eyes.

"You need to behave!" the voice in my head screamed, and a cold sensation ran down my spine.

"I cannot afford another disappointment," the voice whispered into my ears. "You are my only hope my dear, dear Elair."

"You will be perfect, the best of our collection," another voice, this one male, said.

"Sit perfectly still," someone whispered, and I heard the sound of children screaming all around me.

"Nothing else matters to us," a voice told me and from behind, and I felt a hand trace my bones. "Remember, Elair... nothing else," a deep voice said before I felt my entire body being shaken. I opened my eyes and found Maddox with his hands gripping my shoulders, and I stared into the blazing amber stones in his eyes.

Once he realized that I could see him, Maddox took me into his arms, and I turned rigid and stiff... almost like a stone.

"I need to run," I said, and Maddox grunted. He let go of me and looked at Ari for approval.

Ari nodded her head solemnly.

"Afterward, we have something to discuss. I'll get to my readings right now," she said before Maddox nodded and dragged me out of the office.

We were out in the woods when Maddox let go of me and turned around.

"Shift," he simply said, and I folded my arms over my chest.

"I didn't mean run with my wolf," I retorted, and Maddox whipped around and looked me straight in the eyes.

"What were those things?" he asked me.

"How the hell am I supposed to know? I am just as confused that I have strange markings on my arms, okay?"

"A part of you recognizes it, and I can see the fear in your eyes. You're afraid of it, and that means you do remember it."

"Well, of course, I'm afraid, Maddox! My skin is glowing. I'm here with a man who claims to be my mate when I feel little to nothing. I have flashbacks to scenes I can't remember, and not to mention, I have been separated from the family I promised I would protect! So I'm sorry if I can't be the perfect and honest little mate you want me to be!" I shouted at him. He gave me a cold look.

"I am trying everything to make you as comfortable as you can be. I called Ari to help you, I've allowed your brother to stay here, I've let you call your own mother for comfort when that in itself can track my entire pack's location down. Not many can say I've given them the leniency to do so."

"That's because they're all from here. They're indebted to you, love you, adore you, worship you. I don't have any connection with you! I can't feel a goddamned thing, and it's frustrating! I can see what you want from me, Maddox! I'm not fucking blind, and I'm not an idiot. I may not feel it, but I can feel you and what you want from me isn't my little episodes of sexual tension." I ran a hand through my hair and sighed.

"You act so high and mighty when you're just afraid. You're afraid of more than just the fact that I've taken you here… more than what you've said about being separated from your family and from being in this situation," Maddox said. He stepped towards me until he was a fair distance to tilt my head up and have me stare straight into his eyes. Our height wasn't too far apart, so the movement was barely noticeable as Maddox growled lowly.

"You're afraid of anything and everything new. You're nothing but a coward, a mate I can't even look at until she owns up to her foolishness," Maddox said, and I stared back at him. His eyes were blazing, and I felt a smile creep up to my lips. I couldn't help it. I laughed loudly at him.

"It must be so easy to tell a stranger she's a coward when you know nothing about her," I said after I managed to stop laughing. "I'm glad we had this talk, *Alpha*. I know where we stand, now. I have something to discuss with Ari. If it concerns you, this little misplaced and technically rogue wolf would like to head back and talk about something important," I said, my voice devoid of emotion. Maddox didn't say anything as I turned on my heel and left him alone.

When we return, Ari has a distressed look in her eyes.

"Maddox, I'm going to have to perform a cleansing on her," she said as she gave me a worried look. Maddox grunted, causing Ari to raise an eyebrow as he walked over to the table and fixed the documents on it.

"Okay, what the hell happened within a span of thirty minutes that caused this severe gap?" Ari asked as she looked between Maddox and I. I shrugged before walking over to Ari.

"Mikhail told me you can perform an unlock. I want it done," I said, and I heard a glass break. I glanced at Maddox and found that my mug of coffee has fallen in pieces on the floor. I looked back to Ari, who was shaking her head.

"That boy needs to learn to shut his mouth," Ari said with a sigh. "I can't perform an unlock with the way you are now, and I certainly can't do it when Maddox is glaring at me instead of just telling me not to perform it on you."

"It's my decision to make," I said, and Ari released a heavy breath.

"You're both acting like children. I can see why both of you are angry. The two of you won't ever admit to any wrongdoings, but like it or not, the two of you are bonded together. I'm doing my best to repair whatever the Sentinels have done to you," Ari said, glaring at me before glaring at Maddox's back as well. "I do this for your best interest, Maddox. You cannot lie to me, I have been the guidance your father had so needed."

"If you want to lose her, then I suggest you give Elair to me, and you reject her to spare us time," Ari said. By now, her voice had turned into a harsh booming voice that had Maddox and I giving each other intense glares.

Ari sighed before turning on her heel.

"I will cleanse Elair later tonight. For now, fix your childish issues. I will speak to Mikhail about his behavior, and we will discuss the rest of that other issue tomorrow. I will not move unless the two of you are logical and behaved," Ari said before her heels clicked on the floor, marking her exit.

Maddox and I still glared at each other before we turned away and awkwardly stood together.

*Goddamned Alphas and their stupid attitude problems.*

*Goddamned werewolf genes and their mate bonds!* I internally screamed.

"The two of you are like bickering children," Ari said when we entered a little sectioned off area that looked like a mini chill-out room. I groaned as I plopped down onto a pretty white couch.

"He pushed it," I muttered, and Ari rolled her eyes at me. "What?"

"You two have no idea how lucky you are to have each other. Granted, your bond is broken, and he is as mysterious as it gets," Ari said before motioning for me to hold my hands out. I did just that, and Ari stood in front of me holding one hand facing towards my chest. A cooling sensation sprouted from the center of my chest, and I breathed a sigh of relief.

"I can't stay the way I am right now. He's better off without a mate," I said with a sigh. "I literally know nothing outside the duties of my squadron."

"And this unknown territory scares you? I doubt that's the only thing you fear. Either way, you should know, Maddox isn't easily fooled. He sees through people... fast, and he won't let his mate be any exception to his scrutiny," Ari said to me as the cooling sensation began to spread throughout my body.

"I'm not only afraid of that. I'm afraid of... I don't know. I'm afraid of failure."

"Because you were never given the liberty to fail before," Ari told me.

"How do you know that—"

"Trust me, I can read everyone like an open book, and I know the Sentinels. If Maddox can observe, I can literally read every minute detail of every being and object around me," Ari said. "I see the visions you have, and I've seen enough to interpret it fairly right."

"I'm not even sure what's going on in my head right now," I admitted, and she sighed.

"Give Maddox time, he'll come to his senses. For now, I suggest you try not to aggravate him. Do... a little teasing if you will. Just to hasten the process."

"I've been doing that all week," I said with a roll of my eyes, and Ari raised her eyebrow.

"That would explain the hickeys," she said, and I felt a rush of heat burn my cheeks.

"Gee, thanks," I muttered, and Ari laughed before she put her hand away. My body felt soothed and relaxed as I stood up.

"Maddox can be very straightforward. He will be very, very patient with you, but don't take that for granted. He's matured fast, but... I'm afraid he knows nothing about women other than how to *please* them. The boy grew up in my care, and I was probably not as strict as I should have been."

"I don't really care. Wait, just how old are you?" I blurted out of complete curiosity.

"I knew you'd ask at some time." Ari smiled.

"You feel awfully wise and, not to be rude, but old seems the right term," I said as we walked together.

"I'm old enough to have seen all your ancestors," she simply said before I spotted Mikhail and... What's his name again? Oh, right. Scar, the scary one, was waiting for her. Ari nodded in their direction before facing me.

"Don't let it bother you, Maddox has a book about me on his shelf. A sort of history book written by a close friend of mine. Read it for fun if you want. Feel free to ask me any questions you have. It's inevitable for you to find out, anyways," she said, but I felt a quick pang of heat hit the crook of my neck that distracted me from asking any questions I had at the moment.

"Uh-huh. What exactly did you do to me just now?" I mumbled, and Ari simply smiled at me, not answering my question.

"Good night, Elair."

"Night," I said just as Ari walked over to the two men and I walked away, rubbing my neck, on the way to face the damned Alpha I was stuck with.

*Yay, me.*

# Chapter Thirteen

Things were weird between Maddox and I. Maddox had decided to play the Silent Treatment on me, and I had decided to show him that I did not give a single fuck.

Funny, right?

Just two days ago, we were making out in the lake leaving hickeys all around our bodies and now?

We're about as pissed off as feral rats... if that was possible. I'm not good at comparisons.

So I have devised this amazing plan to go out with Winter tonight. Hopefully, unnoticed and long enough for Jasper and Maddox to worry. Well, Winter actually had errands to do, so Jasper probably wouldn't be all that worried. But me?

I have a club to hit that will hopefully get Maddox to come to my 'rescue.'

Where did this idea come from? It was from Celine, my younger sister. Where else?

"I'm having boy problems," I whispered into my phone as I circled Maddox's office.

Maddox was out training the pack while I decided to be the angry mate and stayed in for the day doing nothing but yoga poses.

"What?" Celine gasped, and I rolled my eyes.

"Yes, Celine, I have guy issues. Relax."

"OMG! So like, is it because you guys have bad sex or is it becau—"

"I'm not going to discuss sex with my younger sister until she's legal. Thanks," I said, and I knew Celine's rolling her eyes as well.

"She should make him jealous!" a voice in the background yelled. It was my other sister, Allie, who, by the way, is only fifteen.

"Excuse me?" I asked, and I heard the phone fumble around before Celine scolded Allie.

"Stop! This is my phone, Allie. Bug off," Celine said, and I chuckled at the sound of their voices.

"But you know I'm right! Elair's pretty, what's the big deal? There are lots of other guys out there! Bigger fish!" Allie shouted, and Celine hushed her.

"Shut up!" Celine said in a hushed tone.

"She does have a point..." I trailed off, and I heard Celine's sigh.

*"True, but you have to be hot as in on point hot... and I mean, I'm-totally-angry-at-you-watch-me-grind-someone-else hot."*

*"Ew, that's a definite no. Grinding is a most definite no. Ugh, just thinking about it makes me cringe," I said, and Celine groaned.*

*"You are the most uptight twenty-two-year-old ever. Even Taylor Swift is less uptight than you."*

*"You don't actually know her!" Allie yelled, and Celine shushed Allie again.*

*"She's a superstar! You don't even know her!" Celine responded, and I ignored their quarreling.*

*"Woo, I can totally pull this off. Angry so-called sexy Elair. Okay." I pep-talked myself.*

*"Uh-huh. Which actually happens often. Have you seen how stiff guys are when you train them in that neon sports bra I made you wear last summer? God. You should have seen Greg's—"*

*"No, I am not talking to you about adolescent boners, either," I told Celine, and I could practically hear Allie scream her pleas of disgust.*

*"Kill me," Celine said. "How the hell do you play perfect older sister all the time? This is impossible!" Celine told me, and I laughed.*

*"How do you play preppy cheerleader? I can never understand," I said with a sigh.*

*"Whatever. We practically look the same, but anyways, just head on over to the bar and drink your ass off enough to get him to do the you-know-what."*

*"Okay, I'm not trying to get him in the mood to fuck. I'm trying to get him to talk to me again."*

*"Same shit," Allie shouted in the background, and I rolled my eyes.*

*"Fine. Whatever. Thanks for the advice," I said.*

*"Uh-huh, anytime, Sis!" Celine said before I hang up.*

So, that was that. But... I didn't want to have to go all inappropriate again since I've pulled that trick off twice. I needed something... innocent but not too much.

I just pulled on a decent looking quarter sleeve body hugging dress that ended only an inch away from my ass, but hey, that's what thongs are for. I pulled on some cute nude heels and applied a fairly thin layer of clear gloss. Less was definitely more tonight.

I sighed as I looked at my reflection. If I raised my hands up, my ass would be on total display. I was going to avoid that action at all costs. I checked the time and pulled the dress down a bit, I needed a coat to cover this up...

a long ass coat.

My heels clicked as I went out of the bathroom, only to have the door opened and have Maddox walk in on my club-ready outfit. I masked my surprise with a simple roll of my eyes before making my way to the closet and opening it up. I made as little movements as possible to reach for a coat.

I was not going to spoil tonight with—

"Where are you going?" Maddox asked, interrupting my thoughts, the low growl in his voice resonated throughout the room.

"None of your business, Alpha," I said without looking at him. I found a long enough coat... but it was placed too fucking high up for me to grab without displaying my ass too fucking soon.

"It is when my beta's mate accompanies you," he said, and I rolled my eyes.

"I'm going to hell, care to join me?" I asked sarcastically to piss him off and hopefully get him to stop questioning me. Moments pass with silence, and I suddenly felt the urge to squirm as I finger through the material of my coat.

All of a sudden, I felt a radiating heat from behind me, and I knew it was Maddox. *No... not gonna give in. You need to give him hell tonight, Elair. HELL. H-E-L-L.*

"You're doing this on purpose," Maddox whispered lowly into my ear.

"Oh, hell no!" I said as I whirled around, but Maddox growled and pinned my hands up above me on the nearby wall. My goddamned dress hiked way too high, and guess what was on display?

*Oh, right. That cute nude thong I pulled on. Great.*

Maddox growled, and his eyes were ablaze as his gaze traveled down.

"You're basically asking me to mark you right now," Maddox said as his eyes turned a dark color.

"Excuse—" Before I could even start, Maddox crashed his lips onto mine, and one of his hands trailed down the dress. I squirmed until he used his hand to feel the skin around my neck. I gasped as a warm sensation spread from it, and I felt Maddox smirk against the kiss.

"Helari's handiwork," Maddox muttered, and I raised an eyebrow. Before I could question him, Maddox lowered his head and licked the spot on my neck, and I mewled.

I actually MEWLED.

"Stop," I said in a strained voice, but Maddox didn't listen. He continued to lick and suck that sweet spot on my body.

"I will wait for you," Maddox said against my skin while his other hand held my hip in place as I squirmed against him. "Always." My right hand was on his back and the other on his head, grabbing his thick raven locks.

"Stop," I said in a whisper, but as Maddox lightly nipped on my skin, I suppressed a heavy moan that made me cover my mouth in embarrassment. "Shit," I cursed, and Maddox chuckled.

"Don't worry, I won't mark you," Maddox said, and I felt something weird.

Weird because I felt my shoulders slump, and I guessed Maddox could tell because he breathed in my scent and pressed against me harder.

"Did you want me to mark you?" Maddox said in a low growl that strangely sounded seductive for once. I didn't answer as Maddox licked the spot, and his left hand traveled down to the end of my dress.

His right leg pushed my legs apart, and he pushes his knee against my groin. I moaned at the friction between us, and Maddox used his left hand to lift the material. Maddox sucked on the skin on my neck, and I gasped as he held my squirming figure in place.

"Damn it," I muttered in a soft, hushed voice. Maddox groaned as he continued to suck on the delicate skin on my neck, leaving me in a mess of sensations.

Maddox pulled away in an instant and looked at me and my disheveled figure. My dress was stretched, revealing too much of my neck, and the skirt barely hid me now that I was weak-kneed. Maddox touched my neck, and I shivered at the contact.

"Looks like Ari finally cleared a spot for me," Maddox said, and I didn't question it. I felt like I'd been promised some awesome candy that has been taken away from me.

I growled lowly at him, and Maddox smirked. Before he could say anything stupid, I grabbed the back of his head and dragged him to me.

"Don't you ever leave me hanging," I said before I brought him down against me and crashed my lips to his.

A battle for dominance began between the two of us, and the room was filled with nothing but moan after moan. To any outsider, we would only look like we were kissing, but we were fighting out our frustrations. I touched Maddox's chest as we molded our lips together, and Maddox, in turn, pulled at my hair. Our battle eventually led us to the bed. I straddled him for a total of five seconds before Maddox spun us around. Maddox kissed me briefly before he moved onto the spot on my neck.

Frustrated with the cloth of my dress, Maddox, like the wolf he was, tore the dress and kissed my neck. I moaned as Maddox tilted my head up for another kiss before going back at it.

"You have no idea... how hard... this is..." Maddox breathlessly said, and I pulled him to me.

"I think I do," I said as I rubbed my left leg against his groin. I smirked as Maddox let out a strangled groan and pulled him down for another kiss.

My body was a mind-boggling mess, and for once, I was able to push my damned brain away long enough for me to enjoy this sensation of pure lust.

Just as Maddox was about to switch our positions over once more, a knock at the door sent us crashing back into reality.

"Alpha Cross? Is Elair ready?" Winter's voice awkwardly asked. Maddox looks to me, and I looked at our position.

Maddox was on all fours on the bed, trapping me underneath him. My hair was a mess, my dress was torn at the top, partially revealing the cutesy matching nude bra I had on, and my skirt was pushed up enough for anyone to see half of my assets.

"She's just changed her mind. She says she won't be going," Maddox replied calmly. I raised an eyebrow at him, but instead of growling at me, Maddox swooped down, cupped the back of my head, and planted a deep and lingering kiss on my lips.

"Oh... Well, I'll see her tomorrow instead. Thanks, Alpha," Winter said from behind the door, and Maddox didn't reply as we heard her footsteps fade away.

"Does this mean we're good?" I asked when I was certain that Winter was gone. Maddox looked at me and sighed before lifting me off and placing me in his lap.

I was straddling him, and he was seated leaning his back against the leather headboard. Maddox tucked a hair of mine behind my ear and pressed our foreheads together.

"I'm trying to be patient," Maddox told me. "But I don't want you to fear a damned thing. I can't get rid of your fears unless you try," he said, and I bit my bottom lip. Maddox suddenly growled, and I released.

"I'll try," I said, and Maddox picked up my right hand and kissed every knuckle before using his free hand to bring me down to his level.

He took a deep breath as we stared centimeters apart from each other with our eyes blazing at each other's intense gazes.

"Good," Maddox said before bringing me back down to him again.

# Chapter Fourteen

Since waking up without Maddox has lately become a regular thing, I wasn't surprised when he left me with just a tray of food by my side and a little note telling me he was in the conference room to finish off the plans for the attack. There was only this day left after all.

We strike tomorrow.

Feeling too lazy to see him, I got up and stripped out of my ripped white dress and pulled on some white workout leggings and a gray sports bra. I work slowly into a few yoga positions. Funnily enough, as I was doing my little handstands and crow positions, I didn't feel calm. I felt strangely exhilarated... like I had more to look forward to despite the absence of any real plans for the day. I groaned as I leaned against the wall to perform a backbend and touch my toes. I heard the sound of some long unmoved bones click and crack with the action. I held my position and sighed in relief when the door opened, revealing Maddox wearing a pale blue button down with a pair of ripped jeans.

"Yoga?" Maddox asked as I stretched out of my position and back on balancing myself on my own two feet.

"Why not?" I asked as I walked over to the bed and picked one of the strawberries on the tray, placing it into my mouth.

"Ari is coming. You'll be in pain for at least a few days. Are you absolutely sure you want to go through with the unlock?" Maddox asked me, and I sighed as he walked over and kneeled in front of me.

"I'm sure I'll be fine. We were supposed to do it last night," I said reassuringly.

"We had other plans," Maddox said with a contented sigh. "You don't have to go through with it." He reached for my cheek.

"I want to go through it, Maddox. This goes beyond the bond I've lost," I muttered, and Maddox shook his head.

"Then let's get this over with. Ari's waiting for us downstairs."

Wearing a plain black shift dress, I made my way downstairs to meet Ari. Maddox and I made our way to a room I had yet to see, and I was surprised to see that it was an all-black room that contrasted greatly with the usual wooden theme of Maddox's cabin-styled pack house. There were windows on the side, but the heavy-looking velvet curtains got rid of any light that trespassed. The only real source of light was a large spotlight at the center of the room. Below it was a rounded slab of pure white marble that reminded me of a few gruesome images in my head.

"What is that?" I asked, and I watched Ari walk towards me. She was dressed in a plain white dress and had a little black dagger in her hands.

"It's necessary. Mikhail told you that the whole ritual thing is similar to the etching process, right?" Ari asked, and I shrugged.

"Something like that," I muttered. Maddox squeezed my hand softly, and I sighed. "Let's just get this over with."

Ari nodded and motioned to the round slab of marble. I walked over to it and laid down at its center. I trailed my fingers around it and felt the intricate carvings. It was like a giant rounded maze below me. Maddox stood to my right and squeezed my hand harder before moving aside. Ari appeared at my side and sighed as she hovered a hand above my eyes. I looked straight up and focused on a single light.

"Spread your hands to your sides. If you can touch the edge of the slab, then do so," Ari said, and I nodded as I did as she said.

"I will have to press the blade down on both your arms," Ari said, and I smirked before nodding. "If anything becomes too painful, say it at once."

I felt a quick sharp pain in my right wrist followed by another on my left. I looked to my left and found that Ari's other usual servant, Scar, was doing the same thing. He had an expressionless face as he drew blood from my arm. The blades weren't pulled out until a sufficient amount of blood dripped from them and landed on the slab, drawing lines of blood on my arms.

After the blood has been drawn, I stared up into the light and waited. The strong smell of moonflowers hit my nose, and a cold sensation traveled throughout my body.

"I'll start the unlock now. Look up, Elair, and nowhere else," Ari said, and I nodded as I stared at the orb of light above me.

Helari began to chant something in a language I couldn't fathom, and I watched as the light above turned into a blur. I felt a burning sensation run down through my arms, and I resisted the urge to look at them.

"Focus on the light, Elair," Ari's voice said, and I bit my bottom lip as I forced my arms to stay still.

I felt something bind them to the table, and within moments, something knocked my breath out of my lungs. I felt myself strain against the new binds on my hands, and my chest was lifted off the slab. My breath hitched in my throat, and I felt a large surge of pain spread from my chest down to every nerve on my body. A warm fluid fell from my nose, and my breath came out in small pants.

My vision fell into nothing but white light.

*"She must be absolutely perfect,"* a powerful voice said from behind me. *I heard the familiar sound of Aunt Eleanor's heels clicking on the floor.*

*"Oh, but she will be. So young and innocent... Her very first session will be wonderful,"* her voice said.

*"Aunt Eleanor... I'm scared..." I said in a quivering voice, and I heard her chuckle softly. "I... I can't see anything!"*

*"You will be fine, Elair. Different, refined... absolutely perfect."*

*"I wanna go home!" I cried out.*

*"Don't be selfish, Elair. You will be part of something greater than Blood Moon."*

*"She's rejecting the change, Madame Eleanor."*

*"She's adapting. Give her time," Aunt Eleanor's voice said.*

*"Last time, your daughter failed to adapt. What if sh—"*

*"Failure does not exist in my family. Camille has always been too weak. Now, get out. My darling Elair will be the perfect offering for Faustus," my aunt said.*

*"It's been years, Eleanor. She's perfectly ready," another voice said from behind me.*

*"Her final session is today. Do not fail me, my darling," Eleanor said.*

*"When have I ever?" I asked her, but I couldn't see a damned thing with the lights blaring in my face.*

*"Faustus, this is my niece, Elair," Eleanor said, and I walked towards a figure whose back was turned towards me.*

*Faustus turned around and revealed a surprising appearance. He was young. He looked no older than twenty years old, but the glow in his eyes revealed a danger to him. He wore a plain white suit with brown leather shoes, and his platinum blond hair was neatly combed. He offered his hand to me, and I simply stared at it.*

*"Don't be afraid. I've overseen your training since you've arrived," he said, his voice cheerful and welcoming. I looked at Aunt Eleanor, and she nodded as I walked over to him and took his hand.*

*"Marvelous work, Eleanor. How effective is she?" Faustus asked.*

*"Very," I interjected as I put my hands behind my back, the all black leather suit I was wearing squeaking with my movements.*

*"Well. I'd love to see you prove it," Faustus said as he walked over to me and tucked my loose hair behind my ear. He was my height, but his icy blue eyes were fierce and intimidating. "You will be ready soon. The squadron will be a fit place for you until I call."*

*"Yes, sir," I responded.*

*"Faustus will be fine. After all, you have yet to know your true role in my organization, but we will meet again under better circumstances," Faustus said before my vision turned into a dark haze.*

"She's burning up. Scar, slice the restraints. Mikhail, grab the stake. Maddox, I need you to hold her in place. Move, fast," Ari barked out orders, and I felt my bones clicking around.

A ripping sound echoed all around me, and I heard the sound of whispers practically scream into my ears.

*Perfect.   Killer. Murderer. Broken. Lost.   Cursed. Chosen.*

The words were repeated over and over, and I felt a sharp pain strike down my back. The restraints on my hands were removed, and I immediately bent over, but I still saw nothing but white.

My vision cleared slightly to reveal the stone slab and my legs covered in blood. The slab and its intricate lines were covered in the blood staining my body. I screamed in agony as a sharp pain entered the back of my neck, but instead of a scream, I heard a terrifying growl. It sounded nothing like a wolf. It was definitely not normal.

I felt someone hold my shoulders, and I immediately turned my head and snapped my mouth in an attempt to bite whoever was holding me. My mouth caught nothing but air, and I growled loudly.

"Mikhail, now!" Ari shouted, and I felt a strong hit at the back of my neck.

I screamed and heard the sounds of the whispers grow louder and louder. Something pierced through my neck, and I felt a cooling feeling spread down my spine. I welcomed the sensation, and my body relaxed. My arms and legs felt soaked in a warm liquid that I knew wasn't something I wanted to open my eyes to.

But I heard the muffled sound of Maddox's voice, and when I blinked my eyes, I found that he was right in front of me, holding my face in his hands.

"Don't look anywhere other than my eyes," Maddox told me, and I suddenly felt faint.

"Aunt Eleanor..." I heard myself say in a hoarse voice. "She said a name..." I continued.

"What name?" Ari asked, and I turned my head towards her. Ari's hands were covered in blood, and her eyes were glowing with a striking blue and yellow hue.

"F-Faustus," I said, recalling my trance.

"Helari," Scar said, his voice a hell lot lower than I thought it was.

My shock momentarily distracted me from the bone-shattering pain I felt throughout my body, and I watched as Scar loosened his tie. I also noticed Mikhail and the smirk on his face.

"My oh my... so the rat has returned," Mikhail said, and Scar grunted.

"We will discuss him later. Right now, I need you both cleaned up and for you two to clean this mess. Maddox, wrap Elair with this." I felt a cloth being wrapped around my body. "Take Elair and have her go up to rest. I'll be with her in a moment. The stake I've embedded into her neck will regulate her, and her body will eventually absorb it."

"Stake?" I asked and was surprised by how weak it sounded.

"Later," Maddox said. My vision blurred, and I felt my weight being gently lifted off the slab.

"What... about... my... blood?" I said.

"I'll have someone clean it. Rest." Maddox said, and everything else faded into a hazy memory.

# Chapter Fifteen

*I was making a run for it in the woods. The leather jacket of my combat outfit hit a few branches as I sprinted off. I was wearing our classic outfit of a crimson leather jacket over an all black attire. My heavy combat boots crunched with every step I took in the woods as I ran my routine. Guns at the ready, I circled the perimeter.*

*"You've progressed very well," a familiar voice said from behind me. I turned, ready to fire, before sighing.*

*"Who—"*

*"You know who I am, but, of course, spells can get a bit tricky. Rememorari," the voice said, and I blinked my eyelids.*

*"Faustus," I simply said.*

*"I'm glad the spells still work," he said with a smirk, and I arched a brow.*

*"What spell?" I asked him, and he sighed before tucking a strand of hair behind my ear.*

*"My darling, Elair... Ari has hell to pay, and you will be perfect. Farvel," he said, and I felt every part of my body turn frigid. "The attack Maddox intends to proceed with tonight... I want you to do exactly as I say..."*

I woke with a start and felt the breath get knocked out of my lungs. The back of my neck was sore, and I gingerly lifted myself off the bed. I was in Maddox's bedroom, and I sighed in relief when I found that it was only night. Meaning, I still had time to train tomorrow morning before the attack. The only surprise was that I was dressed in a really big gray sweater that reeks of a certain Alpha.

"You alright?" Maddox asked from behind me. I turned and found that he had just showered. His hair was damp, and he got a fitted silvery gray tank top and a pair of black cargo pants on.

"How long was I out for?" I asked him, and Maddox sighed before walking around to the bedside table.

"Ten hours... and twenty-seven minutes," Maddox said.

"Uh-huh..." I muttered as I rubbed my neck.

"Does it hurt?" Maddox asked, and I shook my head.

"Just irks me. Something's there," I said, knowing how ridiculous I sounded.

"Ari placed a regulator of some sort into your neck. You won't feel it, but it's hooked into your system," Maddox said as he pulled a tray off of the bedside table and places it beside me. He took off the silver covers on the three plates, and I practically drooled at the sight and array of food.

There was a bowl of cream of mushroom soup, a plate of steak and vegetables, and a small bowl of mashed potatoes. On a smaller plate was a little mini cake that looked like a chocolate mousse.

"Was there an event?" I asked, and Maddox chuckled.

"It's tradition. The night before an attack, we have a little feast. Just in case people don't come back," Maddox said as he played with a loose lock of my hair.

"Huh, what's your average casualty?" I asked.

"Zero. Consider Helari a great perk in times like this," he told me, and I rolled my eyes as I picked up my spoon to eat the soup. Why even celebrate if you expect zero casualties? But it wasn't illogical, I guess.

"Have you eaten?" I asked, and Maddox shrugged.

"I had a meeting with the final council. I don't want anything to go wrong. You'll be leading one of the sectors with Iain. I'm not taking any chances," Maddox said, and I nodded my head.

"Okay, I'm gonna let that pass tonight since I have a mind-bending headache going on right now, and I can't negotiate otherwise," I said as I put my spoon up towards Maddox. He raised an eyebrow at me, and I rolled my eyes. "Eat, you bastard," I said. I watched as he kept his eyes on me and took the spoonful of soup into his mouth. I tilted the spoon and pulled it away before dipping it back into my bowl.

"You're being nice tonight," Maddox said.

"Don't take it for granted," I said, cocking my head to the side.

"I'm glad you feel fine," he chuckled before he cupped my cheek. I stared at him, probably because I felt a little spark with his touch.

"I don't understand how I still don't feel much different," I admitted, despite the tiny spark I felt. It just wasn't enough, and Maddox sighed.

"Don't worry about it," Maddox said as he rubbed my cheek with his thumb. "Keep eating, I'll have someone bring me food later. I have a few documents to send in for the night," he said before lifting himself off the bed.

"Could you grab me some history book about Helari?" I asked, and Maddox raised his eyebrow. "She told me about it the day we had our little anger episode," I added. Maddox nodded his head before disappearing into his office and re-appearing with a little leather book that has aged so much that it looked like it had been through hell and back.

"This thing is centuries old. Helari hasn't renewed the preservation spell she normally casts on it so be careful with this one," Maddox said as he handed it to me. He ran a hand through my hair and tilted my head upwards. "Helari will be here tomorrow morning. She waited on you for a bit to make sure the regulator was fine," Maddox told me, and I nodded my head.

Maddox paused for a few seconds, and his gaze dropped to my lips before he looked into my eyes again. I rolled my eyes and grabbed the back of his head.

"Quit hesitating and kiss me," I muttered before pulling him down to me for a deep kiss. Maddox groaned and pulled me in even deeper.

I could feel every worry and frustration he's had since the moment the *unlock* began. Maddox put his knees on the bed and continued to kiss me as he laid me down gently. I smirked when he pushed the tray of food away just far enough to give us space. I ran my left hand through his damp hair, and he groaned as I trailed my right hand down his back and pulled him closer. I felt a rush pulse through me as Maddox tilted my head up further, baring my neck to him. Maddox trailed his mouth away from mine and moved down my jaw to my neck.

"Maddox..." I moaned, and he set his lips onto the sensitive part on my neck. Maddox worked gently, sucking and nipping whilst avoiding breaking skin, and I felt the muscles on his back strain from the effort.

I wrapped my legs around his hips, and he groaned as I trailed my arms all around his back. Maddox growled seductively into my ear, and I felt his canines elongate and trace the spot where my mark would be.

"We... have... to stop," Maddox said in a strained voice, and I laughed breathlessly as I pulled my hands away from his back and towards his face. I cupped his face in my hands and pulled him up to my own. His eyes were dark and full of lust.

His teeth are still partially elongated, and I felt an impulse to do something I would have never done a few weeks ago. I pulled him down to me and did the weirdest thing. I licked his canines and smirked as I felt the growl vibrate through his lips.

"Later," I said in a soft whisper, and I felt Maddox smirk against my lips as well. He placed a quick yet deep kiss on my lips before pressing his forehead against mine.

"Tomorrow," he said before kissing my forehead and pulling away from me.

I felt a bit of disappointment as he left me, but he turned his head and smirked at me before heading back to his office. I grinned to myself and suppressed a giggle before realizing what was going on. I did a double-take and bit my bottom lip.

*Damn... this guy's got me good.*

# Chapter Sixteen

"Are you feeling alright?" Ari asked me as I undid the braid in my hair. We were currently in the living room area, and I had just come back from an early morning training session.

"I'm feeling great. Still not used to the slight... protrusion at the back of my neck, but I'm good," I said before sitting down on a little wooden stool. Ari released a soft laugh before brushing my hair away with her leather-gloved fingers.

"Great. It seems to be doing fine, that's a relief," Ari said with a sigh before softly muttering a word that I couldn't fathom. The back of my neck suddenly felt cool, and it spread throughout my body.

"What was that?" I asked as the sensation died down.

"It's a restoration spell. I have to do it every once in a while until the *scal* disappears off your body."

"What the hell's a *scal*? And... it's visible? What does it look like right now?" I asked, and Ari smirked before giving her hand out to me.

"Phone," she said, and I quickly pulled out my phone from my pants and handed it to her. With a quick click, Ari handed back my phone, and I stared at it. "That's the *scal*. It's where the regulator stays. Well, regulator sounds a bit terrifying, it's called a *sere*. I use it most of the time to, well, regulate an abnormality."

"Abnormality, huh," I said as I stared at the picture.

It was like an encrusted silver piece that was stuck to the back of my neck. It was tiny, but it had a little hole in it. As I was about to ask a question, Ari pulled out a thin almost glass-like needle out of a small leather box.

"And that is...?"

"The *sere*. Your body absorbed the one I put in last night. It's like medicine. The first nights will be a bit of a hassle since the *scal* will absorb it overnight, but with time, it'll adjust, and you can put one in every few months or so until it disappears. Well, let's hope it'll only be there for little more than a few days."

"So... this is important?" I asked, and Ari nodded her head just as I heard the sound of the *sere* sliding into the weird thing at the nape of my neck. It sounded like a quick crystal sound, and I heard the little thing lock into place.

"Uh-huh. I can get rid of any magical mumbo-jumbo the Sentinels left on you," Ari said, and I laughed.

"Never thought someone known as an ancient power would ever say the words mumbo-jumbo," I said, and Ari laughed at me this time.

"I have to adapt too, you know?" Ari said. "Have you been feeling something... *more* now with you-know-who?"

"I have... impulses. More so than before," I said, and Ari smiled proudly at me.

"Good. Hopefully, we can get that sorted by the next full moon."

"Uh-huh. Let's just hope we get the whole battle plan sorted... right now." I said, and Ari laughed before nodding her head.

"Trevor, I need you to pay attention to the borders. Leave any children to Scar. He'll be with you on that front. Everyone else is open prey," Jasper shouted as Maddox stood firmly in front of everyone. The sun was beginning to set, and everyone seemed to be high with tension.

Each sector was separated into ten lines of what appears to be fifty. This made a total headcount of five hundred plus the leaders: Maddox, Jasper, Iain, Trevor, and six others. There were four women amongst us, and I've learned them to be Jillian, Rina, Loraine, and Naomi.    All of them have had a quick word with me. Jillian was the first to speak up, and I did apologize for the whole shooting thing that went down when we first met. So there's that. Rina and Loraine were mates, and the two of them were some of the nicest people I've met.

Naomi was more standoffish although Maddox had told me that she liked me. I have no idea how I'm supposed to be able to tell, but she did offer me a bottle of water, and Jillian told me that was the most I could hope for.

"Mikhail will be at the front with Jasper. You are instructed to kill on sight. Women or children that surrender are Mikhail's to handle," Maddox shouted, and I watched as Helari emerge behind us.

She was wearing a plain white dress that flowed to her knees, but she was barefoot. Her long black hair was down, and her eyes were aglow.

"If anyone encounters the Sentinels, you'll know them by the aura they emit. Kill them immediately. Children or women... the Sentinels have stripped them of their humanity already. Spare them, and it's *you* who will die," Helari said in a cold and harsh tone. "There's a danger of their leader being there. If you should encounter him, inform Maddox immediately. I will be with Maddox's sector. We will strike the pack house for any clues on the Sentinels' whereabouts."

"The Sentinels are highly dangerous. If they overpower you, avoid direct conflict. Dodge them, running will get you killed," Maddox said. "My mate will join us tonight and will accompany Iain's sector. They will attack from the back. The Sentinels will most likely retaliate through there. Stay in focus and do not lose sight of your sector," Maddox added with finality, and I watched as everyone solemnly nodded their heads.

"Tonight! We dance with death!" Jasper shouted, and Maddox smirked as everyone cheered on.

Maddox growled loudly, and everyone followed, including us leaders. The sounds of bones cracking, cloth ripping, and shifting could be heard from the two sectors at the front. They were heading straight into the shift. Meanwhile, the rest of us would strike from the back.

"Here we go..." Loraine whispered with a smile as she and Rina shifted to join their sectors.

Maddox nodded in my direction before he shifted into his brilliant black wolf, and his sector transformed as well. Helari paused, and with her right hand held up, a bunch of shadows formed at her feet and seemed to swallow the remaining sectors.

"*Oviere,*" she muttered before the darkness swallowed all of us.

Everyone seemed to disappear, and I felt a rush of cold air hit me. With one sudden bat of my eyelids, I found myself with my sector in unfamiliar territory. Iain walked around, and I stood parallel to him. He was issuing commands via mind-link, and I watched as our sector ran out and spread themselves all around our designated area.

"I can't mind link you so keep on guard," Iain told me, and I nodded my head before I pulled my guns out of their holsters.

A loud howling sound informed me that we've begun, and I felt my every senses heighten. The sound of paws hitting the ground towards us was loud and clear, and I smirked as I prepared my aim. Iain growled loudly, shifted, and ran forward. In a blink of an eye, another wolf crashed into him, and I watched as one prepared to go towards me.

"Bad choice," I muttered before shooting it right in between the eyes.

A growl directly behind me had me swinging around with a kick to the floor. I tripped a big gray wolf down, pointed my gun at his neck, and shoot him twice before turning back to where I was shooting down another wolf that was coming for Iain.

A loud sound of bone breaking hit my ears, and I watched as Iain finished off the first wolf and moved on to attacking the next. There are now growls and snapping sounds coming from all directions, and I ran forward. The sound of dead leaves snapping beneath my heavy combat boots attracted the attention of several wolves. Iain and I had formed a strategy of me luring the wolves whilst our sector closed in on them.

I counted the number of pants I heard from behind me before shouting.

"Five! On your left!" I shouted, and I heard the sounds of my sector's running paws close in. I stopped running, causing my boots to skid and drag on the slippery ground before I turned and pointed my gun at the wolf in front.

I shoot twice, out of habit, and he dodged, but my bullet managed to hit his left paw. I watched as he stumbled but landed on his four legs, snarling at me. I smiled at him before aiming straight in between his eyes, shooting just as he was ready to pounce. I dodged his body as he fell dead behind me on the forest floor. The rest of my sector was hard at work, and I made a run back to where Iain was, only to find three wolves cornering him.

"Hey! Need help?" I shouted, and I heard Iain bark at me before I took aim and shot one of the three wolves, grabbing their attention.

Iain seized the opportunity, and I watched as his brown mass of fur hurled itself towards one wolf, biting it in the neck and snapping it almost as fast as he bit the poor thing. The wolf I shot wasn't dead yet, so I aimed at its neck and shot it three times more before aiming at the final wolf. Iain glanced at me quickly before pouncing on its back and biting the nape of its neck, pulling it back. With the wolf's neck bared to me, I didn't hesitate as I pulled the trigger once.

I sighed as our sector reformed, and Iain barked at me twice, wagging his tail. I grinned in response to him before reloading my guns and shoving the empty magazines at the back of my holster belt. Guns freshly loaded, Iain nodded his head at me, and I watched as the sector moved forward.

It looked like Maddox just called us in.

Iain bowed his head towards me, and I climbed on his back. He was large enough to carry me, and I didn't bother holding onto his fur as we followed our sector through the woods. Iain barked two times on both sides, and two other wolves came to our side. The sounds of whimpers, howls, and snaps were all around us, and when the pack house came into view, the dead bodies that littered the forest floor no longer came to us as a shock.

Their pack house was still brightly lit, a modernist styled stone cabin that seemed to be made of three large floors. I watched as the shadows of the battle going on revealed the horror of what was inside that house. There were blood-stained curtains and bodies strewn aside. I looked away from the image as I hopped off Iain's back and watched as our sector spread out once more, preparing to kill anyone that was running away. The smell of blood was strong and the distant sound of bones snapping and people screaming were under way.

I heard the sound of a terrified scream, and I watched as a little girl, only about the age of five, runs out of the pack house. Before any of us can act, the wind lifts up all the leaves off of the plain forest floor that surrounded the pack house. Out from the pack house walked Helari who remained barefooted as she walked towards the little girl.

"*Hu petaris*. Come to me," I heard Helari said. Although she spoke two sentences, they almost seemed to have been said at the same time, and the girl, in all her fright, fell to the ground and crawled backward away from Helari's small figure. "*Wiviadere*. Listen," Helari muttered, and in an instant, the girl suddenly froze.

It was as if the little girl was caught in a trance. I watched as the girl slowly and calmly stood up and approached Helari. Helari held her hand out, and the girl took it.

"*Farvel,*" Helari said, and I felt a sudden heat strike the nape of my neck. Helari glanced at me but quickly returned her focus to the little girl. "*Fenian lyger*. Stop, little girl," Helari said to the girl, and I felt the little spark of heat stop.

"*Eovre frei, lyger. Relesereo...* You have been freed," Helari said, and all of a sudden, the girl fell limp into Helari's arms.

Helari sighed, and with one move of her hand, Mikhail was by her side. He took the girl from Helari and instantly disappeared out of sight. Helari then looked at me and beckoned me to come to her. I did as she willed, and she sighed once more.

"That bastard has always known how to get on my nerves," she muttered, and I raised my eyebrows. "It's Faustus. The bastard screwed with the minds of children and the wolves we killed tonight. It's unbelievable... the amount of damage done to their minds. Their poor souls were almost ripped right from their bodies," Helari said with a sad look in her eyes.

"Faustus..." I muttered, trying to think about what and who he was.

"Unfortunately, he wipes memories away from those he encounters, too. I have no doubt he's the one behind the disappearance of your mate bond. I feel very worried, Elair," Helari said, and I looked at her as she stared straight into my eyes. "*Vedel hæl.*"

"What?" I asked, and Helari shook her head.

"These happenings are some very bad omens. Stay close to me, Elair. It seems Faustus is still here," Helari said, and I nodded my head.

"Where's Maddox?" I asked, and Helari smirked at me.

"In the bloodbath. He can be a bit... gruesome." I paused before I heard the sound of paws running our way.

I pointed my gun quickly at two of the sources and spotted the shadows of five wolves hurling at us. I aimed and shot two wolves at the same time, hearing soft whimpers before I shot them down. Helari used one swipe of her hand across the thin air, and I heard the bodies of the wolves hit hard against the trees of the large forest.

"Handy," I muttered, and I heard Helari chuckle.

"We got everyone," Iain said after getting dressed in a normal shirt and jeans. I nodded my head.

"Good to hear," a familiar voice said from behind me just as I pulled my guns back into their holsters. I felt the warmth of Maddox's hands wrap around my waist and inhale the scent of my hair.

"You reek of blood, Maddox," I said, slapping his hands away. He laughed, the action causing his chest to vibrate against my back. I turned around and faced him, finding his forehead bleeding slightly. "Where'd you get that from?" I asked as I picked up a towel I tucked into my pockets to wipe the blood away.

"It's not mine," Maddox said with a shrug, and I rolled my eyes as I wiped his sweat-covered face. I grimaced as Maddox shook his head, causing his sweat to go flying everywhere.

"Okay, ew," I said as I finished wiping his face. Maddox chuckled before gently touching my face with his left hand.

"I'm glad you're okay," Maddox said.

"Why wouldn't I be?" I asked, and Maddox rolled his eyes just before we heard Jasper call.

"Hey, Maddox! Come here for a sec!" Jasper yelled. Maddox sighed before kissing my forehead and jogging towards Jasper.

I sighed as well and looked at the pack. A few of us were injured, but it was nothing too bad. There didn't seem to be any casualties, and from what I heard, Helari has already healed half of us. I watched as Jillian and Iain talk to each other in between kisses while Loraine and Rina had a drink together.

Where on earth they found stashes of beer was absolutely beyond me.

The bodies had all been burned. Macabre wanted no trace left other than the letter that Ari left on the pavement as the pack house was set on fire. If you wanted to know how exactly we burned the bodies... take a look at the large mass of fire at the center of this forest.

I felt something cold hit my right arm, and I immediately turned to the source, only to find Naomi, the silent one from earlier, handing me a beer. I nodded my thanks before taking it from her. She nodded before disappearing into a crowd of other wolves celebrating. As I was about to take a drink, a soft whispering sound caught my attention.

"*Hu petaris min silder.* Come to me," I heard. I immediately felt a strong and heavy feeling overpower me.

I turned around and dropped my hands to my sides. The drink in my hand fell slowly to the ground as I walked towards the source of the voice. As I continued walking, I found my vision growing hazy and dark. The wind has started to blow stronger, and my feet stopped in the middle of an empty clearing.

"Faustus," I heard my voice say, and just as I blinked my eyes, I saw a figure standing before me.

"How glorious," the person said. I felt my head being tilted up and found myself gazing into a pair of ice-cold eyes. He studied my eyes before letting go of my head and walking around me.

I felt my body freeze in place.

"You're not ready yet. The damned wolf has yet to mate with you. No trouble, I am patient. *Rememorari*, Elair. Remember, you have a purpose, my dear. *Eovre andet.* Do not fail me," he said before I felt myself nod my head.

"Of course," my voice said, and I saw Faustus smirk before touching the back of my neck where the *scal* was.

"Good, we've caught Helari's dearest attention. *Farvel* for now, my child. You shall remember me again in time," Faustus said before kissing the back of my hand, and in a blink of my eyes, his figure disappeared.

I stared at my hand and watched as dark shadows seemed to penetrate its center. Before I could react, I felt a great pull at my back, and a mind breaking pain hit me. The air was knocked out of my lungs before I landed on the forest floor with a thud.

Muffled voices called me, but my vision completely went hazy, and I fell into a deep and dark slumber.

# Chapter Seventeen

It's been six days since the attack. and six days since I've woken up to Ari placing another *sere* into my neck while Maddox gripped the life out of my hand. Apparently, someone had slammed me against a tree and messed with the *scal* in my neck. I didn't even remember why and how I ended up like that. I sighed as I ate my bowl of Honey Nut Cheerios in front of Maddox's desk. The confusion was killing me.

Maddox glanced up at me from his paperwork, and I raised my eyebrows.

"Any problem?" I asked, and Maddox shook his head.

"It bothers me that you were speaking in Helari's mother tongue while you were knocked out," Maddox said, and I sighed.

"I told you... I barely remember anything. And from what Ari says, I was talking about that Faustus guy again—"

"And the mating ceremony, which is a week from now," Maddox interrupted, and I swallowed a lump in my throat. That had totally slipped my mind.

I have a week until we do the hoo-ha. *Someone, help me.*

"Uh-huh, speaking of which... Can it be postponed?" I asked, batting my eyelashes. The corners of Maddox's mouth slowly turned up into a smug grin.

"Of course not," Maddox said as he stood up and walked over to me. He took my bowl of Cheerios away and placed it on the corner of his desk before swooping down and taking my bottom lip in between his teeth and tugging on it slightly.

He quickly pulled away with a low growl.

"I can't wait to claim what's mine," he said, his gaze burning into mine before he abruptly turned to leave. "Shower," he said, and I rolled my eyes.

"Shower," I mockingly said, scrunching my nose.

"I heard that!" Maddox yelled.

"Yeah, well, let's not forget that you're mine, too!" I shouted before I pursed my lips, grabbed my bowl of Cheerios, and angrily slurped down the milk in my bowl.

I left the bowl on his desk before I made my way to the bedroom and stretched my legs. I was wearing a pair of black leggings with sheer panels along the sides, and I matched it with a yellow sports bra under a loose black tank top that had long cutouts down the sides. I pulled my body into a handstand then slowly lowered my legs so that they now hovered behind my head. I sighed and concentrated on my body movements as I slowly pushed the weight of my body back so that I was now on my stomach. My hands then pushed my upper body up, causing my head and toes to touch.

I sighed in relief before I relaxed my legs and softly let them down on the floor and pushed myself up to a standing position. I stretched my arms, tightened my ponytail, and made my way towards Maddox's desk to clean up my bowl when I heard his phone vibrate on his desk.

"Maddox! Phone!" I yelled, and I heard the shower stop. I looked at the caller ID and gawked at it before picking it up and answering it. "Mother," I greeted.

"Hey, Elair, can you ask Maddox where that boy Iain is? We got here five minutes ago and—"

"And she wasn't supposed to know yet," Maddox said as I felt his wet hands wrap around my waist. He kissed my neck and took the phone from me. I pursed my lips before Maddox winked at me and answered the phone. "Iain said he's only a few minutes away. He's the one with the red shirt on and driving a black Ford Escape."

"Oh, I think we've just found him. I'll see you both later then," my mother said through the phone before she hung up. I glared at Maddox as he turned around to face me.

"What?" Maddox asked, feigning innocence. I folded my arms over my chest.

"Really?" I rhetorically asked, and Maddox chuckled.

"I think you need the help your mom can give you before we consummate our relationship, mate," Maddox said, and I grimaced.

"She will most likely bring at least three of my siblings with her. Which means I have to play babysitter, which means—"

"I'll have an easier time restraining myself until the mating ceremony," Maddox interrupted, and I bit my bottom lip. "Wesley is with her," Maddox added, and I felt my spirits lift.

"Roland is probably with her, too... and Charlie, but hopefully, not Landon. Landon would go crazy over the fact that there's a huge TV in the lounge area."

"Roland, Charlie, and Landon... should I be worried?" Maddox asked, and I rolled my eyes.

"They're the youngest of the litter of Richelieu pups. Roland is two, Charlie is seven, and Landon is twelve. And just so you know, Charlie's short for Charlotte," I said.

"How many of you guys are there?" Maddox asked with a smile.

"Twelve, but I don't even think my parents are considering stopping anytime soon. Which is weird, considering I'm in my twenties. I have a little brother that is literally decades younger than me."

"The bigger, the better, right?" Maddox asked.

"In terms of family then yes." I agreed, thinking about how much fun it was to take care of them— except of course when they fought with each other. That was just plain hell.

"And so while we are on the topic of children, how many do you think you'd have?" Maddox asked, bringing me out of my thoughts.

"Hypothetically speaking, if I have children, I'd want... and do not laugh at me... five or six," I said, feeling a little embarrassed. Maddox laughed, and it was only at that moment that I realized he was only wearing a fucking towel.

"Well then, looks like we've got a lot of work ahead of us," Maddox said humorously, and I chucked a throw pillow towards him. Maddox laughed as he dodged it and took me into his arms so that my back was against his chest.

"Dick," I muttered, and Maddox chuckled as he kissed both sides of my neck.

"You look too delectable in those pants," Maddox whispered as he ran his teeth against my right ear, and I felt a shiver run down my spine.

"And you need to get dressed," I said as I spun around Maddox's hold and pushed him against the bed. "Unless you have plans to make out with me before my mother gets here," I said with a suggestive wink as I straddled him.

"I'd love to, but they'll be here in five minutes, supposing Iain has already picked them up," Maddox said.

"Fine," I said before Maddox pulled me down so that our foreheads were touching.

"Five minutes," Maddox repeated, and I smiled as I pushed him down onto the bed.

"Elair!" Charlie greeted as she hurled herself at me. I laughed as I picked her up and hugged her.

"Elair! Could you help me pick up — nevermind!" my mother yelled, and Iain walked in with four luggage bags in his hands. "Celine, carry your brother for me, will you?"

"Need help?" I asked.

"Not really. Your mom's holding a baby while trying to manage the other two boys who've started running around.

Remind me never to give chocolate to children as a welcome gift. Your sister's here too. She's a fun one," Iain said, and I laughed at him just as I felt a familiar warmth on my back. I turned my head and found Maddox ruffling Charlie's hair.

"Hi!" Charlie greeted happily, and Maddox smiled at her.

"Hey, did you have a fun trip?" Maddox asked, and Charlie, not one to be shy at all, nodded her head enthusiastically. Maddox opened his arms to carry her, and I carefully handed Charlie over to him.

Charlie wore an adorable little baby blue dress with a pair of white leggings on and some matching shoes. No doubt my mother had wanted her to look extra adorable on this trip. Her bright big blue eyes showed her love to everything in the cabin. Particularly because Charlie was born in winter and absolutely loved anything to do with log cabins. We were on vacation in one of my uncles' log cabins when she was born. Not a very pretty story to tell, now that I think about it.

"Are there other kids here?" Charlie asked, and Maddox nodded his head as he carried her into the living room.

"I'll have them come over later," Maddox said, and Charlie celebrated in his arms.

"Is Wesley too little company?" I asked, and Charlie shook her head.

"Wesley's okay, but he doesn't like having tea parties with me. He always eats my cake and then he runs and gets all dirty in the garden." Charlie complained, and I smirked.

"Elair! Elair!" I heard a familiar little voice call me.

"I'll be right back," I told Maddox, and he nodded as he put Charlie down and I quickly made my way back to the foyer.

I spotted Wesley scrambling to get away from my mother who was wiping off the dirt from his shirt. Once she let go of him, he immediately ran towards me. I laughed as I kneeled down low enough for him to give me a hug. My mother smiled as she walked over to me. Her hair was put into an intricate braid that wrapped around half of her head and ended with a ponytail. She smiled warmly at me. I stood up, and my mother wrapped her hands around me.

"We've missed you," my mother said, and I smiled as I hugged her back with Wesley still hugging my legs.

"I missed you too," I said as we let go of each other.

"It's so cold here—" Mother began, breathing in my scent before she did something totally weird. She held my shoulders so that we were an arm's length away as she stared at me with an amused smile.

"Hey! Don't forget about me, damn it!" Celine said as she hopped out of the car with Roland in her arms.

"Of course, not! I'm glad your mate didn't stop you," I told my sister, and she smirked at me.

"Oh, please, Chad can't stop me from visiting you even if he tried," she said as she hugged me as well.

"You absolutely reek of that Alpha. I'm glad I didn't bring Ender... or your father. Goddess knows what those two would do," Mother said with a wide smile, "But I am glad to see you two are getting along."

"I know you are," I said just as I felt Maddox's warmth behind me. He wrapped his arms around my waist, and my mother put a smug look on her face.

"Hey, Alpha!" Wesley greeted as he looked up at us, and Maddox chuckled softly to himself.

"Hey there. You know, Winter's inside with a few kids from the pack. You might wanna head in and have some coffee," Maddox told my mother, and she smiled at him. Celine smirked at me with a raised eyebrow, and I rolled my eyes. The two of them were practically beaming at the fact that Maddox was so close to me.

"That sounds amazing," she said. Just as Maddox took my hand and turned us both around, my mother decided to mind link me.

*Just so you know, Elair, I'm expecting grandchildren soon,* she said, and I felt a nervous shiver run down my spine.

That was definitely not a topic I wanted to bring up with her.

# Chapter Eighteen

My mother helped me make breakfast the day after they had arrived. I sighed contently as I babysat my siblings. Charlie and Wesley were both having fun watching a movie and roleplaying as a dinosaur and a princess in the living room. I was cradling Roland in my arms, who was fast asleep.

"Having fun?" Maddox asked me, and I murmured my answer. "Seems like all Richelieu children are blonde and blue," I chuckled at that before Maddox took a seat beside me, leaning over to look at baby Roland.

"Uh-huh. This one's just like the rest of us," I softly said as I watched Charlie fold her arms over her chest and shout at Wesley who was running around with his arms tucked to his chest. I was guessing he was acting like a T-Rex.

Roland slowly fluttered his eyes open, and his big deep blue eyes immediately captured mine. He looked to me and then to Maddox who smiled widely at him.

"Can I hold him?" Maddox asked, and I nodded as I gently turned and placed Roland in Maddox's arms. Roland was silent and watched Maddox's face before he squirmed in his blanket.

I laughed as Maddox lifted Roland out of the blanket, holding my brother up before laughing as Maddox raised him up and down. Roland laughed and squirmed in Maddox's grip before Maddox placed him close to his face. Maddox nudged his nose with Roland's, and my baby brother giggled with delight. I heard the sound of a camera shutter, and my gaze immediately landed on Celine who was sitting just across us on a lounge chair.

"Oh, Mama is gonna love this picture," Celine chuckled, and I sighed.

"Uh-huh," I muttered before I looked over at Maddox and felt a sudden urge to touch him. Before I even knew what was going on, I had rested my right hand on Maddox's shoulder as I gently touched my baby brother's cheek with my left hand.

An image quickly flashed before my eyes. It was a dark room with a soft wind blowing the curtains aside, and I immediately froze up. I got up abruptly, and Maddox stared at me with concern. Worries aside, I couldn't even describe how adorable it was when Roland followed his gaze and looked at me too.

"Bathroom," I quickly said, and Maddox nodded before I practically made a run for the nearest one, which was right by a little hallway.

I locked myself in the bathroom and stared at my reflection. The same blue eyes stared at me, but I looked healthier. I stared at myself intently. I barely wore any makeup today other than mascara because, Goddess help me, blonde lashes are the worst. I sighed as I stared at myself in the wide mirror of the bathroom.

*What the hell had just happened back there?* I thought. I looked at my hands and found that they were shaking. I swallowed a dry lump in my throat before quickly washing my hands.

"*Rememorari.* You will remember me," someone whispered harshly into my ear, and I immediately jumped back, hitting my back to the wall as I did so.

I stared at the mirror and found a dark black mist coming from behind me. I turned around to face the wall but saw nothing. I looked back at the mirror, and there was nothing either. I was going crazy.

No.

That was not it.

I'm just... I'm sure it was nothing. Unless, of course, I was going insane.

I ran a hand through my hair and sighed before I left the bathroom, only to crash straight into Maddox.

"You okay?" Maddox asked, and I nod my head.

"I'm fine," I said, my voice coming out harsher than I expected it to be. Which was why instead of letting me be on my merry way, Maddox grabbed me and held me in his arms.

His hands were at the small of my back, and my hands were on his chest. I felt the soft beat of his heart and took a deep breath before I felt a strange warmth surge from my fingertips. Maddox released one of his hands and used it to tilt my head up just slightly for me to stare at him. The slight caress of his fingers touching my skin was tingly, and my breath hitched, but Maddox didn't pay any attention to it.

"If anything bothers you, tell me. I don't want you to feel any type of discomfort before the full moon," Maddox said, "Okay?"

"I feel like a child," I said as Maddox chuckled, dropping his hand. The warm tingly feeling on my chin felt cold all of a sudden.

"I don't doubt that. Your mom and Celine wanted to head out into town for you to buy ceremonial clothes. Are you okay to go out? I'll have Iain and Jillian come with you," Maddox said as he reached for my hands. We were still standing close to each other in the little hallway, and I nodded my head.

"Yeah, I have a feeling that this will be a lot more fun for them than me, though," I said with a sigh.

"No doubt about it," Maddox said with a laugh, "The car leaves in fifteen minutes."

"Are you coming?" I asked, and Maddox shook his head.

"I have business to attend to, but I think Helari will come with you. She says she'll meet you at the mall. She said something about keeping watch over you and handing over more things for that regulator in your system," Maddox said, and I nodded, ignoring the sinking feeling I felt when he said he was busy.

"Okay," I simply answered before Maddox smiled and walked off.

I looked at my hands and bit my bottom lip.

What the hell was going on with my body?

I have been dragged to every goddamn motherfucking store in this goddamn mall.

What in the world was the point in trying on fifty different nightgowns for a single night? It was just a 'mating' ceremony, and I said 'mating' with air quotes because Goddess knew what hell I would have to go through that night. Yes, I was fully aware that I was twenty-two and should be more mature about sex, but it was not very appealing to me to have blood seeping out of my neck as the whole mating process ensues. That was the very reason I said 'ew' for everything along the lines of mating.

At the moment, I was sitting down in yet another boutique of clothing, as my sister and my mother ran around all over the place looking for white dresses. Meanwhile, my poor tired feet and I were seated on a comfy white leather couch beside Jillian who was enjoying the trip so far. Iain has been decidedly left outside to roam the mall because there was no point to him actually being in the boutique.

"Luna's have it so hard," Jillian said, and I nodded my head.

"Why on earth do I have to have a ceremonial dress? Can't I just wear some normal dress?" I asked aloud, and I immediately regretted it.

*No!* my sister and mother's loud voices mind linked me, and I cringed.

"I think it's because it's also the day that you're finally going to be a part of the pack, so that's exciting! It's like our version of a wedding," Jillian giddily said.

"At least I'll finally hear you guys mind linking around," I said with a sigh as I stood up. "I'm gonna go check a dress out as well. I might as well go find one I like," I said, and Jillian nodded as I walked off into the direction of a row of expensive-looking lace dresses.

Nope, not the lace.

I walked away from it and moved a hell of a lot away from my mother and sister who were scanning the nighties section. I skimmed through a few of the longer dresses and sighed as I went through hanger after hanger of garments.

"Need help?" a familiar voice said from behind me, and I rolled my eyes as I turned around to face Helari who was carrying a sleek matte black shopping bag.

"Help would be great," I said.

"I think this will look good on you," Helari said as she handed me the bag. "There are also other *seres* in the filigree box there for you. I think you can do it yourself. It's a bit weird at first but, I can't always be there to give it to you." I nodded my head.

"Thanks. I think I should just tell my mother and sister that we're done here. It looks like a shopping bag anyways," I said with a shrug.

"That is a good idea. Shall we?" She asked, and I rolled my eyes as we walked to grab my family.

An hour or so later, we're in Celine's guest room just minutes after I put on the dress. It got the seal of approval from my mother and sister, and I took it off the moment I wore it.

My mother insisted that only the girls present were supposed to know what it looked like before the day. It wasn't like I was going to gush about it, but the material of the dress was just plain beautiful.

But like I said.

I wasn't and would not gush about it.

Although it was pretty.

And I felt comfy in it.

And I would feel really, really bad if Maddox ripped it off me like Celine's prediction.

I would probably just walk out of the room if that happened.     Like... why? Why would you rip such a—

Like I said.

I wouldn't even talk about it anymore.

"You know, it would look even better if you let your hair down," Celine said as we walked down the hallway. I had the little shopping bag in my hands as we went up to the room Maddox and I shared.

"I wasn't planning on doing anything to it, anyways," I said as I twirled a lock of my hair around one of my fingers.

"Good. Also, mother wants to know when you wanna head to the spa with her since she wants to have a little time to *talk* about things," Celine said as she nudged me hard with her elbow.

"No, I think I'll be fine without the talk." I glared at her. "I also think I'll be fine without any other fancy treatments. It's a ceremony, not a wedding. I doubt it'll be anything fancy. There are people who mate without the whole luxury of—"

"Okay, okay, Sis, I get it. No need to get all defensive on wanting a simple—" Celine interrupted, but she was cut-off by her own cell phone. She fished it out and smiled to herself. "It's Chad. I'll talk to you later, okay, Sis?" she asked, and I nodded as she answered the phone and hurried back to her room.

Once I was alone, I headed straight for the bedroom and let out a disappointed sigh after realizing that Maddox wasn't there. I gently placed the shopping bag in the back of my closet before taking out the silver filigree box. I took it into the bathroom and lifted my hair quickly into a high ponytail. In front of the mirror, I felt for the *scal* at the back of my neck and opened the box. Inside was a set of eight *seres*, which still looked oddly ancient. It was only now that I noticed the tiny inscriptions on the crystal-like needles. Each needle was laid and secured neatly onto tiny ridges within the vibrant blue velvet interior of the box. I took one out and cringed at how long it was.

It was the length of my pinky, and it felt extremely light and cold to the touch. I held it like a pen before using my left hand to feel for the hole in the *scal*. With a quick movement, I effortlessly slid the *sere* into it... But as soon as it locked in, I felt a sudden headache that was so strong, I had to grip onto the edge of the counters to stay balanced. I looked into the mirror, and my eyes widened.

They weren't blue. They were pitch black. I felt my heart race before I closed my eyes.

When I opened them, I found that my plain blue orbs were back, and I sighed in relief. This whole mating ceremony must've been stressing me out more than it should. I closed the filigree box gently.

"*Eovre ande,*" a harsh whisper suddenly said into my ear. I spun behind me and gripped the sink tightly as I stared at nothing but the walls of the bathroom.

There was no way that I had imagined that. I felt a slight burning sensation from the *scal* on my neck before I felt a cold shiver run down my spine. I heard a low growl escape from my throat, and I suddenly felt the cold sensation run through my entire body. I suddenly felt the urge to shift and run as far away as I could. The urge was overwhelming. Every part of my being felt like it wanted to just—

"Elair?" Maddox's voice interrupted my thoughts as he called from outside the bathroom.

In an instant, every sensation I felt disappeared. I stared at the mirror at how normal I looked and immediately touched my face to make sure I wasn't running a fever.

"Yeah?" I answered a lot calmer than I had expected it to be.

"Dinner's ready," Maddox said.

"I'll be right out. Go ahead," I said. I heard our bedroom door shut along with Maddox's footsteps disappearing and sighed in relief.

"You're fine, Elair. Fine... No one wants to hear you freak out about things you can't prove," I talked to myself before shutting the bathroom and heading down to dinner.

*I will be fine.* I remind myself repeatedly, ignoring the heavy feeling at the back of my mind.

# Chapter Nineteen

*5 years ago*

*I woke up to the cold, harsh feeling of winter. The tiny little cabin I had lived in for the past two months, really only a bit larger than a tool shed, had everything I needed. A tiny bathroom had a little wall without a door that separated the dinky shower and toilet. The bed was a plain mattress on an old metal bed frame with one pillow and a thin blanket that was pushed against the corner where the fairly large window was. There was a tiny stove to cook on near the door facing the bed. A small fridge was to the left, on the other side of the door. I washed my face and opened the closet, grabbing only a single black robe as I stripped down and shrugged it on.*

*The robe was just a plain thick black robe tied quickly at the waist. It was made out of a thick velvet material and reached my ankles. I walked out of the cabin, the sound of ice* being crushed by my footsteps filling me with a strange feeling of satisfaction, just as I took off the robe and shifted into my wolf. The liberating feeling of having the cold earth mix with snow underneath my paws and the even more intense scent of the mountain area immediately calmed me down.

I silently made my rounds, sniffing the air and taking in the cold mist. My family had no idea where I was, and I had no means to contact them. I would return three nights from now for a quick break with my family. I made a sprint for the mountains and caught the scent of something unusual.

It was the smell of a human. I cautiously passed through the mountains and listened. Interactions with humans needed to be kept to a minimum, but I had to guard the area. I sniffed the vicinity and walked up the mountains. The snow was thicker up here, and even my wolf's breath appeared in a cloud of mist before me.

As the scent became stronger, I felt a warm sensation run through me before a strong wind blew down on me. I closed my eyes as the wind became harsher before I felt a hand on my head.

"Min silder... my dear child," a voice said, and I opened my eyes to see a blond haired man I recognized. I felt no animosity towards him as I sat down in my wolf form and he smiled.

I panted and nuzzled his hand as he looked woefully at me.

"It seems I have no choice in the matter, my dear child," he said, and I tilted my head before he looked at me and sighed. "The pain will be temporary, and whatever you know of me will disappear."

*I was about to whimper when the man's eyes turned into a deep blood red. I felt my control over my body being pulled away from me, and I felt like I was suspended in air. I fell with a loud thump onto the ground. My jaw was open, and I was panting as I looked at the man.*

*"Nuntiare satren tevra. Renounce your bond," he coldly said, and I felt a harsh pain pulse through me. I whimpered and whined, howling in agony as the surge of pain ate at my very being.*

*"Eovre andet, min silder. You still have a purpose to serve, my child," he said, and I whined as another pang of pain hit my wolf, and I couldn't resist. My body and mind seemed completely bound to his every word. "Don't worry... your master will return for you. Farvel, Elair," he said just as my vision blurred.*

I took a deep breath as I sprinted through the mountains. Maddox was right behind me as we patrolled his territory. His jet-black wolf barked as we moved left and right, dodging the trees in our way. I barked back as I came to a stop to face him. His eyes widened, his momentum carrying him too far just as I pounced on him, pinning his wolf to the ground. I howled victoriously before Maddox whined below me, and I got off him, proudly walking away and sitting down on the ground. Maddox shook his fur, and I barked at him in disgust.

We had decided to go for a run together this morning since I had been busy for the past few days taking care of my siblings and dealing with my mother. I loved the company, sure, but sometimes, a breather was needed. Maddox barked at me to get my attention and pulled his body even further up the mountain. I panted before shaking my body and sprinting off. My paws caused harsh crunching sounds on the thick forest floor as I stepped on the leaves.

Maddox ran alongside me as we got up higher. The time for snow was near, and I had always loved the feeling. My mother prayed that we get to have the first snow during the ceremony. She thinks it's a good sign. I personally couldn't care less, but hey, that was just my opinion.

Once Maddox and I reached the top, I smelled the faint scent of food and heard my stomach grumble. Maddox barked at me, and I knew he was laughing inside with the glint in his eyes. I barked back at him just as he sprinted forward at an incredible speed.

I shook my head as I dashed towards him to find a cliffside that overlooked Maddox's territory. Not that you could see a slight hint of it. It was just a large forest to the average eye. I sat down and admired the beautiful view of the terrain. Thick bunches of trees and the large lake was just a sprint away. There was a stream traveling down to the lake from the mountain as well, and the cliff revealed the source of the stream... a beautiful waterfall just by the edge. Maddox had entered into the cave where the waterfall began.

I waited and admired the view as I heard Maddox come out of the cave. He nudged my side with his nose, and I turned to find him with a large basket in his mouth. I raised my eyebrows, and Maddox nudged my neck again. I rolled my eyes as he sat the basket down and used his snout to open one flap. With one move, he had a pile of clothes in his mouth, and he gently put it down in front of me. Then he sat down expectantly, panting.

You know how a dog sometimes wants to play so they leave a stick at your feet and stare at you with their big eyes? Yeah, that was how Maddox looked like right now. I pointed my nose at him and urged him to turn around with my eyes, and he did just that.

I shifted back into my human form before grabbing the clothes and pulling them on. As weird as it was for Maddox to pack me a full set of clothes, I couldn't exactly hang around naked. So I pulled on the underwear, the big gray sweater dress, some leggings, and slipped into little plain ballet flats before I walked over to Maddox's wolf, who was at a height just below my shoulders.

Maddox barked, lay low, and looked at his back before looking at me.

"What? You don't expect me to get on your back, do you?" I asked, and Maddox barked before wagging his tail. I glared at his amber eyes before he attempted to lick my face, and I dodged him. "That is disgusting," I said, and Maddox barked again before I climbed onto his back.

Maddox panted as he stood up, grabbed the basket in his mouth, and reared his back, preparing to do something stupid. In one quick movement, Maddox leaped off of the cliff, and I felt my stomach do a flip as we fell down. I bit my bottom lip and hang onto Maddox as I braced myself for the water. Instead, Maddox managed to land on his four legs on a large slab of stone at the foot of the waterfall.

Placing the basket down, he nudged it towards me, and I rolled my eyes as I opened it up and took out a pair of shorts for Maddox. Before I could even question him, Maddox jumped into the water and dived deep before emerging to the surface as a human. His black hair was now completely wet as he swam to the edge of the rock.

"You could've just let me jump," I said as I threw his shorts at him.

"I could've, but I didn't," he said as I turned away from him.

"Yeah, yeah, whatever," I muttered as I picked up the basket and smiled as I pulled out two packed boxes of food. "Is this my mother's cooking?" I asked as I turned around, knowing Maddox had already pulled on his shorts.

"Who else would make those?" he asked me back, and I rolled my eyes.

"Whatever," I said as I took off the shoes and sat on the side of the stone, swinging my feet in the water. Maddox sat by me with the packed food and handed one to me.

We ate in comfortable silence before we packed up and headed back. Maddox still had work to do as the alpha, and my family probably wanted me to be there to talk about the ceremony.

Just as we were about to run home, a scent filled my nostrils that had me releasing a feral growl.

"What's wrong?" Maddox asked in a concerned tone.

"Don't you smell that?" I asked as I sniffed the air, and Maddox followed suit, but he looked confused. "Shit."

I didn't hesitate as I made a run for the source of the scent. It was definitely a rogue, and the scent was a marking from my squadron in the past. Back in our squadron, we would have witches embed scents into our prisoners. This was one of them. Meaning this particular rogue was especially dangerous. I made a quick sprint, dodging tree after tree and jumping over boulders. At a clearing nearby, I spotted a mass of brown fur and announced my presence with a loud growl. I may be in my human form but I could sure as hell growl.

The wolf turned around and growled back at me.

*Damned rogue.*

I didn't have my guns on me, but I didn't want to shift. Sighing to myself, I got ready for a fight. I saw the amusement in the wolf's eyes, and I smirked.

"If you think you can run from me, you're wrong. And if you think I won't be able to kill you in this form, you're also dead wrong," I said just as the wolf reared its back and bared its teeth.

The wolf launched at me, and I dodged to my left. I turned immediately to face it and took a quick breath as the wolf sprinted off. I rolled my eyes and sprinted as well, fighting the urge to shift.

"*Rememorari, Elair. Eovre andet, min silder,*" a loud whisper rang in my ears. I forced myself to ignore it and continued running towards the wolf. "*Remember that you have a purpose, my child.*"

Once the wolf came into sight, I picked up a rock that was just about the size of my fist and threw it as hard as I could at its foot. It whimpered as the rock managed to scrape its right hind leg, and I took the opportunity to catch up with it. I got there and sighed as I reached over the wolf's other hind leg.

If this guy has been marked by my squadron, then that meant this little wolf here couldn't be killed quite yet. In one swift movement, I broke the wolf's leg with my hands. The sound of bones snapping ripped through the forest, and the wolf howled in pain.

"Oh, shut it, will you?" I said just as the wolf whimpered in an attempt at gaining pity. I was about to say something when I heard footsteps from behind me that had the wolf whimpering loudly and scrambling with its front legs to get away. Someone clapped, and I widened my eyes as another heavy feeling enveloped me.

My mind felt hazy, and I felt like my consciousness was being pushed to the back of my mind. It took me a few seconds before I regained a sense of who was behind me.

"Bravo, Elair. Bravo!" a male voice said, and I watched as a form of a man was formed out of pure black shadows.

"Faustus," my voice said as my body kneeled. My right leg was on bended knee, and I bowed my head.

"Kill the poor thing, Elair, but don't touch him," Faustus commanded, and I stood up and faced the wolf without a word.

"I'm no witch, Faustus. You're asking the impossible."

"Focus. Remember… *min silder*, my sweet, sweet child," he said, and I sighed as I looked at the wolf.

I lifted up my right hand and took a breath as a familiar feeling of exhilaration rushed through my body and into my fingertips. The *scal* on my neck was burning up, but I focused on my fingertips and the wolf.

"Good. Now kill him," Faustus said lowly into my ear before placing his hands around my shoulders. I let my right hand go limp as it pointed to the ground, and the sound of the wolf's whimpers immediately died away. Instead, it was replaced by the sound of its neck breaking.

"I could've done that with my own hands," I said as I put my hand down.

"Yes, but *min silder*, the mate bond has made you stronger. Perhaps... I should unlock it for you and hasten the process. It would certainly make it easier," Faustus said as I turned to face him. His ice-blue eyes pierced straight through me as he cupped my cheek.

"My dear, dear child, your aunt and I have never been so proud to have trained you," he said, and I felt a heavy feeling engulf me. Faustus lifted his right hand, and I watched as, out of the blue, blood began to be drawn across his hand like an invisible knife had cut him.

It flowed out from his hands and onto the ground, and I felt a burning sensation run through my chest.

"By blood, I bound your fate to mine, and by blood, I destroyed the bond of wolves. By my blood, I restore it, and by my blood, I will destroy it again." Faustus recited. His eyes were aglow as the burning sensation ate at me until I screamed from the pain.

A thousand knives felt like they were piercing through me as I fell to the ground and curl up into a fetal position. My breath came out in pants before I heard Faustus' footsteps come near me.

"Enjoy your moments with your mate, my child. It will not last long. *Farvel,* and forget me again," Faustus said as he disappeared into the woods, and I lied on the ground, forcing myself to try to fight to remember his words.

I screamed as I fought his commands, but I couldn't. As my consciousness took over and struggled to keep the memory I just regained, it felt like my brain was being crushed into a thousand pieces.

"Maddox..." I said breathlessly.

*I have to tell someone before...* My thoughts trailed off as my memory faded to black, killing off my consciousness... and I fell asleep on the ground.

# Chapter Twenty

My eyes fluttered open and widened as they came to a realization that we were still in the middle of the forest. A dead wolf laid close by, and I watched as it slowly shifted back into its human form. It was a man who I assumed was about forty. There was no point in checking on him, though. He was already dead. His neck was clearly snapped. Though I had no clue as to whether I did that, I was assuming that I've had a blackout scenario... as my Aunt Eleanor would have called it.

As I stared at the body, an amazing scent began coming towards me. It immediately made me want to run towards it.

"Elair! Are you okay?" Maddox's voice yelled from behind me. I turned, and immediately, my body felt as if it was under high tension.

My senses all seemed pushed back as my wolf kicked in and a single word came into focus.

*Mate...*

I thought to myself, and I watched as Maddox emerged from the trees and was immediately in front of me, cupping my face up to look into his eyes. His touch sent tingles down my spine, and I suddenly felt faint. I had the sudden urge to just pull him down onto my lips and kiss him. I immediately froze up at the thought. *What the hell?*

"What's wrong?" Maddox asked, and I shook my head.

"Nothing. I took it down," I softly said, motioning to the dead wolf behind us.

"I'll have someone clean it up. Let's head back to the pack house now," Maddox said, and I obediently nodded, trying to process why I was suddenly so submissive and silent.

It was probably because I was in shock. As Maddox turned around to leave, I grabbed his hand, and he turned to look at me with wide eyes. I paused and watched as he smirked and squeezed my hand as we walked back to the pack house together.

I was in the shower as I heard Maddox walk around the room. I've left the water running for fifteen minutes now as I've been trying to process what was going on with my body. I stepped out of the shower and wrapped myself up in a towel before taking another towel to dry my hair. I placed my hands on the counter by the sink and stared at my reflection. I felt as if I forgot something... like a heavy feeling was crushing my chest. Unable to pinpoint what it was, I resumed my usual routine and left the bathroom in just a towel.

"We'll have dinner in five minutes. Do you want anything in particula…" Maddox began, but he trailed off as he looked at me.

"What?" I asked with a raised eyebrow before realizing I was only wearing a towel. "Oh, right. Gimme a sec," I muttered before sliding the closet door aside and pulling out my clothes.

Maddox turned around so that his back was faced towards me, and I smirked. *Always so kind*, I thought to myself. I pulled on my underwear and a pair of plain black joggers that were fairly comfortable and a military green tank top. Then I shrugged on a long black cardigan and shoved my feet into a pair of plain black flip-flops.

"Done?" Maddox asked just as I had combed my fingers through my wet hair.

"Let's go," I said, and Maddox turned around with a grin before we headed down to the dining area.

As we were eating in the dining room, I felt a familiar set of eyes on me, and I realized it was coming from Helari. She seemed to be calling me, so I walked over to her, leaving my siblings bickering about which TV show was the best and which cartoon character was the strongest. Kids these says…

"Seems like you're having a lot of fun," Ari said, and I nodded my head as we sat down in the living room.

"Never a dull moment with my family," I said, and Ari smiled

"Elair... I need you to be honest with me." Ari suddenly said in a serious tone. I looked at her and saw that she had her eyes closed. "Have you seen Faustus lately?" she asked, and I raised an eyebrow.

"No, I only see him in those weird dreams and flashbacks I have. Why?" I asked, and Ari opened her eyes and revealed a worried look.

"I can sense him here sometimes. He's somewhere in this territory. His presence has been lurking around, and it's irritating my servants... particularly Mikhail. That boy has a grudge against Faustus. I'm afraid of what Faustus is planning and what he's done to you," Ari said with a sigh.

"The full moon is in three days, and there is darkness lingering everywhere. If you even feel a slight change or something even the most minutely different about anything... tell me immediately," Ari said, and I nodded my head.

"Of course," I said, and Ari smiled before her shoulders fell into a more relaxed position.

"I can sense that the bond is almost fully restored. I'm glad," Ari said with a wide smile.

"Not excited," I mutter with a shrug, and Ari laughed as we began to talk about random things.

By the time I had gone up to the room to sleep, it was already past two in the morning. I had spent most of the night on a chick-flick marathon with my sister. Classic, I know.

Maddox was still working in his office, and I had decided that I would just sit down and read a book or something. I was reading a few of the old human tales about werewolves. Those were always a good laugh. Nothing better than getting a kick out of what humans thought of us 'supernatural beings.' The book I was now reading was old and yellowed. The paper already felt very delicate, and each page was so stiff that I feared I would have ruined it if I turned a page too excitedly.

I sighed as I flipped through the book before I found a story I had never heard of before. Strangely enough, it was titled Cardis, not that I knew what that even meant. I breezed through it. It was a story of two ancient lovers that bore a child of various supernatural powers. The child was said to be blessed by the Moon Goddess herself, and like all fairy tales, she was one of the fairest people anyone would come across.

She never aged... and one day, the people realized that she was an abnormality. They hunted her down for centuries, and finally, on a night of a full moon, an entire village of humans surrounded her home, a haven in the woods, in an attempt to kill her and destroy the family she had finally had. The lady herself had gone out to perform a ritual by the river. The mob of humans killed her three children and captured her husband. When the lady returned home, she found her home destroyed, and she wept over the deaths of her children.

To save her husband, she disguised herself with a cloaking spell and entered the village that same night. There she found her husband at the stake, bruised and bloodied. The villagers yelled obscenities at her husband and threw rocks at him. Rage took over the woman, and she screamed. In her anger, she released her powers, and her rage engulfed the entire village in flames.

After the attack, she tried to heal her husband but found that even he had feared her. So she gave him a gift, a silver dagger covered in gems to mark that she existed. The dagger allowed her husband to heal, but she disappeared shortly after.

I flipped to the last page of the book and traced the drawing of the lady's figure with my fingertips. As I did so, I felt a slight pang of pain hit from my core. I gasped and gaped for air as the pain began to come in waves and overwhelmed me. I heard the clatter of objects falling onto the floor before I found Maddox staring at me.

"Shit," Maddox muttered as I continued to gasp for air.

"What... the... hell?" I hissed, and I watched as Maddox went towards me and embraced me tightly. His touch immediately calmed me down, and I breathed a sigh of relief. The waves of pain had dulled down into a slight discomfort.

"You're in heat," Maddox said in a low voice. My eyes widened as I softly pushed him away and looked into his eyes.

They were a golden color that revealed his lust. I bit my bottom lip, and he growled lowly.

"This is going to be hell. Yet another werewolf thing I hate," I said as Maddox pulled me into his lap.

"Goddess help me with my patience," Maddox muttered as he switched our positions so that he was lying against the bed frame and I was straddling him. I felt a wave of pain hit me once more, and I fell against him, my chest heaving from the large gulps of air I started to inhale.

"We are not doing the—"

"I'm not going to do anything you don't want me to," Maddox said, interrupting me. I nodded my head in relief.

I was not going to have a sexual adventure right now. No mother fucking way.

"I hate my life," I mumbled, and Maddox chuckled as he held me, his touch allowing me to focus away from the pain... although the sparks of electricity I felt when he touched me were certainly making my wolf think of different things.

"Do you want Helari to—"

"Nope," I said. The last thing I needed was for anyone else to know that I went into heat.

*Ugh.*

Never in my life did I think I would even experience the hell that female wolves endure. Who the hell wanted to be in pain and have sex? Why would anyone think that this was a good idea? It just sounded like a really sad excuse to get laid.

"Are you comfortable?" Maddox asked, and I knew he was trying really hard as his voice was strained whenever I pressed myself against him.

The more my body touched, him the less I felt the pain. Which was why I had no complaints when Maddox intertwined our legs together and left me on his chest. He had lowered himself down onto the bed so that we were now both lying down together.

"I'm as comfortable as I can get, I guess," I said as Maddox cupped my cheek. I looked up at him and watched as our faces neared each other's.

Our lips brushed slightly, and my breath hitched. Maddox leaned over, and I captured his lips with my own. I ran my hands through his hair as I pulled him over me so that he hovered above me. I pulled him down by hooking my arm around his neck. Maddox growled into my mouth as I used my legs to press his lower body against mine.

*Rip it off like a band-aid, Elair,* I thought to myself. *Rip, rip, rip, rip it. Rip it off like a—*

Maddox slipped his tongue into my mouth, and we began our usual battle for dominance in our kiss.

*Fuck it*, I muttered in my mind.

I moaned as Maddox trailed his hands behind my back. The pain from before died down just as fast as it came as Maddox began kissing my jaw. He didn't try to mark me. Instead, he just kissed me down from my neck. He broke away to pull off my tank top, tossing it aside as he kissed the top of my chest. He came back up and gave me a deep kiss that took my breath away as he pulled back and gazed down at me.

"Perfect," he said, and I rolled my eyes. My instincts told me, and I pulled him back down for a kiss. I pulled away and dragged him to me so that my mouth was by his ear.

"I didn't tell you to stop," I said in a breathless whisper as I kissed him from the edge of his jaw down to his chin. "So don't," I said, and Maddox's eyes flashed an even darker color before we resumed our business.

Maddox had been kissing me lower until he got to the waistband of my pants. He searched my eyes for permission, and just as I was about to give it, a knock on the door came to our attention.

"Alpha, Luna! There are Rogues rushing in from the western borders! We've sent three of our sectors out there, but Miss Helari says that there's something off."

"We'll be right out," I answered for Maddox who smirked at me. Maddox kissed me quickly before pulling back.

"Stay here. I'll have Helari come to you," Maddox said as he got off the bed.

"No fucking way! I'm—"

"You're still in heat. I don't want any other wolf smelling you the way you are now, especially not a rogue," Maddox said in a loud growl.

I rolled my eyes as I sat up.

"Fine, but you better get your ass back here in five minutes. Otherwise, I'm going to end up looking for someone else to do this whole shenanigan with," I said, and Maddox growled possessively, making me laugh. I pulled myself off the bed and picked up my tank top. "Kidding. Go," I said as I pulled the waistband of his pants towards me and ran a hand down his chest with the slightest bit of self-control.

With my free hand, I pulled him down for another deep kiss, and I darted my tongue into his mouth, causing him to moan into my mouth.

"You're going to kill me here," Maddox said as I pulled away and shrugged.

"If that gets you back faster, then I'll gladly continue," I said with a sly grin on my face, and Maddox chuckled before he pressed one last kiss to my lips and headed out the door.

As soon as he left, I felt a strange weight fall onto my shoulders. I shrugged the feeling off. I probably just missed him from the heat.

It was nothing.

# Chapter Twenty One

"I think she should do it," Jasper argued for me as we discussed the rogues from earlier this morning.

They attacked at just around two in the morning, and Maddox had gotten home extremely pissed. The wolves in charge of the borders were put to sleep with a spell, and Helari had to perform a cleansing where the rogues had gone. The rogues themselves seemed to have been branded and were quickly thrown into the dungeons. I was glad that my family had gone out for some sightseeing around Oregon although I doubted there was much to see. They'd probably decided to head all the way to Portland for all I knew.

"I think I should do it, too," I said with a smirk, and Maddox sighed.

"You should really stop siding with her," Maddox told Jasper, who simply smirked in reply.

"From what I heard, she's ruthless, so I think Elair can manage to get the info out of these folks," Jasper casually said, and I nodded my head.

"I think so, too."

"I know you do, that's why I'm asking other people what they think," Maddox said, and I rolled my eyes at him.

"I haven't done anything since the attack, Maddox. I think I can handle getting info out of a rogue or two."

"There's only one night until—"

"We know!" Jasper and I argued at the same time, and we high-fived each other. Maddox sighed and looked at the others in the council.

Trevor and Carson both had amused looks on their faces. Naomi didn't seem to care about the situation, and Iain didn't seem bothered. Rina and Lorraine seemed excited.

"I'd love to see it happen," Trevor said, and Iain nodded.

"I'm all for it." Rina began. "It's not everyday that the luna tortures—"

"We're avoiding that word," Lorraine told Rina, and she rolled her eyes.

"Okay, whatever. Either way, I think Luna Elair can handle it," Rina said, and I cringed ever so slightly at the sound of that title. *Luna Elair? Really?*

"No one else has a problem with it other than you," I quietly said to Maddox, and he sighed again.

"Fine. Head to the dungeons. We'll all be there in case anything happens. Helari should already be there," Maddox said in defeat. I silently did a fist pump for myself and saw Maddox glare at me. As everyone left the room, I hugged

Maddox from behind, and he sighed. "Don't get too aggressive. Your eyes went blood red the last time this happened."

"No problem," I reassuringly said, and Maddox nodded as I let go of him and skipped off to join the others in the dungeons.

I have never been so glad to wear leather boots. Helari had already made the cells all bloodied and messy. Walking on pools of blood wasn't exactly my cup of tea.

Helari seemed really tense. I could feel it in the heavy weight in the air and the way that the whole group had gone quiet. Everyone in the small council that Maddox had was with me. The stench of fresh blood was everywhere. This cell was pure stonewalls with just enough light to see the four rogues secured with thick chains and straps onto inclined torture beds.

"Doesn't seem like there's much left for me to do," I muttered, and Helari sighed as she turned to look at me. She had splatters of blood all over her.

To be honest, she looked quite horrifying especially with the cold look in her eyes.

"I haven't tried to talk to them. I've only done some more damage. The build up of stress should make it easier, but more than anything... I wanted to make them pay," Helari said in an icy cold tone. I raised an eyebrow, and she shook her head. "Whoever sent them wanted to send a message. These guys are meant for ritual purposes. They've got inscriptions down their backs. I've read them, and each one is different. Stay cautious."

"What is that supposed to mean?"

"The ritual inscriptions involve you. If it helps... one of them was singing the same song as before."

"I don't think I wanna hear it again," I said.

"You won't. He's out cold, anyways," Helari said as I made my way to a table filled with tools. I took the usual container of wolfsbane and a set of plain daggers before examining the three rogues.

My blood ran cold.

"Elair, you okay?" Jasper asked, and I didn't respond. Instead, I walked towards one of the rogues, a male with long brown hair that's been soaked through with blood and sweat.

I placed the wolfsbane down on a little stool in front of the rogue along with the daggers. The rogue stirred slightly, and I sighed.

"Any of you have a gun?" I asked, and I heard the shuffling of feet and some rustling of pockets.

"Me," a female voice said, and I turned around to face Naomi who pulled out a gun from the back of her thick jacket. Trevor, Rina, Loraine, and everyone else gawked at her except for Ari who just smirked as she watched Naomi toss the gun towards me. I nodded my thanks.

I caught it with my right hand and checked the cartridge. It was a normal handgun, probably something that Maddox had stocked for those involved in main security. There were fifteen bullets in it, and I sighed as I pushed the cartridge back in and cocked the gun at the rogue's foot. I didn't even have to take a breath. I aimed and fired.

The loud agonizing scream of the rogue-filled the room immediately, and I rolled my eyes.

"Wakey wakey, Dallas," I said and watched as the rogue's eyes widened. He squirmed in his binds, and I prepared the gun for another shot. "Last time I saw you, you were still in training back in the squadron," I said, ignoring his heavy breathing as I examined the handgun. He coughed and groaned.

"Faustus... he's found you," Dallas said, and I rolled my eyes.

Dallas had been a part of my squadron. No one in the squadron was ever close. We were all focused on our duty. We worked together, and when one of us fell, we accepted their sacrifice and moved on. Things were easily run that way, and Dallas was one of my squadron members. Never quite on par but never far behind me.

"So I've heard," I said with a shrug as I pulled the slide of the gun, and the bullet locked in preparation for a shot. Dallas' face was bloody, but he smirked at me.

"Good," Dallas simply said, and I sighed.

"I just wanna know why you were here last night," I said, and when he didn't respond, I pointed the gun at his knee. "You know my methods, Dall," I said, and Dallas lets out a laugh that sounded more like a wheeze. I pulled the trigger.

The sound of the gunshot echoed all over the room, causing the other rogues to stir to life. Dallas' scream revealed his agony, but I stared blankly at him, examining his face.

"Faustus... told me... to tell you this. *Sileio skeiva, eovre andet enfarvel,*" Dallas said in a hoarse voice before laughing maniacally just as the other rogues in the room growled rabidly.

"Elair, what's going—" Jillian said, but despite all the growling and Dallas' laugh, the ground seemed to shake. I turned around and looked at Helari whose odd-colored eyes have both turned blood-red.

"Let me translate that for everyone. Your friend Dallas is saying 'he knows you have a purpose. Don't forget.' If you're telling me that Faustus can communicate with Elair in my language, then you have some nerve," Helari said loudly. "*Eovre en-gairun. Hes asvretum ti vren irvon,*" Helari said as the ground stabilized, and she looked to me. "I don't care what information they think they have. Kill them before they do their jobs. He's useless and deserves to go die with his friends." The wolves began to growl in response. Their anger seemed to reverberate in the cells.

"*Vedel hael.* Yet another bad omen," Helari mumbled to herself as she began to walk out of the room.

I sighed as I realized that Helari was right. The look in Dallas' eyes was full of something dark and lost. As if his mind had been broken. He'd already been tortured... but in a way that only witches can derange the mind.

I took the gun in my hands and walked away to the center. There was no need to get bloody, anyways. I aimed at Dallas and shot. I then pulled the slide of my gun and did the same to the other two before I silently walked out of the room, the mini council following behind me.

"What did you say to him?" I asked Helari who walked in front of me out of the dungeons.

"I told him he was useless and to die with his friends. *Eovre en-gairun...* that's how you tell someone they're useless in my language," Helari said with a smirk, and I nodded my head.

"There are bad things ahead of us. I suggest you enjoy the peace we have for the meantime. I can hardly act like a normal human. Faustus and I have a terrible history. Perhaps I should stop acting so casual. I'm not even mortal, and I have a family to protect," Helari said, and I raised an eyebrow. The council behind me muttered words to each other before they began sprinting off, probably from Maddox's orders.

"What do you mean?" I asked, and Helari smiled at me.

"Mikhail and Scar are two of the first people that came into my service. They are as good as my blood, and like them, I take in as many children as I can. I know how bad it can get when one loses their family. It's painful... and it's even worse to know that you aren't accepted," Helari said.

"I read a story last night. It was called—"

"Cardis, right?" Helari asked me, and I nodded my head.

"Yeah, that."

Helari smiled sadly at me.

"I don't have to tell you that it was my story, right? Cardis was the name of my husband back then," Helari told me, and I tried not to react, but that would make Helari ancient. "Let's take a walk, shall we? Maddox will come across our path, anyways," Helari said, and I nodded as we walked into the woods.

"How are y—"

"My story never actually started in that damned village. If you must know, my husband and I never met again after that.

I healed him and left him. He wrote this book in a letter only three years before he died. His daughter came to work for me, but we were no longer related. She handed me the letter, and I allowed its publication. The rest is history."

"How'd he know about your back story?" I asked. "I mean, it said something about being blessed by the goddess, but you know..." I trailed off. Helari laughed as we walked together, and I paused.

"Cardis has always been one to talk fancy words. I'm not blessed. In fact, if anything, I'm cursed. Faustus made sure of that when he tortured Cardis. Human as he was and human as our children were, I loved them all. I left my entire organization in the hands of Mikhail and Scar, and the one day that I went back to visit them... Faustus attacked," Helari said with a sigh, and I felt her anger seep from her being. "Cardis' daughter... is an ancestor of Maddox's," Helari said.

"What?" I asked, and Helari chuckled slightly.

"I doubt Maddox knows the truth, but when the option was available to her, I was the one who took care of the preparations to send Maddox's originating pack here, to the Americas," Helari said with a shrug. "How Cardis' family ended up with wolves is a mystery to me. The goddess works in strange ways, but Maddox reminds me much of my lost son. I had three children. Two of which were girls that were no older than seven. My son was fourteen and almost ready for the world back then," Helari said with a wistful look.

"It's not my place to explain... but Maddox had never known his mother. When I came to visit, I felt the need to guide him. His father, however, was undeniably an asshole. He caused trouble wherever he went. It earned them the title of

'macabre' and made me responsible for restraining him."
Helari explained, and I nodded my head as we sat down on a
couple of tree stumps.

"Maddox has known me since he was ten, and after
hundreds of years of trying to forget my lost family, I allowed
myself to treat him as my own. I value you just as much as he
does for being his mate... and for being someone who can make
the boy listen. I would do anything to protect his happiness as
he would protect yours," Helari said, and I suddenly felt the
urge to shrink away.

A lump formed in my throat, and Helari sighed. There
was something trying to claw away at my mind. There was
something I had to say. My lips quivered, but Helari didn't
notice.

*What is it?*

*Why is this feeling gnawing at me like—*

"Elair," Helari called, and my thoughts were pulled
aside.

"Hmm?" I asked, and Helari shook her head.

"The mate bond seems like it's completely healed,"
Helari said, and I bit my bottom lip.

"Hmm..." I mumbled, trying not to make it seem like a
big deal.

I mean, meh.

It was not like I went into heat or anything.

It was not like I had the urge to jump Maddox's bones.

It was also not like I had the urge to kill myself after I
thought about the two things I just talked about.

Like I said... *meh.*

"That's good," Helari said with a smile. "At least something is going well. Let's hope for the best. I'll do my best to keep everything safe and sound for the next days to come," Helari said, and I nodded my head.

"Safe and sound, huh? Sounds good to me," I said, and Helari laughed as we made our way to the pack house.

# Chapter Twenty Two

"Okay, so we've gotten your nails cleaned and polished, and we got you a facial. Should we get you a new haircut?" Celine asked.

"I'm done," I said with a sigh.

"Oh, come on! You didn't even put nail polish on!" Celine exclaimed as my mother laughed.

"It's a mating ceremony, not a wedding," I said as I rolled my eyes. "Besides, it's not like Maddox will get all 'pretty,' so why should I?" I asked, and my mother giggled.

"Let your sister make the choice, Celine. She just isn't the type to do much of things like this," Mother said.

"Whatever." Celine rolled her eyes.

"How about we go get some coffee and then we can talk?" Winter suggested, and I nodded my head.

"Sounds great," I said as we walked away from the shops.

We were at the Bridgeport in Portland again, and I swear, I could've made do with a small shop closer to Maddox's territory. However, my sister whined, and Winter had to run a few errands. In fear of anything bad happening today, Maddox had the whole place surrounded by pack members that were very discreet in their roles in guarding me.

I did, however, pick them out of the crowd. It was pretty fun. Everyone would always widen their eyes whenever I approached them to tell them they were doing a good job. It was only awkward when they bowed their heads and called me Luna Elair. I didn't think I'll ever get used to that.

We entered the Bridge City Cafe and waited as Celine and Winter ordered their drinks.

"Are you ready for tonight?" my mother asked, and I nodded my head.

"Ready enough... I guess," I said with a shrug.

"Well, at least you'll be a part of his pack now," she said.

"It's probably the only thing I'm looking forward to," I said.

"Oh, don't be like that, sweetheart. I'm sure Maddox will treat y—"

"Mom, please. I don't wanna hear anything about that kind of stuff," I said, cringing to myself. My mother laughed, and I groaned as Celine and Winter brought over our drinks.

"Sounds like you guys are having a fun conversation," Winter said with a smirk.

"Kill me," I said with a sigh as I took my coffee.

We spent a few hours in the coffee shop talking about things other than the ceremony, like how Ender was doing.

Ender and I had never gone without communicating for so long. We normally kept in touch with letters despite my far locations during my time in the squadron. Ender had always been the clingier twin, and as his older twin sister, I always tried to make sure that he was comfortable. Now, he was leading most of the meetings and handling the Blood Moon Pack as the alpha. My father was ready to step down, and I was glad to hear Ender doing well.

"Oh, crap! I forgot to get something!" Celine said as we exited the café.

"What?" I said, raising an eyebrow.

"Oh, yeah! I forgot about that, too!" Winter exclaimed.

"I think I should help you two with that," my mother said, and she smirked at me. "We'll only be away for ten minutes. Do you mind being alone until then?" she asked.

"I'm more than capable of handling myself, Mother," I said.

"Alright, let's go get that thing then," my mother said.

I raised an eyebrow as they all scurried away.

*What the hell was that about?* I wondered as I walked off, passing through shops. Just then, I heard whispers in the wind.

I looked around and spotted a few of the Macabre Pack, but none of them seemed to notice. I closed my eyes and took a deep breath, focusing on the voices.

"*The fountain...*" one of the voices said. I looked around again but spotted no one in particular.

Calmly, I made my way to the fountain. My blurry reflection was all that I saw. Just as I was about to look away, I saw a dark figure beside me in the water. I looked to my side and saw no one. I looked into the water again, and I found the figure standing right behind me.

"*Rememorari,* Elair. You have a purpose. *Min aitien hes dun, hu petaris, relesereo opiere ti lyger,*" a loud voice said from behind me. It was then that the words made sense. 'Remember, Elair. My patience is running thin. Come to me and release your power, little girl,' it said.

I froze up and felt a cold shiver run down my spine. I stared at my reflection and looked into my eyes. They were glowing red, and I felt a sense of calm overpower me. My subconscious felt suspended into the back of my mind.

"When the night is over and the ceremony has been completed... you will return to us," the voice whispered, and I felt myself smirk at my reflection.

"You know, you don't have to wipe my memories away all the time," I said as I turned around and came face-to-face with the shadow. The shadow dissipated, and Faustus revealed himself to me.

"My brother is very perceptive of my presence," Faustus said with a smile.

"You mean, your brother, Mikhail? You two look alike though I doubt he'll notice you here," I said with a shrug as we began to walk.

"The members of Macabre—"

"I cloaked us the moment I deciphered your ridiculous message. They should still be thinking that I'm just walking around waiting for the others to return," I said with a shrug. "You'll remove the mate bond after the ceremony, right?" I asked.

"There is no need for it anymore. The plan continues, and you will be perfect for the job. Don't worry about a thing. I will handle the rest," Faustus calmly said. "I will create a distraction as the dawn sets. You can disappear then."

"Good," I said, and Faustus smirked.

"*Farvel, min silder,*" Faustus said, and with a blink of an eye, his figure disappeared.

I balled my hands into fists. *Got you*, I thought to myself. Thank Goddess he didn't notice. I looked around and spotted the members of Macabre and sighed. The things a little spell could do. I looked at the sky. It was almost sundown. The time I had left to prepare was short. I didn't have much time.

I walked to the fountain once more.

"Let's do a little test run, yeah?" I mumbled to myself.

I stared at the running water.

"*Sefreo,*" I muttered, and the surface of the water slowly began to freeze.

"Elair!" Celine's voice called. I turned, the ice cracking as I released my hold on it.

"Yeah?" I asked, and Celine grinned.

"Let's go. Iain's here to pick us up," Celine giddily said, and I nodded as we headed back.

I was going to end Faustus' hold on me tonight.

"I need to talk to Maddox," I said as I walked into the pack house.

"He's in his office, the one down the hall," Jasper told me as he walked over to Winter. I then made my way towards Maddox's office.

The heels of my boots clicked on the floor, and I sighed as I opened the door to his office. I paused when I spotted someone else there... a woman.

"Come on, Maddox, there's no way my father would agree to an allegiance without having us—"

I cleared my throat, interrupting the woman's voice. Maddox looked at me, and I could practically feel him relax. The tension in the air was almost palpable.

"I need to talk to you," I said.

"You heard her," Maddox told the woman, and she glared right at him and then at me.

She had a bob haircut dyed in a crimson color that matched with her lips and strong eyeliner. Not gonna lie, she was fairly pretty, but she looked like she was thirty with the outfit she was wearing. Who still wears cheetah print dresses?

Okay, I wouldn't judge anyone, but that was not—

"Who the hell are you?" she asked with a hint of sass, and I rolled my eyes.

"I don't have time for this. Is she a friend of yours?" I asked Maddox, and he shook his head.

"Hardly, she came by because her father wants us to form an alliance, but her wishes are different from her father's. She's a complication at best," Maddox said, and I smirked as the red of the girl's hair traveled down to her cheeks. Someone was pissed.

"I'm from the—"

"Look, I don't have time, so shut the fuck up right now and leave," I said in a cold voice. When she didn't move, I shook my head. "Do you understand English? I said leave," I said. She was about to open her mouth, and I rolled my eyes as I pulled a gun out of the waistband of my jeans. I pulled the slide, aimed, and fired right by the side of her face.

The bullet grazed her cheek, and she gawked at me.

"Like I said, get the fuck out of this office before I shoot your pretty little red head. I doubt anyone will even figure out you've bled to death when I'm done," I said, and I grinned as her lips quivered and she ran out faster than a cheetah could have. Funny cause she's wearing a dress. Okay, fine.

Anyways...

Once the door shut, I made my way over to Maddox, and he immediately placed his hands on my waist.

The action sent a delicious sensation down my spine, but I did my best to shake it off. I couldn't have any distractions right now.

"Maddox, we have an issue. I need to say it before he realizes," I said, and Maddox raised his eyebrows.

"What is it? Who is *he*?" Maddox asked possessively.

"I think it'd be better to discuss it if Helari was here," I said.

"Okay, then," Maddox said as he removed one of his hands from my waist and used it to pick up his phone. He dialed a number, and without even putting the phone to his ear, he dropped the call.

I raised my eyebrows, and he smirked.

"She'll be here," he said, and I nodded my head. "Do you want to tell me what's going on before she gets here?" he asked me.

"Well, in one word..." I trailed off as I looked at his desk. "*Lothrian,*" I said, and the papers on his desk began to lift. Maddox's eyes widened as the papers didn't just fly off, they floated up and suspended in the air.

"Well, then," Maddox simply said, and I rolled my eyes.

"Well then is right. I don't have much time. With the ceremony tonight, Faustus has probably begun preparing."

"Faustus? I told you not to worry about hi—"

"Maddox," I said in a commanding tone as I let the papers file in order in the air and land in Maddox's desk. "He's going to take me tonight, and I won't be able to defy him like I did tonight. I'll be too weak to resist his hold on my soul. The fucker's been trying to mess up my head since the day I entered the squadron."

"I'll tell you about it later, but right now, I need Helari to trace Faustus. He'll know we've interfered if I do it myself," I said, and Maddox cupped my cheek.

"Alright," he said as the door to his office opened, revealing Helari with her servants, Mikhail and Scar.

"What's the problem?" she asked, and I stared at her.

"*Eovre vedel hael.*" There are indeed bad omens. I stated, and Helari raised her eyebrows.

"*Ercharie,* Elair," Helari said. I looked at Maddox and used one of my hands to summon a white flame at the center of the room.

"Faustus," Mikhail growled lowly, baring his teeth.

"Calm down," Helari said. "Let's listen to her story before jumping to conclusions."

"Alright then," I said with a shrug. I led Maddox onto the couches, and we all sat except for Helari's servants.

"This is going to take a while..." I trailed off.

# Chapter Twenty Three

I sighed as I casually poured myself a bit of whiskey into a glass.

"So how long does this break away from his control, last?" Mikhail asked sternly, and I turned to face them. Maddox, Helari, and her servants were now seated on the two couches facing one another.

"Approximately an hour or so. Which was why I can't waste any time at all. Faustus always knows where I am, so he leaves behind a trail for you to track. I can't do it myself. He'll find me. In fact, I don't think anyone can other than you." I looked at Helari. "You can trace him from it without being noticed."

"Very well. This will take no time at all, so sit down," Helari calmly said, and I watched as Maddox got up, took my glass of whiskey, and drank a bit of it. I raised an eyebrow, and he wrapped an arm around my waist, gently leading me back to the couch, my glass still in his hands.

I sat down and sighed as I offered Helari my left hand. She took it and closed her eyes. When she opened them again, her eyes were aglow and were looking into a place beyond what the normal eye could see. I felt a warm tingling sensation from my palms. After a few seconds, Helari closed her eyes again and opened them to reveal her odd-colored eyes.

"He's a bit too far off right now, but I should be able to find him once he calls for you," Helari said, and I breathed a sigh of relief.

"Alright, I can feel my hold on my consciousness waning so let me just *show* you what I need to say," I said. Helari nodded, and I looked over at Maddox, who gave me an encouraging nod. I leaned into him before I speak, "*Rememorari erhistor.*"

I closed my eyes, and I felt a soft breeze surround us. When I opened my eyes, I found that we're in my room... well, my cell.

It was nothing but stone and dim light. I spotted myself, a small, frail body curled into a dark corner.

"Is that you?" Maddox asked from my side. I looked at him and nodded. Helari was on my right with her servants standing behind her, and Maddox was to my left.

"I was ten years old," I said. I watched as the old me leaned her head against the cold wall. "I was being punished for refusing to kill my opponent in a combat session," I said and walked over to the little girl.

She had puffy eyes and red cheeks that revealed her tear-stained face.

"When did Faustus first—" Helari began, but she was interrupted by a male voice.

"Elair," the voice called out, and the little version of myself stood up and began sobbing.

"I didn't know. I didn't mean to disobey. She was my—" she started, but she became quiet as Faustus walked in. He gave her a kind smile and wrapped her in his embrace.

"Ssshh... Elair. *Min silder*, there are no friendships here. You know that," Faustus said. "She was about to kill your aunt, and you shouldn't feel bad for her. She's gone now."

"But—"

"You will not sleep here tonight, my child. Your aunt has forgiven you, and tonight, we continue the ceremonies as planned," Faustus said as he tilted her head up. My past self revealed a set of determined eyes. "*Renare lyger... farvel hes ti opiere*. Strong little girl... forget your powers," Faustus said, and the scene disappeared.

"You were bound to his commands," Helari said.

"I'm bound by blood. The night of the mating ceremony is supposed to complete the binding process," I said. "I have no clue on the details, but I trust that by the time the night is over, I would have been long gone," I said, and Helari nodded her head.

"Troubling, to say the least," she said, and I felt Maddox hold me closer. "I will see what I can do. Mikhail, go and do your best to prepare for Faustus' arrival. Scar, come with me. Tracking is what you do best," Helari said, and the two men walked to the door and opened it for Helari.

"As for the two of you, there are only two more hours until the mating ceremony. I suggest you place a new *sere* into the *scal*, Elair. Should your consciousness fade away, the *sere* should be able to help fight some of Faustus' hold on you... for now." She smiled as she walked away, the two men closing the door behind her.

"Trouble in paradise already," Maddox said, worry etched into his face. I turned around to face him.

"Whatever happens tonight, I'm glad I got to feel what it was like to have a mate," I said, and Maddox's face turned into an expression of concern.

"And you won't forget it," he said as he cupped my cheek. I leaned into it and enjoyed the warm tingles it sent down my spine.

"I will forget the time I spent telling you all about Faustus. I have only a few minutes left," I said, and Maddox nodded. I wrapped my arms around his neck and gently pulled him down so that our noses touched.

"I will do everything that I—"

"Sshhh..." I placed a finger on his lips and closed my eyes. *"Min tevra, wiviadere, en-farvel... vren renare siourvran, sileio skeiva,"* I said, knowing he would never decipher that. It meant 'my love, listen, don't forget... you are powerful, but he knows it, too.'

"Wha—"

"A little charm for the night." I lied with a soft smile before I felt a darkness come over me. I felt faint and weak as I fell into Maddox's chest. "Take care of us tonight, Maddox. I doubt I will be able to do anything," I muttered as my eyes grew heavy with sleep.

"I swear, I will," Maddox said just as the darkness consumed me.

# Chapter Twenty Four

What was I doing sleeping on the couch in Maddox's office when I have like an hour left until I have to *get ready*?

"Um, how did I get here?" I asked as Maddox looked up from the paperwork on his desk.

"I found you knocked out in the living room. I was going to carry you up to the room, but I figured I might as well bring you here since this is the other office I use," Maddox said.

"Great. Is it bad to have signs of Alzheimers before a mating ceremony?" I asked sarcastically, and Maddox smirked as he got up and walked over to me.

"Not really, although I'm a bit surprised you had a gun on you," Maddox said, and I raised an eyebrow as I immediately reached for the back pockets of my jeans. It was empty.

"Maddox..." I said in warning.

"You had the safety off, and you were asleep. How else was I supposed to keep you safe?" Maddox asked as he pulled one of my beloved guns out of his back pocket.

"Why the hell would the safety be off?" I asked. It was not like I used it at the mall.

"I don't know. You really shouldn't ask me. I just found it like that," Maddox said, and I squinted my eyes at him.

"Liar," I said with a sigh as I stood up. Maddox stood as well and immediately wrapped his arms around my waist. "Maddox, are you okay?" I asked.

"Yup, just wanting to hold you before the ceremony." I rolled my eyes, and as I did so, my eyes landed on Maddox's wall.

Maddox released me from his hold and sighed.

"I'm going to go ahead and prepare for the ceremony. You staying for much longer?" Maddox asked me, and I shook my head.

"Y-yeah, go ahead," I said and didn't even turn to watch Maddox as he left. Instead, I moved towards the wall. I used my index finger to touch it.

There was a bullet hole.

I turned on my phone's flashlight. There was a bullet embedded into it, and as I shone my light on it, I examined the bullet.

*What the fuck?*

I sighed as I pulled on the dress. It was a beautiful white dress with long silken sleeves and a skirt that flowed down elegantly to my knees. It was silk and made my body look like it was masked in liquid pearl. I simply let down my hair in its usual waves. I didn't wear any form of footwear, and to be honest, I looked like I had just gone out of a relaxing bath.

I took a twirl in front of the mirror. The silk moved with my movements and just felt absolutely wonderful on my skin. I had to thank Helari for it later. I sighed as I opened the box of *seres* on the nightstand and took one out. I only had two remaining. I stood in front of the mirror and felt for the *scal* at the back of my neck. I carefully slid the *sere* in and sighed as I felt it cool down my body.

"Ready?" Helari's voice asked, and I looked at the door only to find her peeking her head through it.

"Yeah," I said with a shrug as she made her way in.

"Good," Helari said with a smile. "I have to say, the dress looks great on you," she said.

"Thanks, I have you to thank," I replied before releasing a heavy breath. "I'm feeling nervous, and I don't know why," I blurted out, and Helari chuckled softly.

"Don't worry about anything. It's a full moon, and the pack is celebrating. Not to mention your family is here," she said.

"True," I said before fiddling with the material of the skirt. "Let's just go get this over with."

Helari nodded, and we walk together out of the pack house and down into the forest.

"I hate people. I hate attention," I said, and Helari chuckled.

"Well, you're bound to be the center of all attention tonight. Don't worry. I'm sure you already know the words you have to say." Helari reassured me, and I bit my bottom lip.

"Ah, fuck it, it was going to happen some time," I muttered.

We walked to the waterfall at the edge of the lake, and I fought the urge to roll my eyes as I spotted the area. It was lit with paper lanterns all around, and all members of the pack had surrounded the circular slab of stone that Maddox and I had gone to before.

The sky was dark, and rightfully so as it was almost twelve midnight. The full moon seemed larger than ever, and the stars glimmered all around like never before. Two of the pack members had already shifted into their wolves. They stood at what looked to be the beginning of the aisle formed by the gap in between the rows of pack members. They watched as I walked down the aisle littered with blood red and white rose petals.

On the slab was a marble stand that held a ceremonial bowl with detailed carvings made of polished black stone. At its center was a bright blue flame seeping through beautiful clear crystals. Helari made her way to the front, and I stood to her left with Maddox in front of me.

He wore a casual all white outfit consisted of a plain white shirt and a pair of white jeans. He was barefooted as well. Although he wore a serious expression, the moment our eyes met, I saw the glimmer of excitement in them.

We turned our attention to Helari, and she smiled.

"Members of the Macabre pack," Helari began, raising her hands, the sound of the waterfall seemingly fading away at the sound of her voice. "Tonight, we secure the bond of two capable leaders. Macabre, tonight, we are to officiate the joining of your alpha, Maddox Cross, and your future luna, Elair Richelieu. May the goddess bless this union and strengthen the Macabre Pack!" Helari said as her voice radiated power.

Maddox placed his right hand over the flame with his palm facing the sky. I placed mine on top of his with my palm facing his, clasping his hands. Maddox squeezed mine, and I sighed as the light of the full moon began to focus on the bowl. The blue flame rose, but there was no heat or burning sensation. The flame eventually wrapped itself around our hands.

"Elair Richelieu, as alpha of the Macabre Pack and your mate, will you renounce your pack to join and lead the Macabre Pack as a new member and its luna?" Maddox asked.

"I, Elair Richelieu, renounce the Blood Moon Pack to be joined with her mate and be his equal as a new member of the Macabre Pack and as his luna," I said. Maddox beamed at me, and Helari smiled as well.

I looked at my mother and siblings and saw their happy faces.

*There is no other person in this world that can be happier than I am at this moment*, my mother mind linked me, and as I closed my eyes, I felt my connection to her and my siblings fade away.

*Can you hear me?* a voice asked through the mind link. I smiled as I opened my eyes to Maddox's blazing amber eyes.

*Loud and clear*, I mind linked back, and Maddox smiled as he lifted our hands in the air.

The two wolves howled in the back, and the rest of the pack shouted in joy. I was about to face the rest of them when I felt my body being hurled towards someone and then lifted off the ground.

I stared wide-eyed at Maddox who has lifted me off the ground bridal style. I was about to struggle when Maddox carried me through the cheering crowd and off into the forest.

"Um..." I trailed off. "So where are we going?" I asked as Maddox still walked forward.

"It's a s—"

"Don't you dare fucking say it's a secret. It's cheesy and lame," I said, and Maddox chuckled.

"Well then, we're going to hell, since you invited me earlier."

"Oh, great, finally. How long does it take to get there?" I asked, and Maddox laughed.

"Five seconds," he said, and I raised an eyebrow. I looked around and realized we were climbing the mountain from before to jump off the waterfall.

"Cool," I said with a smirk.

As we made our way up, I slowly snuggled up to Maddox and breathed in relief as we slowly reached the top.

"Silent all of a sudden?" Maddox asked, and I rolled my eyes.

"Well, I'm enjoying the fact that I'm being carried up a mountain. It's a once in a lifetime opportunity," I casually said, and Maddox smirked as we finally made it to the top.

My eyes widened at the sight of a beautiful large teepee with a mix of flowers covering the top of the white canvas. The inside was covered with beautiful bright glass lanterns filled with candlelight, and the ground was covered with layers of blankets and topped off with a soft white velvety material that looked all too comfortable to lie on. There were pillows all over, and more than enough space for... I don't really have to say, do I?

"Like it?" Maddox asked.

"Meh," I said with a shrug, and he laughed as he placed me down, the feeling of the soft ground soothing the soles of my feet. "We're bound to get all those white sheets dirty from our feet, though."

"Oh, we were bound to get them dirty, anyways," Maddox said with a smug look on his face. Before I could react, he wrapped his arms around my waist and pulled me to him so that our faces were mere centimeters away from each other. "Mine at last," he said against my lips, and I rolled my eyes.

"Hmm... Not sure how I feel about that," I said as I pulled his shirt so that we're pressed against each other further. "You're mine," I said as I bit his bottom lip.

He growled softly before moving his right hand up to tangle them into my hair.

"That works for me," Maddox quietly said as he gently tilted my head and placed his lips on mine. I wrapped my hands around his neck and moaned as we deepened the kiss.

We started walking to the teepee and broke away from each other. Our eyes were a mix of lust and impatience. Maddox pulled his shirt off and placed his hand on my back, kissing me as we lie down on the sheets. I broke away first, and Maddox stared at me as I used my legs to flip us over.

"Much better," I said, and Maddox smirked as I leaned down and captured his lips. I began to trail kisses along his jawline and down his neck, sucking on the sensitive skin where his mark would be.

Maddox growled lowly against my ear, and I smirked as my fingers trailed down to the waistband of his jeans.

Maddox and I lay tangled in each other's arms in the little teepee. Our clothes laid forgotten on the side, and we're wrapped in between the layers of blankets that cushioned us from the cold ground.

"Feeling okay?" Maddox asked.

"Did I sound like I wasn't?" I asked, and Maddox laughed as he tucked a lock of my hair behind my ear.

"Hmm... Maybe we could get you to repeat tha—"

"Ssshhh, I'm enjoying my chill session," I said, and Maddox chuckled.

"Well, I don't think we're going to *chill* for long," Maddox said as one of his hands traced my skin underneath the blankets, leaving goosebumps and sending sparks down my spine.

"You need to stop before I jump your bones," I said in warning as I stared at him. His eyes were filled with amusement, and I found my gaze flitting towards his bare neck.

Maddox seemed to notice where I was looking since he cleared his throat.

"Do it," Maddox said in a low voice, and I raised my eyebrows.

"Already?" I asked as I pulled myself up to look into his eyes. They were already dark and full of longing as if it would do him the greatest honor. He pulled me into his lap, and I was thankful I wrapped myself in a separate blanket. I was not going to get sexual while marking him.

"It'll heal almost instantly… and I want you to do it," Maddox said as he caressed my cheek. I placed a gentle kiss on his lips. "And it means I have more time to seduce you," Maddox said, and I rolled my eyes.

"This is gonna hurt, you know?" I said, and Maddox smirked as he pulled me down so that our foreheads were touching.

"Does it look like I care?" he asked, and I grinned before kissing him once more. Maddox groaned as I trailed my hands down his body, exploring every crevice of his chiseled skin.

I moved my lips down, and Maddox caressed my back as my canines elongated.

"Mine," I said.

"Yours," Maddox responded before I bit into his neck. Maddox strained underneath me and grunted, but after a while, he stopped and took a deep breath. I knew it was excruciating. He seemed so tense, and the taste of blood in my mouth wasn't too appealing.

I promptly released him and looked at my handiwork. Maddox's amber eyes were bright even in the dark light, and I watched under the bright candlelight as the bleeding wound disappeared and immediately began to heal. The mark was of my canines. It was like a faint scar of welts against his skin. I traced my fingers around it, and Maddox's breath caught in his throat. He stared at me, and I felt an electrifying sensation run through me.

*Beautiful,* Maddox's voice said in my head. I stared at him and smirked.

"Oh, so that's what you're thinking," I said, and he grinned.

"What else could I possibly think of?" Maddox asked as he pulled me down to him. He captured my lips in a deep kiss, and I used my hands to keep me balanced.

*Probably marking me*, I mind linked back, and Maddox laughed into our kiss. We broke apart, and I watched as his eyes turned a dark lust-filled color. Was that a yes?

"Would anyone's mate say no?" Maddox asked in a low and dangerous voice. I smirked as his wolf instincts kicked in.

"So what are you waiting for?" I asked, and Maddox growled as we switched positions at almost lightning speed.

"I have no idea," Maddox said as he placed his face on my neck. "But I do like to tease," he said as he kissed my neck. A moan escaped my mouth, and I covered it immediately.

"Dick," I muttered, and Maddox chuckled as he sucked and nipped gently at my skin.

"You've already seen that," Maddox said, and I widened my eyes.

"I cannot believe you just said that," I replied, and Maddox laughed.

"Hmm..." Maddox mumbled, and I felt tingles run down my spine. I felt his teeth trace my skin and elongate with his breath.

# Chapter Twenty Five

I woke with a start, my neck was sore, and Maddox was sleeping soundly beside me. I smiled as I spotted the mark on his neck before touching my own. The skin was still sensitive.

The sun had already gone up, and almost all of our candles went out over the night. I gingerly sat up. I found the dress I wore yesterday and sighed in relief as I slipped it on. I stared at Maddox before kneeling back down and studying his face. He looked completely calm and unguarded.

Maddox's eyes fluttered open, and he immediately beamed at me.

"Morning," he greeted.

"Morning, wanna go for a run?" I asked. He grinned before he got up and shifted into his black wolf.

Of course, he said through the mind link as his wolf panted at me, his tongue hanging out.

"Okay, then," I said as I slipped out of the dress and shifted into my wolf. I shook my fur and barked at Maddox.

Are we running or what? I asked, and Maddox's wolf barked back as he took off into a sprint. I let out a huff before sprinting in his direction. I caught up with him and barked.

Thanks for the warning, I mind linked, and Maddox's wolf barked twice at me.

You're welcome.

I mentally groaned as we dashed through the forest and down towards the lake. Halfway through, I heard a strange sound and stopped.

Elair? Maddox asked, and I felt the worry that filled his head. He trotted towards me and tilted his head.

There's something... I trailed off as I sniffed the air. I caught the scent of a familiar person. Over there! I mind linked as I darted to my left and sprinted off. Maddox followed closely behind me.

Smell that? I asked, and Maddox barked.

Clearly, he responded, and I continued to follow the scent.

Once I get close enough, I felt a dark feeling swallow me up.

Maddox, go—

I heard a loud whimper and turned around. I watched as Maddox's wolf fell limp to the ground and a figure emerged from the darkness.

"Eovre andet," You have a purpose... a female voice said from behind him. Maddox was awake, but his eyes revealed his pain.

Run! Maddox yelled through the mind link, and I heard his wolf yelp as the figure stepped out of the shadows.

The figure was that of a woman, and my eyes widened upon recognizing her. Her eyes were dark blue, her hair blonde and pulled into an elegant style, and she stared at me with disdain.

"You broke the rules, Elair," she said, and I widened my eyes. "And you will pay for it." I launched my wolf at her only to find me suspended up in the air.

She looked at me and then at Maddox's wolf. From her side, she pulled out a dagger, and without so much as another glance, thrusted it at me. I watched as Maddox whimpered in his wolf form as the point of the blade raced towards me.

"Elair, wake up!" Maddox yelled, and I opened my eyes to his blazing amber ones.

"What?" I asked, and Maddox sighed in relief before embracing me.

"You were having a nightmare," Maddox said, and I swallowed a dry lump in my throat. Just as I was about to speak, Maddox froze up.

*Alpha, Luna, sorry to cut your day short. We have incoming,* Jasper mind linked. I stared blankly at Maddox.

*Got it. Everyone in your places. Helari's already at the front. Send Naomi to the east with Iain. Lorraine will stand guard with Winter at the pack house.* Maddox ordered, and I watched as he got up and rummaged through the pillows in the teepee.

*So much for romantic,* I thought, and Maddox chuckled.

*Don't forget, I can hear you now*, Maddox said, and I rolled my eyes.

*I know fuckface*, I replied as Maddox handed me a set of clothes.

"I had these prepared in case something was to happen. You can find your guns back at the pack house, right?" Maddox asked.

"Of course," I said as I got up and put on my clothes. I grinned at Maddox's choice— a thick black leather jacket, my usual combat boots, a plain black tank top, and some jeans.

Maddox eyed me as I dressed up.

"Not gonna change?" I asked, raising my eyebrow. His white jeans were the sole thing he was wearing at the moment.

"I prefer my wolf," he said, and I nodded my head.

"Are you gonna bring me to the pack house or are we just gonna stare at each other?" I asked, and Maddox smirked at me before shifting into his black wolf. He barked and lowered himself as I climbed onto his back.

We made it to the pack house, and I found that there were wolves on guard already. I got off Maddox's back, and he barked at me.

*I'll head to the front. Take care of yourself, okay?* Maddox mind linked, and I smirked.

*When don't I? Get your ass up there and do your job, Cross*, I said, and I sensed the amusement in Maddox as he turned slowly, glancing at me before taking off.

I ran into the pack house and made my way up to the bedroom. As soon as I got there, I put on my leather holster and placed my guns at my sides. I brought more than enough magazines and pulled my hair up into a ponytail.

I made my way downstairs and saw the elderly and the youngsters of the pack already settling in.

"Luna," a voice called from the side. I turned to its direction and found Jillian with a few children.

"What's the problem?" I asked.

"Your mom and siblings are in here, but we're going to lock down the pack house. It'll be inaccessible until you and Maddox return." Jillian informed me.

"Alright, are we missing anyone?" I asked, and Jillian shook her head.

"We gathered everyone right after the ceremony," she responded, and I raised my eyebrows.

"How did you guys—"

*Elair, head straight towards the southern border*, Maddox mind linked me, and I sighed.

"Nevermind. Take care of them. I'll be right back," I told Jillian, and she nodded as I quickly got out of the pack house.

Last time I checked, the pack house wasn't centered around the borders. It was leaning more towards the western side. I sprinted as fast as I could through the forest and began to hear what seemed to be the sounds of the intruders. As a werewolf, it was easier to make the run from the pack house to the southern border. I imagined being human would tire me out within two minutes of full on sprinting.

I reached the southern border and was immediately hit with a pang of pain in my abdomen.

*Shit, Maddox,* I thought to myself as I used the mate bond to sense him.

I went for my intuition and sprinted to my right.

*Maddox!* I screamed through the mind link.

I dashed my way through trees and jumped over shrubs as I sensed the mate bond grow stronger. I heard the familiar growl of Maddox's wolf and a few voices shouting.

"It seems my little one has made it," a male voice said as I entered the clearing.

I found Helari, Scar, and Mikhail who was holding Maddox back. Everyone's eyes were on me, and my gaze landed on two figures.

"Aunt Eleanor?" I called out, and I watched her grin.

She had deep blue almost violet eyes, and she wore a sleek black coat that fell to the ground. She had her arm around a male with pale ice-cold eyes and an amused look on his face.

"*Min silder,*" he greeted, and I raised my eyebrows.

"Oh, for fuck's sake," I said with a sigh, "Can everyone please stop speaking crazies? It's like you all expect me to be able to understand what you are saying."

*Elair, stay calm and focus,* Maddox said, and I could feel the subdued anger in his voice. I glanced over at him and at Mikhail.

"Leave this place, Faustus. We have no reason to—" Helari began, but Faustus interrupted her.

"Oh, do be quiet," Faustus said as he used one hand and beckoned me to come towards him. I felt a pull in my chest, and my feet were lifted off the floor as I was dragged in front of him.

"I was very disappointed in you, Elair, but impressed, all the same," Faustus said, and I glared at him.

"I have no clue what the fuck you're talking about," I said through gritted teeth, and Faustus grinned.

"It seems you are losing your grip, Elair. That is understandable. After all, you had no idea what the mating ceremony would do to you. Besides, I see that you and your mate have succeeded," Faustus said as he did a motion with his fingers. My head moved on its own and bared my neck to reveal my mark.

"Let her go!" Maddox said as he shifted into his human form. Yet surprisingly, he was clothed in a skin-tight black armor. It was no doubt Helari's doing.

"So you did assign a pawn. How cute," Aunt Eleanor said, and I felt something constrict around my throat. I gasped for air before I was dropped to the ground struggling for air.

"What are you doing to her?" Helari asked in a solemn tone.

"You'll find out soon enough," Faustus responded, and Aunt Eleanor made her way towards me. "I am somewhat thankful Elair was smart enough to hold onto her consciousness. It made the journey here a bit more exciting... but I have no time to waste," Faustus said.

"Proceed, Eleanor," he said, and Aunt Eleanor untangled herself from him and began to chant incoherently. Her eyes became blood red, and it felt like a large punch hit me from above.

My back arched from the pain, and I tried to scream, but I couldn't.

Maddox's growls were loud and clear, and I watched through tears as he tried to hurl himself towards me, only to find himself unable to even get an inch closer. Helari immediately began to work her spells, Mikhail stood at what seemed to be the barrier, and Scar had taken off his black gloves and took out a set of knives.

"Nothing, I'm afraid, will be able to stop me this time," Faustus said, and Mikhail let out a feral growl.

"You have hell to pay," Mikhail said, seething with anger.

"We have hell to pay, Brother," Faustus said with a smile as he looked eerily at me. The pain has subsided, but as I tried to get up, Faustus used a wave of his hand, and my body was hurled towards a tree. I was smacked horizontally against it, and I heard the sound of my bones cracking.

Maddox let out a scream of pain that mirrored the exact amount of pain that coursed through me.

"I am... going... to kill... you..." I said breathlessly, and Faustus laughed maniacally.

"Poor little mate, broken little mate," Faustus said, changing the lyrics to the damned song. My eyes suddenly felt as if they were on fire. "By blood, I bound you to my soul. My demands are yours forever to obey."

"Go... to hell!" I hissed as I felt my bones heal. I got up, and Maddox growled.

I pulled out one of my guns from its holster and, as fast as I could, fired in Faustus' direction.

I gawked.

The bullet aimed right at his head stopped just in front of him. He smirked as he turned to face me.

"It would be a waste to just turn you into a mindless follower. Perhaps breaking you again is the best course of action," Faustus said as he nodded his head. My shooting hand twisted, and I heard the sound of my bones snapping.

I screamed in agony and fell to the ground. My breath was ragged as Faustus' eyes began to glow. Out of them emerged the shadow of a wolf-like creature.

"Now then, my child, let us show your friends what exactly *macabre* looks and," Faustus began as he looked over at Maddox, "feels like."

I watched as the shadowed wolf rabidly growled and launched itself at me.

# Chapter Twenty Six

I was launched towards a tree helplessly as Faustus used his creature to break every part of me again and again. He relished in the pain that Maddox and I shared. I tried to block the mate bond, but I could hear Maddox's pain above my own. The wolf had bitten my arms and shattered my skin and bones. As I lay broken on the floor, the wolf stepped on my back and bit down on the back of my neck. I felt it pull something back, and Helari screamed in my place.

The *scal* was being pulled out of my own body forcibly. I screamed, blood gurgling my voice and the warm feeling of blood seeping from my neck. I used all my strength to try to block out my bond with Maddox, but it was pointless as black dots began to blur my vision and my breath became ragged.

The creature stopped for a moment, and I watched as blood pooled where I lay down and the stench of my bleeding flesh wrapped around me like a suffocating blanket.

Helari launched her own shadows and powered through Faustus' barrier. I watched her as she tried to keep a composed face, but the worry in her eyes and the sheen of sweat on her forehead showed otherwise.

"How many children, Faustus? How many had to die for this power?" Helari screamed, and Faustus tilted his head.

"Now, that's a secret... but if you really want to know, I'd say I slaughtered just a little below a million, and half of them were her doing," Faustus said as he looked at me. "Pity I can't reveal the full effects of my work on you yet," Faustus added, and his creature circled around me as I healed. It knew when I healed and attacked me as soon as the process was completed.

"Say... my dear child, why can't you shift?" Faustus asked, and I felt the pain course through me. He was forcing me to shift.

"Faustus, stop this!" Helari screamed, and I felt the agony as my bones shattered. I wasn't fully healed and yet my bones were being forced to regenerate.

The pain was excruciating.

It was as if every part of me was being crushed, snapped, and shoved against each other. I felt a sudden pain that was different from anything else. I coughed out blood and choked on it. My breath was growing weaker, and I felt my vision blur every now and then. Faustus raised his eyebrows before smiling and laughing maniacally once more.

"Oh, dear... already?" Faustus wondered, and I felt a mind-breaking headache come over me. The shadow wolf stopped right in front of me and stared into my eyes.

It growled at me, and I felt anger surge through my veins. My blood suddenly felt like it was boiling. I growled right back at it, and Faustus grinned even wider.

"I think it's about time we show them what we've created. Thank you, Eleanor," Faustus said, and I watched as Eleanor lifted the barrier.

Scar made one quick movement, and his knives immediately impaled the damned shadow creature against a tree. Helari immediately attacked Faustus, a blur of dark shadows launching themselves at him. Maddox made a run towards me, and Mikhail moved at lightning speed to snap Eleanor's neck.

I didn't have any more emotion in me to grieve her death.

"*Relesereo opiere.*" Release your power... Faustus said, and I felt a sudden numbness.

I felt someone shaking me, but my eyes landed on Faustus who was laughing out of control despite Helari's shadows shredding his clothes and drawing blood with them.

"I will return once more, my child, but the damage has been done... and I doubt anyone of you can fix that. *Rememorari, Elair, enfarvel vren min silder,*" Faustus said.

Helari screamed commands as I found myself looking at Maddox who had already taken me into his arms, broken and limp as I was.

"Don't let him escape, Mikhail!" Helari screamed as I fell into the darkness that weighed on my eyes. I felt myself lose something... something that would make me lose my mind.

"How is she?" I heard Helari say behind the doors.

"She's coping up," Maddox responded as I lay still on the bed.

I was in our room, but I was placed under extreme care. I wasn't allowed to move at all... not that I could. Maddox had a makeshift desk by the bed and would work by my side. He never left me though I haven't spoken a single word out of my mouth since I woke up the other day.

All I had was the mind link.

*Maddox, could you come here?* I asked him, and he immediately went inside and sat on the edge of the bed. It dipped to the side, and he took my hand as gently as he could, knowing full well that all my bones were shattered beneath my pale-looking skin.

I couldn't even complain about my stupid blond eyelashes or the fact that I looked like I had seen a ghost. I could barely eat anything, and if the stupid tubes stuck into my skin had anything to say about it... I wasn't healing by any means.

I wasn't healing.

Helari had done everything in her power. Mikhail was gone though Helari said he was on track.

Faustus had apparently disappeared without a single trace. There were a handful of dead wolves, but many of the pack did visit me. Iain came with Jillian the other day with flowers to which I mind linked my thanks. Jasper and Winter had come with a few movies for me to watch.

As for my family... well.

I told Maddox to send them home and tell them I was feeling ill. I didn't have the heart to face my siblings or my mother looking like I had been broken and torn apart. Physically, I was.

Mentally, I was filled with a mixture of rage, disgust, and contempt, all of them directed towards myself. I couldn't even recall a single thing about Faustus. Helari explained that nothing was my fault and that Faustus had manipulated me way before I could have stopped it.

I felt stupid.

I felt like I had let myself down.

I wasn't supposed to let anything and anyone get hurt, and yet if I couldn't protect myself, my mate, and now my pack, what the fuck was I supposed to be good for? To be on fucking display? To be a little doll that just sat around all day?

It was killing me inside, and Maddox could see it. He could feel it, and every time it ate me up, Maddox would sit by my side and gently hold me.

I felt the urge to punch myself for my uselessness.

I had never felt as worthless as I have now.

And I could do absolutely nothing about it.

No matter how fucking resolved I was to get up and prepare to fight... I couldn't. The truth of the matter was, my body wasn't healing. My bones were like immovable rocks. I didn't even have the healing capability of a human being. I was exactly like a doll.

*You can't keep being like this, Elair,* Maddox mind linked as he lay by my side.

*I can't do anything else, Maddox. I'm literally incapable of doing a thing. I've become a goddamn vegetable in the simple matter of hours that Faustus broke me,* I said.

*You're not broken if you're talking as much as you are now.*

I smirked, thankful that at least my face muscles weren't damaged.

*What else can I do?* I asked, and Maddox sighed.

*Sleep,* Maddox said, and I released a loud breath.

*Yeah, that works.*

I woke up with my heart racing against my chest, but my brain was unable to recall what caused the reaction. I looked to my side and found Maddox fast asleep. I wanted to touch him... to run my fingers down the side of his jaw.

Maddox's eyes blinked open in the darkness, and he immediately snuggled closer to me.

"Bad dream?" Maddox asked.

*Yeah, I guess. I can't remember any of it,* I responded, and Maddox looked into my eyes.

"You'll get better," he said, but it was like a promise more than a reassurance.

*I hope so,* I replied, and he kissed my cheek. I watched as he promptly fell asleep. His wounds had healed within a matter of minutes when we were out there. I was glad he was fine. After all, he felt all the pain that I had because of the mate bond.

Then again, I envied him, too.

I stared at him and fought the urge to cry. Maddox had no idea how much more pain I felt when he was asleep, and I was left alone with my thoughts. I sighed and forced myself to sleep, hoping that tomorrow my bones would heal and move.

I woke up to a brightly lit room filled with sunlight. I blinked my eyes a few times before I realized that Maddox wasn't in the room. Over me was a breakfast tray sat on an elevated mini-table. There was nothing on it, though, except for a note from Maddox.

*Having a meeting. Mind link when you want breakfast,* it said. I looked around me and sighed. This was my only chance to figure out if I could move or not.

I tried my best to move my fingers. I bit my bottom lip and muffled a scream as I moved around. Tears welled up in my eyes as I struggled to move my legs. I lifted my neck off my pillow and used the force of my body to turn around.

When I turned to my right, I found myself staring at my reflection in the tiny bedside mirror. My eyes looked dull, my hair looked brittle, and my lips were chapped. I had bruises everywhere, and it showed through the little white t-shirt dress that I had on. I swallowed the dry lump in my throat.

*Fuck it, Faustus said something to you before he left, Elair,* I told myself. What the fuck was it?

*R-rememorari Elair,* I remembered, and I was filled with the urge to say the word out loud. I opened my mouth, and a shaky breath was all that escaped it.

"*R-re..*" I began to say, but it only sounded like a whisper. "*Rememorari...*" I managed to wheeze out.

I heard the sound of bones clicking and cracking.

My eyes widened, and I had the urge to look at my hands. I tried to move them and gasped as I was able to hold them up to my eyes.

*Rememorari, Elair. Enfarvel vren min silder. Relesereo opiere. Vedel hael. Lothrian. Ercharie...* I chanted in my brain. I paused and stare at my reflection. They made sense to me. In order they were... Remember, Elair. Don't forget you're my child. Release your power. There are bad omens. Float. Speak.

"*Rememorari,*" I said again in a louder voice. My rough voice sounded more like a loud wheezing sound. I felt a surge of warmth from my chest.

My back arched from the bed, and I felt my body shake and tremble. I heard the sounds of clicking, and I felt my blood boil. My forehead was wet with sweat, and my body felt like a Rubik's Cube being twisted and turned.

*By blood, we are bound, and by blood, I will be destroyed,* I heard a voice in my mind say. It was my voice. It was a memory of some sort. I closed my eyes and bit my bottom lip, fighting the urge to scream as I felt the excruciating pain of my regeneration.

It was like being awaken during a surgery... painful, agonizing, and terrifying.

I bit into the duvet of the sheets as hard as I could as I felt my bones heal.

When I opened my eyes again, I felt something flow through my veins… something familiar yet strange at the same time.

I turned my body effortlessly and lifted myself off of the bed. I took the tubes out of my skin and cringed at the size of the needles that were in me. I stretched my neck and groaned. Feeling the cold hardwood under my feet had never felt so relieving. I grinned as I found myself in full control of my body again. I did cartwheels and back-bending yoga moves. I wanted to run.

I wanted to shift.

Filled with elation, I crept slowly out of the room and sneaked my way out of the pack house.

Once I was out in the forest, I didn't bother to take my clothes off. I willed myself to shift.

# Chapter Twenty Seven

I felt the breath catch in my throat. I had just been standing here, human, for the past ten minutes.

*Shift, goddamn it!* I thought to myself. I stared at my fingertips.

Nothing.

No claws.

No canines.

Nothing. There was nothing but the cold ground under my feet. Nothing but the smell of the forest.

I held my hands up. I imagined my wolf and the feeling of forming bones into that of one. I thought of the thrill of having my wolf freed and ready to run around and explore the mountains, paws padding along the forest floor, and the thrill of being able to release the strength of a beast.

But here I was with nothing.

"Elair!" Maddox yelled, and I heard the sound of several footsteps coming my way.

I hadn't made it too far off from the pack house. I was only a few meters away from the patio. I remained there, frozen and shocked.

I couldn't shift.

"Elair!" Maddox yelled even louder, and I felt his arms wrap around me, squeezing the life out of me as he turned me around and nuzzled my neck. I wrapped my arms around him as well. "You can walk! You're... you're okay." Maddox said, slowly calming down. I nodded my head, and I spotted Helari and Scar along with Iain, Jasper, and Winter.

"What's wrong?" Helari asked me, and Maddox released me from his grip.

"I can't shift," I said. At first, Maddox was happy to hear my voice, but when he processed what I've said, a worried look crossed his face.

"What?" he asked.

"I can't fucking shift," I said as I felt the anger boil under my skin. I stared out into the mountains, and the surrounding air grew electric.

"Elair, calm down," Helari said, and I looked at her and attempted to growl. However, no noise came out of my mouth

I kicked the dirt and ran my hands through my hair.

"What the hell is going on with me?" I screamed and watched as Helari lifted her hand up.

"*Fenian, Elair, eovren skeivia... vre opiere renare,*" she said, and I raised my eyebrows as the language deciphered itself in my head. *Stop, Elair, They know that your power has returned.*

"*Hevaete? Sileio necran min vulko. En-eovre min satren.*" *Why? He broke my wolf. I don't have my connection...* I replied, and Helari's eyes widened.

"How are you speaking in my—"

"I don't know," I responded simply. "I woke up, somehow healed myself with a magic word, and bam! I had a dictionary of words in fuck-knows-what stuck up my brain. Meanwhile, my wolf is nowhere to be found."

"No, she's still there. If you can still mind link me, then she's still there," Maddox said, and I shook my head.

"I can't feel her. I can't... I can't explain it. It's like I'm a part of your pack, and I know I could link you... but I'm not... I—"

"She's in transition," Helari interjected, and I gave her a questioning look.

"What do you mean?" Maddox asked, and I stared at the ground.

"Faustus created his own pawn," Helari said, and I backed away into the forest. "A hybrid, at that," Helari continued, and I watched as Maddox looked over at me. My heart leaped into my throat. I couldn't even speak.

"Elair, calm down," Maddox said as he walked over to me. I wrapped my arms around myself, wishing I was dead.

I was no good to anyone without my wolf.

I was no good to Maddox or his pack.

I was... useless.

I was a failure.

"Elair!" Maddox yelled as he grabbed me and wrapped his arms around me. His right hand was in my hair, securing me to his neck and allowing me to feel the warmth that radiated off of his body. "Stop thinking for a second. I'm still here. We still share the same feelings. I can feel the weight on your shoulders. I'm here. Calm down." He reassured me.

It was only then that I realized the tingling sensation running down my arms. Once it died down, Maddox loosened his grip until he only had his left arm around my waist.

"Elair, come, I think I can help you," Helari said, and I looked at Maddox who squeezed my side reassuringly. I nodded my head before Maddox walked me back to the pack house.

I dressed in a pair of plain blue jeans and a black shirt, not wanting to bother with anything else. Helari insisted I bathe myself so I did, and here I was, sitting in Maddox's office with Maddox working at his desk.

Helari placed her hand on my forehead, and I felt a surge of energy flow through me.

"*Vre opiere renare siouvran, eovre sileio,*" Helari said. I sighed, deciphering it in my head as, 'Your powers has returned. However, you have done so because of him.'

"I'm not gonna even answer to that. I've already been told again and again that I belong to him. It doesn't mean that I can't get out of it," I said.

"*Eo echarie min inuage vae vren tevra.*" 'Speak in my language for your mate's sake.' I raised my eyebrows. Speak in her language my ass.

"*Hevaete?*" I asked. *Why?* Helari rolled her eyes. She stared at me, and an image flashed before my eyes.

It was of Maddox throwing everything around in his office with anger and frustration on his face. I blinked a few times before the vision disappeared. I stared blankly at Helari.

*He will not take my advice to you well.* Helari's voice rang in my head.

*You want me to do what exactly?* I asked.

*Train with me.* Helari told me, and I raised my eyebrows.

*I have no idea what that even means. Why wouldn't Maddox like that?* I asked confused.

"You'll be too busy working, and alphas like Maddox are possessive," a voice I didn't recognize said, and I turned around and saw what looked to be an aged Maddox.

There were silver hairs in his long black hair tied at the back of his head in a low ponytail. He had a black and gray beard, his eyes were a deep brown hue, and he had wrinkles on his face.

"Let me guess... Are you Maddox's father?" I said, and he grinned at me.

"The one and only!" he said before walking a few steps towards me.

"I did not give you the ability to communicate with me for you to abuse it and use it as telepathy," Helari said as she shook her head.

"But it *is* telepathy. And well, Maddox's mate is my family now. Because I couldn't move as fast as I could before or manage this pack anymore, the least I could do is be a father and help my new daughter out."

"When did you get here?" Maddox asked as he got up from his desk.

"Just an hour ago. It reeked of blood over at the southern border. I guess no one bothered to clean that up yet," he replied, and Maddox glanced over at Helari who sighed.

"Consider it done," she said before looking over at me. "Elair, meet Colt, Maddox's father."

"Nice to get to know the apple of my son's eyes," he said with a wide smile as he extended his hand towards me. I shook it and felt Maddox's presence behind me.

"Don't give me any trouble, Dad," Maddox said with a heavy sigh.

"Wasn't going to," Colt replied with a sigh.

You could see the resemblance between the two. But honestly, they seemed like two completely different men.

"Colt, why don't you, me, and Scar go talk a bit about your little journey around the world?" Helari asked, and he nodded his head.

"Sounds good. I have quite a few things you'd love to know," Colt replied before winking at me. "Nice to meet you, Elair. I'll be sticking around for a few days, so make sure Maddox keeps on his toes." I smirked as I feel Maddox wrap his arms around my waist before Helari practically dragged Colt away, offering me a look that practically said she hated Colt's company.

As soon as they were gone, Maddox spun me around to face him.

"Will you train with her?" Maddox asked me.

"I'm thinking about it," I said with a shrug. "How long does it normally take?"

"I have no clue, but I know that Helari's trained others before, and we don't see them around for weeks," he said with a sigh as he led us to the couch. We sat down, and I rested my head on his shoulder.

"It'd be a great distraction from not having a wolf," I said, and Maddox immediately turned to face me. I looked at him, and he squeezed my waist softly.

"No matter what you are or how broken you think you are, you're mine. That'll never change." Maddox said as he pressed a soft kiss to my forehead.

"I know that. It's just... I can feel an empty part of me filled with something foreign, and I can't... I don't know. Can we change the topic?" I asked, and Maddox chuckled quietly before allowing me to snuggle further into him.

"What do you want to talk about?" Maddox asked.

"Your father."

"What about him?" Maddox asked, and I shrugged.

"You seem like you guys don't get along. Not in a bad way, but not in a close way either," I said, and Maddox sighed.

"Well, he wasn't always so easygoing. Helari gave him a purpose in his life. Back then, he just made a powerful pack that ripped its enemies to shreds—"

"Which you guys technically still do," I added, and Maddox smirked.

"Yeah, but he was insane. I mean that in the worst way possible." Maddox explained.

"What about your mother?" I asked, and Maddox turned quiet. His eyes seemed distant and lonely. I turned and sighed as I placed myself on his lap, straddling him. I tilted up his head to stare into my eyes. "If you don't wanna talk about it, don't," I said as I placed a soft kiss on his lips. He shook his head and tucked a loose hair behind my ear.

"No, I should tell you. I've never met my mom. Dad doesn't like talking about it, and I have no memories of her. Although people have told me that she wasn't my dad's mate, Dad never got lucky enough."

"He never found his mate?" I asked, dumbfounded. I've heard it happen, but I never thought it was real, though. Maddox nodded

"It was like he wasn't given one. Even if he was, he never met her. I know for sure. I asked Helari that when I was younger. She told me that my dad's mate passed away before he met her. Rumors say it was his punishment for what he did in the past." Maddox explained. I pulled him to the side, and we lay together. He played with my hair absentmindedly. "I was more afraid I would receive the same treatment from the goddess," he said as he stared into my eyes.

"I'm afraid I'm a lot more trouble than I'm worth," I said, and Maddox shook his head.

"Believe me, being called Helari's bloodhound is a lot more trouble than its worth."

"Helari's bloodhound?" I asked, raising an eyebrow.

"It's the name most people that recognize her give me. It's my job to protect her. She does the same for the pack. At any point that we need to, Helari will relocate us to her base in case a major attack comes. It was what we prepared for the night of the mating ceremony," Maddox said, and I nodded my head.

"How were you guys prepared for that?" I asked, and Maddox looked away for a bit.

"You told me about it," Maddox said, hesitation evident in his voice. I gave him an incredulous look.

"Something about you losing your consciousness. You did scare the hell out of Vera."

"Who the fuck is Vera?" I asked, and Maddox chuckled.

"A flirtatious wolf that had the nerve to question you as my mate. You did scar her face with a bullet graze right here in this office," Maddox said, and I grinned.

"That explains the bullet hole in your wall. She didn't touch you, did she?" I asked, and Maddox raised his brow this time.

"And if she did?" he asked. I glared before getting on top of him.

"I would be very, very angry," I said as I kissed the mark I left on his neck. He groaned softly.

"And if she didn't?" he asked.

"I'd keep going," I said. He was about to question me further when I captured his lips into mine.

# Chapter Twenty Eight

"You should sleep," I told Maddox. He wrapped his arms around my waist and pulled me to him. I raised my eyebrows as he pressed our bodies together.

"I don't really want to," he said, and I pulled the blanket further up to cover my bare chest.

"You should. I know you haven't slept much since that day," I said as I touched his face in an attempt to be endearing.

"I was worried, and it's not easy holding back after a mating ceremony, you know?" he said, and I rolled my eyes as I allowed myself to relish in the feeling of our bodies touching.

"Hmm... then maybe you should show me," I said with a smirk as we crashed our lips together. Maddox pushed me on the bed, and I giggled as he struggled to remove his shirt.

He tossed it aside, and I immediately wrapped my arms around his neck and pulled him down for a deep kiss. I wrapped my legs around his waist and bit his lip. He growled, and I moaned as his hands traveled down my body. I rolled us over so that I was on top of him. I kissed the mark I left him and gently nipped at his skin.

Maddox's eyes watched me as I kissed down his bare chest.

*You're going to be the death of me,* he mind linked, and I chuckled.

*Let's hope not,* I replied.

I have somehow managed to shower without waking Maddox. Miracles apparently did happen.

Quietly, I put on some underwear, a loose military green tank top, and some pretty black leggings with sheer cut outs on the side, and slipped out of the room. I headed down to grab breakfast for Maddox and I. Maddox had decided to sleep in, and I worried for him. Helari told me that he hadn't slept much ever since the attack, and I knew he must be exhausted. I spotted Colt sitting alone with some half-empty coffee cup at the breakfast table.

"Morning," I greeted as I poured out two cups of coffee.

"Morning. Is Maddox still sleeping?" Colt asked, and I nodded my head as I set out to cook, taking three eggs out of the fridge for some scrambled eggs.

"Uh-huh. He hasn't been sleeping for Goddess knows how long," I said, and Colt chuckled to himself.

"Sounds like him though I bet your injured state had more to do with it than his habits," Colt said with a sigh. "Take care of yourselves, okay? Lucky enough you two got each other," he added, and I nodded my head.

"Want anything?" I asked, and Colt shook his head.

"I'm good," he replied, raising his mug, and I smirked as I mixed some milk and sugar into my coffee. I put a spoon of sugar into Maddox's before cooking the rest of breakfast.

Colt put on some relaxing acoustic music, and I continued with my business. I made a plate of scrambled eggs with some buttered toast and added some sausages and beans. Despite, Colt's response, I slid a plate for him, and he smiled to himself in appreciation before I placed all the food onto a large tray and headed upstairs.

I pushed the door open with my back and sighed in relief when I found Maddox still sleeping on the bed. I placed the tray on the bedside desk and decided to do a bit of stretching. Nothing like yoga after being bedridden for several days.

After stretching my legs and arms and being thankful for wearing spandex, I put my trust into my weary arms and legs and performed a handstand. Lowering my right leg down so that I almost did a side split, I pushed my body down and lowered myself as my other leg came down. I swung my right leg to the side and let out soft, calm breaths as I stabilized my body, focusing on my balance and using my arm strength to maintain my form.

"Am I allowed to compliment the view now?" Maddox asked from the bed, and I turned my head as much as I could before laughing.

"Maybe, or you should do your best to join me," I say said just as Maddox got off the bed and pulled on some pants. I avoided looking at him as I tried to curve back up into a handstand.

Before I could finish the routine, Maddox picked me up by the waist and threw me over his shoulder.

"I said join me not stop me, you deaf motherfucker," I said as I playfully hit his back, and he chuckled as he gently placed me down on the edge of the bed.

"Breakfast first," he said as he slid the tray of food towards us and picked up a fork.

"Sure," I said with a shrug as I lifted my legs up, and Maddox eyed me with hunger, but I grabbed a piece of toast and popped it into his mouth. He frowned at me, and I smirked before we began to eat. We finished breakfast and Maddox quickly showered. I put the tray away and laced up my boots.

*Meet me in the dungeons in ten minutes*, Helari's voice rang in my head, and I sighed.

"Helari asked for you, didn't she?" Maddox asked as he walked out, his hair still damp. I nodded my head.

"I don't see any other jobs for the day," I said and Maddox nods.

"Just make sure you come back tonight to sleep," Maddox said as he kissed my cheek. I grunted before reaching for the back of his head and placing a deep kiss on his lips. Maddox lifted me up, and I wrapped my legs around his waist.

*We're never going to leave if you keep doing that*, Maddox mind linked, and I grinned in between our kisses.

*As if you'd hate it*, I replied as Maddox led us to the door and promptly untangled us from each other.

"Then make sure you come back for bed," he said, and I rolled my eyes.

"Seriously, thanks, *Dad*," I said with a huff, and Maddox laughed.

"Hey! If you two are done, this beta and his friends have stuff to do!" Jasper yelled, and I laughed at him.

"Yeah, yeah," I replied, and Maddox grinned at me. The longer sleep certainly made him look happier.

"I'll see you later," he said as he gave me one last kiss on my lips.

"Uh-huh," I replied as he disappeared. I walked down the stairs and immediately made my way out to the dungeons.

"Concentrate," Helari said as I tried to do the impossible— lift a bullet off a damn table without touching it.

I was stuck laying my upper body on the table with my hands stretched out while my ass sat comfortably on a cushion padded chair. This room happened to look exactly like a dungeon from a fantasy tale in the best way possible. The floor was clean and white and lit by a large round light system from a high ceiling. The walls were rounded, and the area was practically large enough to fit an arena.

I groaned, hands outstretched towards the bullet lying at the center

"Well, I am apparently completely incapable of stopping a flying bullet from hitting my face," I said annoyed.

"Why not? You've already seen Faustus do it," Helari said, and I rolled my eyes.

"He's a sorcerer, and you're a sorceress. I'm a *hybrid,* whatever that means."

"What happened to being witches?" Helari asked, and I shrugged.

"Sorcerer sounds cooler," I said as Helari laughed quietly to herself.

"You're a hybrid now, a mix between one of us and a wolf," she said.

"Not really a wolf now that I'm broken, am I?" I asked sarcastically, and Helari rolled her eyes this time.

"You're not broken. You're in transition. Hybrids aren't exactly a norm." She explained, and I groaned once more.

"This magic stuff is not my thing," I said. "I prefer snapping necks and stabbing people. Much more satisfying."

"You'll be surprised to see what power does to people," she said with a smile. "Trust me, it'll be worth the effort. Try saying a few words. It might get your memory functioning."

"Sure," I muttered. "*Lothrian*," I said.

Nothing happened.

"This is stupid." I huffed.

"Don't worry too much. You know how to do these spells. You just need to wake up."

"I am awake," I dully said.

"No, you're obviously here, but the rest of you is a muddled mess," Helari sid. "Sometimes, you need to just relax and say the words like you mean them. It really doesn't get much harder than that." Helari explained. Just as I was about to perform a spell, the door to the room opened, and Scar walked in, nodding curtly in Helari's direction.

"I'm going to have to leave for a bit. Do you think you can do it on your own?" Helari asked.

"I think so," I said, and Helari looked over at Scar.

"Perhaps, I should leave Scar with you. He's silent but helpful," she added before walking away. Scar closed the door behind him and stayed there.

Scar always wore black suits in contrast to Mikhail, and the two of them always wore gloves, Scar looks like a butler, and I never had a conversation with him the way Mikhail and I had. Though I doubt I could say I was close to either one of them.

"Just curious, but what's your relationship to Mikhail?" I asked as I used my pointer finger to play around with the bullet. Scar didn't answer. Instead, he simply stared at me and what I was doing.

"Okay, silence is okay too," I muttered as I stood up and walked around the stupid table. Scar stared at me before walking over and setting his hand down on the table.

He lifted it up, and a plain borderless fragment of a mirror formed from the bottom of his palms. He picked it up and handed it to me. I took it from him and stared at it.

"Thanks," I mumbled as I looked at my reflection.

I watched as he picked up the bullet from the table and threw it into the air. It traveled fairly high up. He placed his hand out, and the bullet stayed in the air. It stayed afloat above us. I stared at it and watched as he balled his hand into a fist, and the bullet dropped back down onto the table with a loud clatter.

"Okay, great. You can do stuff, too. Fascinating," I muttered as I stared at him. "Can you speak or are you mute and I'm just insensitive?" He stared blankly at me, and I sighed. "You just don't like talking, huh?" I added as I stared at the mirror.

I took a deep breath and studied my reflection. Maddox mentioned something about another version of myself, but what if she disappeared because of Faustus?

I stared at the reflection, and Scar stared intently at me before he glanced at the mirror. I stared at the mirror and squinted my eyes. I focused on my eyes, and I felt a soft fuzzy feeling fill my head.

*You need more focus*, a deep male voice said in my head. *Y-you're... close.* I raised my eyebrows and looked over at Scar. He stared at me blankly. I returned my gaze to the mirror.

*How long have you been trying to talk to me?* I asked.

No response. I bit my bottom lip. *Ercharie,* Elair, I said in my head. I stared at the mirror before closing my eyes and taking a deep breath. I probed my mind for things like the mind link but tried to focus on my senses. I took a deep breath. There was a soft thrumming sound inside the room, and I felt the cold temperature of the room.

I sensed the way the air gathered around my body... the way each little moving particle exuded power. I felt a very stiff and unmoving mass of energy in front of me. It was precise and exact but controlled and calculated as if it was afraid it would slip up and reveal any part of him. My right hand raised, I pointed in the direction of the mass, but my eyes remained closed.

*Hear me now?* I asked.

*Clearly*, the voice responded. I opened my eyes and found Scar nodding his head before his eyes widened. He walked over to me, and once we were a meter apart, he closed his eyes. He slipped his hand into his coat and pulled out a vial of clear and crystal liquid. He handed it to me. *Drink.*

*What is it?* I asked, and he simply stared at me. Well, he really didn't talk much.

I placed the mirror down on the table and took the little vial. I removed the little silver topper before pouring the contents of the vial into my mouth. I was about to hand the vial back to Scar when a quick warm sensation spread in my chest. I closed my eyes and felt my senses heighten.

I could feel every crevice in the room, everywhere air went in and out. The quick vibrations of light and the way each little thing seemed to have its place. I opened my eyes again, but this time, I had to blink several times.

In front of me was a full sized mirror that now made up half of the entire room. In it was just my own self, but she was smirking.

*Takes a dose of Hellfire to wake you up, huh?* she said, and my eyes widened.

*Oh, don't look so surprised. I did warn Maddox about Faustus, and we're one and the same. We are just blocked out by Faustus' stupid fucking enchantments.*

"You do know that this is weird, right?" I said.

*I'm you, and you're me. I'm used to it, but Faustus blocked our combined memories because I come with more demons than what even he can control... demons that aren't necessarily good*, she replied, and I thought for a moment.

"I think we can handle it," I said with a shrug, and she smirked at me.

*Of course, you do. I thought so, too, but these things aren't good to experiment with,* she replied. *But you also can't do much without them.*

"What happens to you if I break this glass down?" I asked.

*I disappear, and we join together... obviously. Then we countdown the days until we go insane, or Faustus takes us back before we do, and we end up doing that anyways,* she explained.

I was about to talk, but I saw something in the mirror.

*So that's where you've been hiding,* a familiar voice said, and I felt the chill run down my spine.

*You can't touch us from where you are,* my reflection answered. I looked to my side and found that it was empty, but out of the shadows in the mirror came the figure of Faustus.

*Is that so?* he asked, and I watched as my reflection fearlessly looked into my eyes.

*Don't be afraid of him. He can't do anything unless he's here with you,* she said, and I nodded my head. Faustus looked over at me, and my blood ran cold.

*They can't keep you from me for long. You'll come to me of your own accord,* Faustus said, and my stomach dropped.

*Don't listen to him,* my reflection said, but I sensed the worry in her voice.

*Oh, you both know you will,* he said just as he touched the glass and I felt myself burst out of a dream.

# Chapter Twenty Nine

I opened my eyes and blinked several times. Scar patted my shoulder.

*Mikhail will not fail you*, he said as he took the vial from my hand. *You may go,* Scar said, and I nodded my head as I walked away.

I walked as fast as I could out of the dungeons, ignoring the whimpers and screams of the people Maddox locked up in here. It was not surprising, every pack has its secrets.

Once I was out in the forest, I immediately decided to go for a quick walk.

I would shift if I could, but I couldn't.

It was another reminder of something I've now lost. As I walked through the forest, I still felt the thrum of every little thing. It was different from hearing everything and focusing as a wolf. It was like... constantly feeling a pull towards my body.

*Elair?* Maddox mind linked.

*Yeah?* I asked

*We're having a meeting in the conference room. I need you here*, he said.

*I'll be right there*, I replied.

"Seems like he decided to go back into his hellhole," Helari said with a sigh, and I raised an eyebrow as she drew a circle on the large map placed on the round table. We gathered inside as a group consisting of me, Maddox, Helari, Mikhail, Scar, Colt, and the other pack leaders like Carson, Trevor, and Naomi.

"If that were the case, he would have resumed his business up north," Colt added.

"It seems more like Faustus relocated. None of his squadrons were in their usual locations, and not a single leader was found," Mikhail said. I raised my eyebrows. *Squadron?*

"I can vouch for that. His overseas locations were empty last time I checked. I didn't find a single mongrel to interrogate either," Colt added.

"Mongrel?" I asked, and Colt smirked.

"Squadron leaders," he replied, and I felt my stomach drop.

I didn't think I've ever told Maddox or anyone else, and I certainly felt the need to tell them now.

"What's wrong?" Maddox asked, and I sighed as everyone's gaze fell on me.

"Squadrons one through seven, do you know anything about them?" I asked, and Colt turned his gaze to Maddox and Helari.

"Yeah, I've had a couple of run-ins with them and caught a few of the member mutts. I threw them into the dungeons last summer. They're probably still there. Squadron one is Faustus' leading sector. They are hard to find, and I've yet to catch anyone from it alive. Why're you asking?" Colt asked.

"I can't recall much about Faustus, but I know that squadrons two and four were relocated a few months back to Europe and Russia. Squadron three is in Siberia. Either way, it doesn't matter since most of the time, they mix up the numbers and change them to make sure no one knew which one was where. As for a squadron one member... consider this your first time meeting a live one," I said as the room went silent. "What? You didn't see that coming?" I asked, and Colt shook his head before laughing.

"I thought your squadron meant the circle of allies in the east. That's what your dad told me," Maddox commented, and Helari shook her head.

"Stupid mistake on our part. Those packs are bound by family ties to each other. Blood Moon is no different. Eleanor's bloodline could be traced to the Silver Pack, a once long member of those allied packs," Helari added.

"Elair, we were investigating Blood Moon to locate squadron one," Maddox said quietly, and I felt the atmosphere in the room tense up.

"Our trackers found no one, but we tracked down Faustus' mistress' scent back in your territory," Iain said, and I raised an eyebrow.

"Aunt Eleanor?" I asked, and Helari nodded.

"Her body was never found, Elair. The chances of her being revived aren't slim by any means... not if Faustus bound her to someone. She's too important for him to lose," she said, and I looked around the room. I immediately pulled my phone out of my pocket.

"What are you doing?" Maddox asked, and I shook my head as I dialed Ender's number.

He picked up almost immediately.

"Hey! Haven't talked to you in a whi—"

"Ender, when was the last time Aunt Eleanor contacted you?" I asked.

"Okay... I miss you, too," Ender said with a sigh. "Umm... last time was the day before you got here."

"Did mother tell you anything? Father?" I asked.

"Mother doesn't know much about Aunt Eleanor, remember? She only contacts us when she sends you back to Blood Moon. Father doesn't contact her unless it's an emergency situation so that we can have the squadron sent to our territory," Ender continued.

"Is that so... Hey, Ender, do you think I can come for a quick visit?" I asked.

"Elair," Maddox began, but I held a hand up.

"Of course, the pack has missed you!" Ender excitedly said.

"Great, but before that, tell Reed that I need his help. Oh, and remember that woman I told you about?"

"The woman that makes your bullets?" Ender asked.

"Yeah, her. Contact her for me and send in an order. There's something I need to do. I'll be there by tomorrow afternoon," I said quickly before hanging up.

I looked around and found everyone staring at me.

"Chances are you were investigating Blood Moon because of something important. I have to go check it out. I'm the only one who knows where the squadron checkpoint for Blood Moon is." I explained.

"Damn it. Okay then. Will you leave tonight?" Maddox asked.

"Tomorrow. Are you coming with me?" I asked Maddox. He nodded and looked over at Jasper who gave him a smirk.

"It's only normal for both the Alpha and Luna to go, right? We wouldn't want any past admirers to get to her now, would we?" Jasper said, and almost everyone smiled... except for Scar who never ever seemed to smile.

"Elair, Mikhail will join you on this trip. He's better at finding Faustus than anyone else. Scar will stay with me. We will use our own connections to find out more," Helari said, and I nodded my head.

"Sounds good," I said before we began discussing the plans. Leaving a pack wasn't easy by any means.

We had to make sure everything would still run safe and sound. Once we were done with those discussions, Maddox and I headed off to bed.

"What was your life like in the squadron?" Maddox asked me.

"Hell," I respond quickly.

"Okay?" Maddox mumbled, and I chuckled as I turned to face him on the bed.

"You saw a glimpse of it before. It was dark. You're told to kill anyone if they order you to. Sometimes, if you break an oath, you're sent to the dungeons and you're left in isolation overnight," I said, swallowing a dry lump in my throat. "They made you cling to something then they separate you from it. In my case, I clung onto my family, and Goddess knows how much they used that to their advantage. Those who come to the squadron with nothing to lose would most likely be broken mentally. That way, they don't betray the system."

"Have you ever?" Maddox quietly asked, and I paused for a moment. He was obviously asking about breaking.

"I don't know," I said.

Maddox and I had traveled with Mikhail for just about half a day before we finally touched down on Blood Moon territory. My brother, stood excitedly, waiting to greet me.

"Elair!" Ender yelled as he wrapped his arms around me. I laughed as I embraced him as well.

"Long time no see," I muttered, and Ender squeezed me before letting me go.

"I was beginning to think you'd never visit," Ender said.

"Of course not. Do I look like I'd let anything get in the way of my family and me?" I asked, and Ender chuckled.

"Well, I don't know. When the only person you get to call is everyone other than me, it gets a bit annoying," Ender responded before looking behind me and glaring at Maddox. "And he is here because?"

"Ender, we've already mated. Get over it," I said, and Ender gawked at me.

"What?"

"Mother should have told you," I said.

"Didn't think anyone would actually be good enough for you," he replied, and I elbowed him in the stomach. Ender groaned, and I laughed. "Anyways, let's go inside. I have your things. Since you requested for bullets, I guess you have serious business here. I thought you wouldn't want an entourage to greet you either, so it'll just be me," Ender said, and I nodded my head as we walked towards the pack house.

I forced myself not to go on a mouse hunt for my siblings. Considering it was night time, they all must've been asleep. Besides, I had a job to do.

We walked quickly with Mikhail silently following us and making small comments here and there while Maddox acted all stoic and weird. He was silent the whole time. However, he has been mind linking me a few questions about the area. He was rather businesslike, which I preferred at this moment as we had serious issues to attend to.

We entered Ender's office, a large space that was fairly simpler than my father's. It was still fairly opulent despite its simplicity. It had sleek black floors, smooth fiberglass tables, a large black fireplace right behind it, and a large window with long black curtains that contrasted with the stark white walls.

"Here's the order. She got back to me fairly quickly. No questions asked, too," Ender said as he handed me a sealed silver box.

I opened it up and sighed in relief as I found a neat line of bullets, each one lined with a silver outer shell that released the wolfsbane upon firing. I loaded my magazines and strapped on my holster. I placed two guns at each hip and secured my magazines into their holders.

"Is the checkpoint dangerous?" Mikhail asked.

"If it's been looked after, then it shouldn't be. Then again, we're talking about Faustus. I highly doubt that it's left unguarded," I said. "Hey, Ender, do you still have my extra holsters?" I asked.

"Duh," he said as he threw a set of them at me. I grinned as I slipped them on, attaching more sections of my holster to allow me to carry the knives at my lower thighs.

"Shall we be off then?" Mikhail asked, and I nodded.

"Ender, if anything seems suspicious, take everyone into the inner quarters," I warned, and Ender sighed.

"I'd want more information on what you are going to do, but it seems like you don't have any time left. Leave Blood Moon to me," he said with a reassuring smile. I nodded before turning to Mikhail.

"Let's go."

I guided Mikhail and Maddox through the woods. I had memorized the territory and the path to which I could return to the checkpoint. There was no other way of getting there.

There were no indicators to point you to the right track.

"And you came to memorize this. How?" Mikhail asked.

"If you don't memorize this as a part of the squadron, you can't go home. It was best to memorize the paths," I replied, trying to focus on where I was going.

"How many times did you go through this forest?" Maddox asked me, and I shrugged.

"Countless times. On initiation night, you're supposed to locate the base from an unknown location. By that time, they should have trained you to be able to survive. Finding the base can take a few hours to a few days, and some don't make it. It's survival of the fittest and a method of eliminating the failures." I explained.

"What happens to those who fail?" Mikhail asked in an amused tone. It didn't surprise me, though. He looked kind, but he was also a total asshole.

But that was just my opinion.

"Failures are left to die. They decompose almost instantly. We're spellbound to our leader during the initiation. Those that fail disappear."

"Have you ever known anyone who's failed the initiation?" Maddox asked as we slowly walked getting closer to the checkpoint.

"I've never really cared. I have a cousin who failed it," I said.

"Eleanor's daughter," Mikhail said right after. I stopped in my tracks and turned.

"You know her?" I asked.

"I heard of her," he said with a grin. "Curious?"

"Of course," I replied.

"I heard that her mother, Eleanor, had a mate who died soon after the child was born. Eleanor was superstitious enough to believe it was her daughter who caused her loss. Seeking solace in the world of witches, she crossed paths with Faustus," Mikhail said. "That should be enough for now. Shall we keep moving?"

I rolled my eyes before turning again and continuing to walk.

*Was she your cousin?* Maddox asked me.

*Her name was Camille. Last time I saw her was three weeks before my initiation. She never returned from hers,* I responded before finally reaching the checkpoint.

It was a rocky area, and the rugged terrain allowed for some intense mountain climbing regimen. Training for that type of shit was difficult. It cost us broken bones and twisted ankles more than we can remember. We left them to heal overnight. Oh, the perks of being a werewolf.

Well… of once being a werewolf.

"There's a system of caverns that we can enter from there," I said as I pointed to a cave opening.

"No wonder we couldn't track them down," Maddox said.

"It was our temporary home until we were called back," I explained.

"Seems like it's empty," Mikhail said as he pulled out a sleek silver gun. I nodded as we walk up the steep path going to the cave opening.

"Can't smell anyone either," Maddox added.

"I can't sense anything. It's probably empty. No one other than me was supposed to return after the Full Moon Banquet in Blood Moon. The rest were to follow in three months."

"And why is that?" Mikhail asked.

"I was the squadron leader. I was the only one who knows the way to get to the base," I informed them. Now without my werewolf senses, I had to rely on the damned magic coursing through my veins.

I felt every little thing that moved. I stayed sensitive to everything and felt the slightest of movements.

"Stop for a moment," I said, and we all froze. I closed my eyes and paid attention to the inside of the cave.

Something was dripping... and it didn't have the fluidity of water.

*Shit.*

"Something's wrong?"

I quickly made my way into the cave, and a freezing cold immediately wrapped itself around my body. I felt something surge at my fingertips.

"It reeks of Faustus," Mikhail said as he pulled the slide on his gun.

"It reeks of death," Maddox added.

"That is, of course, what Faustus usually reeks of," Mikhail chuckled.

"What is your relationship to Faustus?" Maddox asked.

"He's Faustus' brother," I said, and Mikhail smirked at me.

"Well then, little wolf, Faustus must have confided in you," he said, and I rolled my eyes as we entered the cave.

"Helari called me a pawn... a hybrid one. I know what that means. You're her pawn, and so is Scar. It's something the leaders of the council do," I said just as we arrived at the entrance of the base, a tall wall of rock that we had to climb to get in. "The only thing I don't understand is how Faustus is able to create his own pawns," I added as I prepared myself to climb. Maddox offered to help me.

I shook my head as I hoisted myself on top of a ledge.

"There's only one way to get up, so follow me," I said as I continued to climb, gripping onto the cold stone as hard as I can.

"I see. Well, if you must know, Faustus and I were both brought to Helari to become her pawns. We're more like knights. Scar and I are sworn to her... and betrayal is never an option. The moment one of us betrays the other, it's open fire," Mikhail said. "You are a special case."

I climbed onto another rock and finally reached the top. I used my remaining force to push myself up, and I immediately helped Maddox. He grunted as I pulled him up, and Mikhail effortlessly swung up and landed on the ledge.

"We can continue our talk later. I believe the smell is getting worse," Mikhail said, and Maddox released a growl.

"Faustus," he said through gritted teeth.

# Chapter Thirty

I froze up before closing my eyes. There was a clear sound of a thick liquid dripping. *Blood*, I thought to myself. Without a word, I made my way towards the door at the end of the hall. Maddox and Mikhail followed suit. The door was made of solid golden metal. It was heavy and made of intricately designed metalwork that contained etchings of the oath we take as a part of the squadron.

The door was sealed with a complex lock system that required a specific combination and method of twisting the knobs. There were three identical golden knobs on the door. Each had elaborate filigree designs, and a ruby embedded in its center. At the left side of the door was an elaborate lever.

I stepped towards it and moved in well-practiced movements. Taking the middle knob into my hands, I felt a strong and strangely powerful aura burst inside it. However, I ignored it as I continued moving and twisting it until it clicked four times. The now open door unraveled a central area of metal work. It was made of simple silver and gold vines that now fall straight down with the sound of bells singing behind them. It was the sign that you've unlocked the first section right.

I took the middle knob again and turned it five times to the right. The central area twisted around and turned the vines of silver around again. I took the lever and pulled it halfway down. Two loud clicks could be heard as the two other knobs pop out for use.

"Looks complex," Mikhail commented with an amused grin.

"It is," I said. Maddox, meanwhile, watched in fascination.

I grabbed hold of both knobs at the side and simultaneously twisted them outwards.

*One, two, three, four, five,* I counted in my head before I stopped. I waited and counted to twenty. A soft click, one that could barely even be heard by the human ear, clicked. I pushed my right hand down on the knob and pulled the left knob up.

The two knobs locked in place, and I sighed as I pressed the middle knob. It secured and embedded itself deep into the door's vines. Metal began to creak against each other, and I stepped back and watched as the twists and turns unfolded the complicated design of the door.

"Brilliantly designed. It seems Faustus does prepare," Mikhail said with a smirk as the door unlocked. The metal slid away, leaving behind the middle knob standing on a golden stand.

"He's a fan of puzzles," I said as I walked into the library. The smell of old books was now covered with the stench of rotting flesh and blood.

There were no flies as it was hard for insects to enter when magic sealed the place. On the ground were seven bodies laying face down in a circular formation on what used to be a plush woven carpet. Each one had etchings on their backs that dripped with blood.

"Fuck," Maddox cursed as he took out his gun. At the center of the circle was a clean blood red envelope sealed with black wax.

I walked past the bodies and reached over their arms to pick it up.

"I think you should concern yourselves with the messages on their bodies," Mikhail said.

Maddox and I immediately took a look.

*The little wolf's been broken,*

*The little wolf's been marked.*

*And when her wolf awakens,*

*The master takes his part.*

"That crazy bastard," Maddox cursed. I pressed the right side of my temples with my fingers.

"Faustus' was definitely here, but he's not around anymore," I said as I ripped the envelope open and unveiled its contents.

Inside was a silver necklace with a small crystal pendant that carried what looked to be a small flower bud. The flower bud had transparent petals. A yellow tint spread from its base almost like a little flame. Mikhail's eyes widened, and the air was immediately filled with tension.

"That belongs to Helari's garden," Mikhail said, and Maddox stared at me.

"Hellfire," Maddox muttered.

"What's it for?" I asked.

"It's poisonous, except when it's boiled and concentrated into a liquid. Take just the right amount, and it can deliver a strong adrenaline rush. It's like an EpiPen for the magically inclined." Mikhail explained. "Taking too little has no effect. Too much and it can destroy the mind."

"We have to get back to Helari. That isn't supposed to be here." Maddox began, but I shook my head. I placed the necklace back into the envelope and tucked it into my pocket.

"We're not done here," I said as I walked towards the doorway we came in through.

I ignored the dead bodies as I grabbed hold of the center knob and picked it up. It came off the golden pedestal, which now sank down to the ground.

The golden knob felt warm with power in my hands. I knew something was wrong with it.

"*Aieinra*," I said. *Burn*. The golden knob warmed up, and suddenly burst into flames, and I felt a burst of heat from behind me. Maddox grabbed me, and Mikhail ran out of the room.

There was a loud explosion before I heard a maniacal laugh from the center of the room.

"*Rememorari, min silder, vren irvon en-gairun vre tornaren ve minastre*," Faustus' voice said from within the flames before it immediately died down, burning the bodies to ash. *Remember my child, your friends will be useless once you return to me.*

"Always so dramatic," Mikhail said. "He's more of a hindrance than we initially thought he was. Helari will be able to locate him with the information we have and the necklace in your pocket."

"Then let's head back," I said.

It didn't take us long to get back. I felt a bit disappointed with the lack of excitement in tonight's events, but I would rather do that than worry about Blood Moon and my family's safety. Reed greeted me as soon as we came back, and I sighed in relief.

"How's my favorite guard doing?" I asked, and he smirked at me.

"Good enough. Donna's been asking about you, says you need to come visit the house sometimes," he told me.

"I'll take her up on that some other time," I said with a smirk.

"What'd you wanna talk to me about?" Reed asked, and I felt Maddox's presence behind me.

*Jealous*, I mind linked Maddox.

*I'm not*, he replied.

"I was wondering if you still have the stuff I left here from my last visit. I think I left it at your desk," I said.

"I think I still have them. I can have them brought to you later. Is this the new mate?" Reed asked, and I nodded.

"In the flesh," I said as the two men shook hands.

"Nice meeting the Macabre Alpha," Reed greeted. Reed cleared his throat before speaking again. "I'll have your things sent to you later. I think Ender wants a report of tonight. Besides, you two must be tired."

"Very," I said before saying our goodbyes. Maddox quickly led me to the guest room.

"I'm exhausted," Maddox said as he lay down on the bed. I took off my holster and laid it on the empty nightstand.

"Uh-huh. Where'd Mikhail run off to?" I asked, and Maddox ignored my question as he dragged me into the bed by my hand.

"Can we just sleep?" he asked.

"I'm asking because he can contact Helari, not because I'm worried," I said as I lay down and turned to face Maddox.

"He's probably going around. Scar and Mikhail never sleep. They have the task of watching over everything and anything Helari tells them to. He won't rest tonight."

"Huh," I said as I watched Maddox's eyelids grow heavy with fatigue.

"We'll get rid of him," Maddox murmured, and I smiled.

"We will," I said, knowing he meant Faustus. I pressed a soft kiss against Maddox's lips, and he smiled before taking me deeper into his arms.

*Blood.* There was blood everywhere.

I was covered in it.

Bodies littered the floor I walked on, and I felt... *nothing.*

There was nothing to *be* felt.

A hand touched my right shoulder, and I immediately turned and aimed my gun at the man behind me.

He smiled proudly at me.

"You've done well, Elair," he said, and I tucked my gun away. "How long has she gone without the wolf?" he asked the woman behind him.

"Two months," the woman responded. She looked familiar with her blonde hair and blue eyes.

"Eleanor, you're distracting her. She hasn't had enough Hellfire. She'll remember you in an instant at this rate," the man said.

"Faustus, she's hardly able to figure out who *you* are."

"That does not mean we can be lenient!" the man, Faustus, yelled, and the woman, Eleanor, grinned.

"How long do you want her subconscious to remain?" Eleanor asked.

"It would be boring to remove it. Let her believe she can change her fate. The damage has been done. Having a brief moment of rebelliousness may provide me some entertainment... before she serves her purpose," Faustus said. "Tell me, Elair, how well can you wield your own powers now?"

I glanced at the dead bodies around me, and without a word, the bodies reanimated. They raised covered in their own blood, and I used a quick move of my hand. The blood on their bodies seemed to be absorbed back into their flesh. Each one was like the perfect human doll... almost as if they were alive. Without a word, I commanded them to kneel before me. Every single one of them stepped forward and kneeled, their heads bowed down.

Faustus smiled proudly.

"Very good."

I woke up, a cold sweat covered my forehead, and my breathing had gone ragged. I looked to my left and sighed in relief when I found Maddox calmly asleep.

Silently, I crept out of the bed and checked the time on my phone. It was five thirty a.m. I stretched my arms out before going to the bathroom and taking a quick shower. The running water left relief in its wake, and I felt myself relax. I pressed my head against the cold shower wall.

There was a time when I could shut down all my thoughts and emotion, a time when it was necessary. I released a long and deep breath.

I touched the mark on my neck.

*Let her believe she can change her fate,* I remembered Faustus said.

It wasn't a dream.

I was there. That was the first time I had ever gone for a hunt. The first time I woke up with no memory of wiping out the bodies all around me.

I looked down at my fingertips. They had already begun to look like prunes telling me that I'd been thinking in the shower for way too long. I quickly washed my body before leaving the shower. Towel tightly wrapped around my body, I looked into the mirror.

With a move of my right hand, the mist all around me dissipated quickly.

I picked up my used clothes and took out the envelope. Reaching for the necklace, I carefully examined the little flower.

I needed my memories... the subconscious Faustus locked away and the demons she says she carried.

"Elair?" Maddox called, and I shook away my thoughts.

"Almost done," I said as I put the necklace back into the envelope and made my way out.

I quickly slipped into a military green long-sleeved shirt and a pair of black cargo jeans. I strapped my holster on and tied my damp hair into a loose bun.

Maddox came to me and pressed a soft kiss on my lips.

"What woke you so early?" he asked, and I shook my head.

"Nothing."

"I can tell that you're lying," he said concerned.

"A bad dream. I'll tell you about it later," I told him as I trailed my finger down the ridges and curves on his chest. Maddox cupped my cheek with his left hand and pulled us together.

A light knock on the door has Maddox growling, and I laughed at him.

"Elair?" a familiar voice asked. I was Wesley's. I smiled as I walked over to the door and opened it.

I felt a cold shiver run down my spine.

There was no one there. I turned to Maddox.

"I'm not in a fucking horror movie, and you heard that, right?" I asked, and Maddox nodded.

I took the gun to my right out of the holster.

There was something very very wrong here.

"I need everyone searching the borders! No one gets in or out!" Ender yelled. Maddox and I immediately walked out into the lobby, and I watched as section by section of Blood Moon's security groups headed out.

"What the hell is going on?" I asked, and Ender faced me, swallowing a hard lump in his throat.

A loud sob came from the door, and I saw my father embracing Mom.

I walked over to them and saw my mother falling apart while screaming a name.

Celine ran down the stairs in a panic. I felt my body grow numb as the name registered in my mind.

"Wesley's          gone          missing."

# Chapter Thirty One

"Reed, take the section heading to the southern border. I'll go with Maddox and oversee things from the east river. Ender, you have to handle things here. I can't contact you through the mind link so keep your phone on you at all times," I said, and Ender nodded.

"I want everyone to be on high guard. All the trackers will be dispatched in different directions. The moment you pick up on someone's scent, inform the rest of us." My father ordered.

The other pack leaders quickly dispatched their troops, and we were now left with my father, Maddox, Ender, and Vaughn. I nervously played with my right pinky, pinching it harder and harder until the little finger turned red. Maddox took hold of my left hand to stop me, and I pulled away from his touch.

"Calm down, Elair. We'll find him," my father said, and I shook my head.

"We don't even know who or what we're dealing with." I snapped.

"We'll find him," My father repeated, almost as if he was chanting a mantra.

"What makes you so sure?" I asked.

"Because we were able to find you," he yelled, and I felt the authority from his wolf. Everyone froze including Maddox. My father was never one to get angry, but I was never one to succumb to an Alpha's orders.

"What?" I asked.

"Ender, would you make sure the door is shut? Vaughn, go fetch your mother."

"W-we weren't supposed to let you know about it," my mother said, her voice shaking.

Her face had turned beet red, and whatever grace I knew her to have seemed to crumble and fall apart in front of me.

We were seated in the conference room, a large open space with only a large glass-encased map of our territory. I sat on a plain black stool in front of my mother while Maddox tried to soothe me by rubbing circles down my back. I had my hands in my hair, elbows lying on my thighs, and my mind was a mess of emotions.

"You went missing eighteen years ago without a trace for the first time," my mother continued. "Eleanor brought you back that night, but you were so... distant, we didn't know what to do. Eleanor told me it was because you saw a rogue and that you would be better off preparing to be an alpha with her. She said that you would be more ready to face things like that with more exposu—"

"You let her take me?" I interrupted her, my voice slowly rising.

"We did," my father answered for her. "You have to understand. Eleanor lost her mate just a few weeks before Camille was born. Camille was sickly and... Eleanor needed someone reliable to run her squadrons."

I stood up abruptly and walked away.

"So you thought it would've been better to send your own eldest daughter into something you two had no idea about?" I asked, the tone of my voice turned colder and louder with every word. "Do you have any idea what happens in the squadron?" My mother sobbed, and I shook my head.

"Did I disappear without a trace?" I asked, and my mother nodded.

"Not a single one."

I bit my bottom lip.

"I can't do this right now. We can speak about this later. Wesley's life could very well be in danger. I have no time for this shit," I heard myself say as I walked out of the conference room.

I didn't process or think about anything. I was focused on finding Wesley.

I heard Maddox call from behind me, but I couldn't listen to anyone trying to comfort me right now. I wasn't going to let Wesley go through what I had.

I wasn't going to let Faustus damage my family any further when they were the only ones I held on to.

I sprinted through the forest. I knew Maddox was trying to get in my head, but I blocked him off. Wesley was all that mattered right now.

*You know where to find me,* Faustus' voice rang through my head, and I stopped. I heard the sound of paws coming from behind me and found Maddox there in his wolf form. He came towards me, and I closed my eyes.

I felt a pull towards my left and immediately made a run for it. Maddox followed closely behind me. We arrived at the cave for the Blood Moon checkpoint. Maddox barked, knowing full well that he would never be able to climb the wall in his current form.

*Have any clothes with you?* I asked.

Maddox's wolf barked at me before running off into the woods. He came back a few minutes later, and I nodded as we made our way into the cave.

Maddox followed me silently as we climbed the wall. It took me half as much time to get up as I did before. When I arrived at the top, I felt the heaviness in the air. I heard sobbing from the inner room, and my breath stopped.

I walked straight into the inner room. The door was still unlocked, and I could feel the cold seep into my skin.

"Oh, look, Wesley! It's your dear elder sister," Faustus greeted with a sinister smile. Wesley was strapped onto a slab of marble. The dead bodies that we'd left behind were now lying at the foot of the stone in a strange circle arrangement.

Wesley had a cloth wrapped tightly around his mouth. He looked at me, and I felt my heart sink. I heard Maddox growl, and Faustus grinned. I immediately took my gun out and fired, but Faustus dodged the bullet. Instead, the bullet hit the wall.

"Oh, dear," Faustus said with an amused look on his face. "I wouldn't try to kill me if I were you. Your brother's life rests in my very hands."

"You're so full of shit," I said as I fired again.

"I've missed that foul mouth of yours. Quite a change from the usual silent mouthed servants we get in the Sentinels nowadays."

"You already took me, so why are you taking my brother?" I asked.

"I'm not taking him anywhere. I just needed a bit of blood. I've already drawn it from him." Faustus said as he lifted up a small vial of red liquid. "Did you know that Hellfire can increase its toxicity when placed in werewolf blood?"

I felt the mark on my neck slowly burn, and Faustus' smile grew even wider. My body froze, and I felt as if the control I had over my body was being pushed out and suspended away. As if I wasn't me.

"I'm glad you two made it. It took me quite some time to figure out how to get rid of Mikhail. He can be quite a pest, but a few traces of dear aunt Eleanor here and there, a bit of blood, and some dead children tend to get poor Helari's attention," Faustus said, and I felt the tension in the air rising. My blood boiled, and I felt my anger surge through the air. "Oh, don't be so mean, Elair. I did teach you to be more humorous when dealing with your enemies. After all..."

Faustus' eyes glowed bright blue as he lifted a finger.

"*Hu petaris*," Faustus said. *Come to me.* My feet lifted off the ground, and my body was pulled towards him. Maddox immediately made a move to grab me, but he was quickly subdued, and I watched as he fell limp to the ground. "You are my creation."

"Elnir..." Maddox growled as he struggled to move.

"You're far too loud. I guess that's why I never found wolves to be too appealing," Faustus said with a smirk as my feet landed on the ground. "Good thing I've tucked your little wolf away, *min silder,*" Faustus said as he pulled a loose section of my hair behind my ear.

"What... do you want?" I asked, struggling to control my voice. Faustus smiled eerily at me.

"Well, step one was to lure you in with your brother," Faustus said as he averted his gazes at Wesley. "Good job, young one. Eleanor was right when she said to take you."

"You have me now. So let go of him." I felt my voice choke, and Faustus turned his gaze back over to me.

"I preferred you when you were silent although I am quite grateful for your consciousness. Not having the full amount of power I bestowed upon you meant I can still control you." Faustus explained just as I heard Maddox groan loudly as he tried to push himself off the ground. Maddox's strained muscles looked like they were ready to explode.

"Oh, I wouldn't do that if I were you. I can make you feel so much worse," Faustus said, and I felt a backbreaking sensation on my spine.

"Maddox... stop!" I said in pain, and Maddox screamed before he stopped. I watched as his body fell flat on the ground once more.

"Good obedient little pup," Faustus said with a smile. "Now then, *lygre*." Wesley stopped sobbing, and his eyes turned pitch-black.

"*Farvel, eovre engairun netru*," Faustus said. *Forget, you are of no use to me now.* I watched as Wesley nodded his head slowly. The bindings that strapped him onto the slab became loose, and he stood up. "Now then, Wesley, I want you to wait outside. If another person comes up that wall, I want you to run and jump. If your sister or anyone else leaves this room and touches you, I want you to jump as well. Do it head first. It will be less painful that way."

I struggled to scream as Wesley made his way out of the room. Faustus grinned widely before reaching into my pocket and pulling out the necklace that I had found.

"Children do make some of the best toys... but I was beginning to get tired of keeping my older toys away. I find having you, *min silder*, right here so much more of a relief. I couldn't let the alpha have too much fun with my beautiful vessel," Faustus said as he trailed his hand down my cheek. I had the strong urge to pull away, but I couldn't. My body was paralyzed.

"Now, as I'm getting tired of exerting so much power over such small deeds," Faustus said as he walked over to a nearby table, kicking one of the bodies to the side, "I'd like you to sit down on the slab."

My body moved on its own and immediately sat down on the marble slab. I watched as Faustus took the necklace and crushed it in his hands. A bit of blood trickled down onto his white suit, and he walked over to Maddox.

"Tonight, I shall have you, the one and only alpha of the Macabre Pack witness your mate for who she really is," Faustus said. "*Rezanai, vulkos.*"

Maddox immediately got up.

Maddox's eyes landed on me, and I tried to give him a reassuring gaze. I wanted to tell him that I was going to be fine.

But I couldn't.

Faustus walked over to me and placed his bloody hand on mine, leaving behind the flower bud of Hellfire in my hands. It bloomed in my hand and turned into a crimson red color.

"*Einre, min silder,*" Faustus commanded. *Eat, my child.* My hands moved to plucked a petal.

The flower immediately died and turned into a dark black mass in my hands, but the single petal I took turned blood red. Without a word, my hand placed the petal into my mouth.

# Chapter Thirty Two

After the petal of Hellfire had fallen onto my tongue, I felt an immense pain coming from my mark. As it began to worsen, Faustus pulled my chin towards him and placed the vial of my brother's blood into my mouth.

I felt the liquid touch my tongue and felt the immediate urge to throw it all up. I felt sick, and I immediately felt immense rage.

Images flashed in my mind… of dead bodies, children, gun shots right in between the eyes, and massacres.

They were all my doing.

I saw visions of myself bathed in the blood of my enemies. I felt the smile that graced my face when I did so. The twisted enjoyment in bathing myself in gore.

The initiation night...

I remembered it now. I remembered all of it— the night I had to run after my prey in the woods, the initiation that involved me dragging another person into the dungeons of the Sentinel, and the torture that person had to endure before I finally put an end to her life.

I recalled the moment when Faustus slit open the poor person's hands and filled a slab of strange lines with her blood.

*Who was it again?*

*Who did I chase that night?*

"Elair! Stop! Please!" the girl in front of me screamed that night, but I felt nothing as my wolf growled at her.

She had blonde hair... and blue eyes. She looked like me.

She looked like Aunt Eleanor.

*Camille.*

It only registered then that I had been hunting her down... I was supposed to bring her back dead.

I remembered her pleas of mercy and pity. I relished in the fear that filled her to her very core. She was weak just as Aunt Eleanor had said.

There was no room for weakness in the Sentinels.

There was no room for weakness for me.

I was brought back to the day I returned to my family

"When you return to Blood Moon, your mate will cross paths with you, *min silder*," Faustus said. I nodded my head. "*Farvel lae vre morie.*" *Forget all your memories.*

I blinked my eyes open and laughed at my stupidity.

"Elair!" Maddox yelled from my side, and I looked to him.

"How ridiculous," I said as I got off the metal slab and walked over to Faustus. I bowed my head. "*Remera min mories*," I told Faustus. *I remember everything.* He smiled widely at me.

"Welcome back, *min silder.*"

I smirked as I walked over to a nearby mirror.

"Elair!" Maddox yelled. I turned around and raised a finger to my lips. Maddox's voice seemed to have gotten sucked back into his throat. He was too loud.

"Honestly, Faustus, sometimes you take far too long to carry out your plans. What were you going to do if I completely forgot about my purpose?" I asked as I stared at my reflection.

"I trusted your fealty," Faustus responded, and I sighed as I looked at my reflection. I turned my neck and spotted the mark on it.

"Trusted too much, I see," I said as I examined the disgusting mark.

"You were a bit too rebellious," Faustus commented. "I told you to take control over your human emotions. It's quite troubling to have it kept with you. I feared your complete rebellion. You are my best creation."

"Glad to know," I muttered as I placed my hand on the mark. I felt a tinge of heat from the mark and hovered my hands over it. Maddox screamed of pain and agony.

Faustus watched me intently as I finished and closed my hands. The mark on my neck quickly faded away and healed back into its normal bare flesh. Maddox was pulsating with pain and was covered completely in sweat.

"Poor little pup... broken little pup..." I sang softly as I made my way over to Maddox. "His owner loves him so... His owner leaves him so..." I turned Maddox over.

"Poor little Alpha, sad and all alone." I placed my hand on his chest. A black mist left my body and immediately entered Maddox. The haze caused his veins to rise and revealed a mark of pitch black traveling up to the mark I left on his neck.

Just then, I heard a scream from outside the door.

"Was that Wesley?" I asked Faustus.

"None other than," he responded, and I reached up into the air with my right hand and formed a quick fist.

Faustus gasped as I pulled my fist down.

"I told you not to involve him, didn't I?" I said through gritted teeth.

"It... it was only a temporary means of getting your attention. No harm done," Faustus said.

"*Renare vren opiere*," I said, and I felt Faustus' wield over my brother wane. I saw three figures outside and immediately recognized them.

"How troublesome," I muttered. I turned around and looked at the dead bodies on the floor before glancing at Maddox. I raised my left hand in the direction of the dead bodies and watched as they began to reanimate. Their eyes looked dead and empty as they were replaced by pitch-black colors.

"Make them busy," I ordered softly as the bodies slowly got up. Helari and her two servants made their way towards me.

"Elair, stop! Wake up!" Helari yelled, and I smirked.

"I'm already awake," I said, as I circled my right hand around the floor.

A black mist grew from the ground, and I was filled with glee as Mikhail and Scar realized what I had done. Wesley lay in Mikhail's arms, and I sighed.

*He'll be fine*, I thought to myself before I allowed the mist to swallow up Maddox, Faustus and myself, leaving Helari and the rest of them behind.

We arrived at Faustus' home, also known as the Sentinels' base. It was reminiscent of an old Victorian house. It was completely cold and dark. The moon's dim white light illuminated the hall. The place was decorated with furniture that looked as if it jumped out of a French chateau, but the dim light made everything look dull and gray.

"*Velian, aigstre*," two squadron leaders greeted at the same time. *Welcome, sir.* I recognized them immediately, and their eyes widened as they bowed their heads in respect. "*Aigstra*, Elair. We did not expect your arrival so soon."

Each one of them was dressed in black robes. One was female, and one was male. The two of them were dressed in black. The female is known as Zenna, and the male was Quentin. They were part of my squadron and were two of my best fighters.

"We were expecting you three more weeks later," Zenna commented. Her cropped platinum and black hair accentuated her bright green eyes.

"Faustus became impatient," I said as I handed Maddox to them. Maddox's body was lurched forward, and the two squadron leaders stared at him. "Second quarter dungeons.

He's my prey alone, understood?" The two leaders nodded as they pulled Maddox up. Maddox was completely groggy and limp from the spell cast on his body.

Zenna and Quentin carried him away, and I turned to face Faustus.

"Seems you enjoy your little plaything," Faustus said as he traced his right hand down my cheek.

"Toys are meant for breaking, and playtime is over," I said as I look out the tall windows.

"Would you like to meet your new squadron?" Faustus asked, and I shook my head.

"I can do that tomorrow. I'll call if and when I need you," I said as I turned on my heel and left.

Faustus walked in the opposite direction. I sighed as I walked forward, remembering the right halls and turns to get to my room. I ran into a few other Sentinel squadron members, and each of them bowed their heads in respect.

I had to climb up several flights of stairs before I made it into my room, a grand bedroom tucked at the end of a dark, almost abysmal-like hallway. I found its double doors and quickly entered the room. The room was dark, and its walls were made of thick black stone. I checked the windows. There was nothing outside... just a plain black abyss as the moon lit whatever areas it can.

There was a clean bed covered in blood red sheets and pillows. The bed frame was an old canopy bed made of bronze with intricate vine details in the pillars and a large heavy black curtain hanging above it. The thick wooden floor was covered in expensive woven carpets. There was a dead fireplace to help provide warmth, an empty vanity, and a door leading to the bathroom.

As I was about to enter the bathroom, two soft knocks sounded on my door, and I opened it in silence.

In front of me was Aunt Eleanor, her hair tied up in an elegant bun and her piercing blue eyes held a cold glow to them.

"Hello, Elair," she greeted with an icy smile.

# Chapter Thirty Three

Aunt Eleanor was the exact image of my mother if not for the harsh, cold look in her deep blue eyes and the stiffness with which she carried her actions.

"May I come in?" she asked, and I nodded my head. I let her walk into the room and took a seat on the edge of my bed.

"I guess you came here for a reason," I said as I waved my hand towards the door. It shut itself, and I crossed my legs

"Has everything come back to you?" she asked, and I tilted my head.

"Of course," I said as I stood up and approached her. "I've done you proud, and now I'm worth far more than you ever thought I would be."

She smirked at me before taking a loose hair from my face and twirling it between her two fingers.

"Faustus wants you to sit with him at the assembly tomorrow. The Sentinels await your presence," Aunt Eleanor said.

"I'll be there," I replied as I flicked my finger towards the door. It opened quickly, and Aunt Eleanor bowed her head slightly before leaving me alone to my thoughts.

I shut the door and make my way to the bathroom. It was fairly large and the elevated white tub covered in gray stone sat by the windows. The water began to fill it up, and I looked at my reflection in the mirror. The gothic setting of the castle was suitable for what it was. From what I heard and read, the castle was once Helari's home overtaken by the Sentinels.

I stripped out of the clothes and set my gun aside. I stared at my reflection for a while. My neck was clear of any mark that Maddox had given me. My eyes had turned almost indigo, and my face had turned paler. I turned around and looked at the back of my neck.

Instead of the *scal*, there was a collection of intricately placed welts on my skin. They were scars that marked my back with etchings of words from the initiation and countless nights of sacrifices and killings. I was marked by the Sentinels, and there was no escaping that.

I had murdered children and families, and with that came the guilt that would burden me forever. But the Sentinels turned that into something else.

They made you desensitized, but more than that… they made you feel like it was the right thing to do.

They made us believe that if you didn't kill them, they would kill you.

If you didn't value your life, they'd kill whatever you valued or take away whatever humanity was left inside you.

I tore my gaze away and went up the small steps into the tub. I took a dip and sighed in relief as the warm water wrapped around my flesh. I stared out the windows and into the darkness.

Maddox was going to die if I left him here. There was no food for prisoners, and there was no pity amongst Squadron leaders. If I was going to get him out of here, I had to do it fast.

I closed my eyes in the tub and sat on the back of my lower legs in a kneeling position.

I felt a cold rush of wind blow against my hair.

With a quick deep breath, I pulled myself down the water.

Voices sounded all around me… muffled and unclear. I opened my eyes and stared into an empty space.

I heard another muffled voice in front of me and reached for it, making a fist with my outstretched right hand. It disappeared into the pitch-black darkness in front of me. I pulled it back, a pile of mist and dark matter in my grip, and I felt the strain on my lungs.

I walked out and made my way towards the closet, pulling on a thick black robe from a nearby hanger. I slipped into a long-sleeved black dress that had a long slit. It was simple and easy to pull on.

I walked barefoot as it was easier to sense movement without coverings.

Besides, I no longer needed to do my own dirty work.

I padded my way out of my room and took a walk. Each member of the Sentinels greeted me respectfully as I walked towards the second quarters. It was quite a long way from my quarters, and when I finally made my way there, it was filled with the noise of a million captured prisoners.

There were weeping sounds, wails, and screams of terror all around. As I walked, each cell I passed turned absolutely silent. Maddox would have been locked up at the very bottom.

After passing by nearby guards and fellow Sentinels whose hands were covered in crimson blood, I finally made it. Most cells required an intricate knowledge of unlocking doors. It assured us that no one would ever make it out alive. If a code was forgotten, the prisoner died. Simple as that.

I placed my right hand on the large silver slab that was covered in intricate metalwork. I twisted my hand to the right before having my palm face the ceiling and forming a fist. The door made loud noises of metal sliding against each other until a loud clicking sound was heard.

The door opened up with a creaking noise before I spotted Maddox sprawled on the ground. He wasn't chained. It was unnecessary here after all. Light from a small lantern illuminated his almost lifeless body. The door shut behind me, and I watched as Maddox groaned and started to move.

"Who's there?" Maddox asked with a harshness to his voice. I didn't respond.

The floor was damp and extremely cold, the walls were made of cold stone, and not a single window was available. The Sentinels weren't accommodating by any means. The only comfort would be the lantern shining above, illuminating the already dark room. Maddox turned his head, and his eyes immediately locked on mine.

He struggled to get on his feet, and I put my right hand up. Maddox managed to get on his knees, and I walked towards him. He stared at me, his amber coal eyes bordering on glaring.

"What has he done?" Maddox growled, and I lowered myself as well.

"Nothing that hasn't been planned," I told him, and Maddox took a big gulp of air. I reached for his neck, and he didn't budge as I trailed my hand around the bloodied mark that had turned dark from the spell I cast.

I closed our distance, and Maddox's breath caught in his throat. Our faces were mere centimeters away from each other. His face looked tired, but his eyes were fierce and rebellious, prepared to fight. It's a type of courage that could get him killed here.

In a soft whisper, I uttered three words that I knew would break his heart.

"Let me go."

Maddox's eyebrows narrowed.

"No." He growled, a low rumble coming from his chest. I sighed before standing up and walking away from him.

"Learn to control your instincts, Cross," I said in an icy tone. I held my left hand out to my side and turned my head to look at him. "I can only do so much until the woman you knew disappears for good."

I held my hand in a stiff position. With all five fingers curled upwards, a black mist bloomed from the center of my palm. I played with it for a bit, the mist pouring out from my hands and curling around my arm.

"You shouldn't eavesdrop on me," I said sternly, and before my eyes land on the door, and I squeezed my hand into a fist. The mist traveled quickly and sharply, whizzing through the air as it went through the edges of the door.

I raised my right hand up before pointing upwards with my index finger and making small quick circles in the air. The door opened up and revealed Eleanor with the mist around her neck. Her voice croaked, the mist making it difficult for her to speak as I choked her.

"*Krau,* Elair, *sileia neie en-heiran,*" Faustus said as he walked down the stairs. *Calm down, Elair, she meant you no harm.* Maddox growled, and I glanced back at him. I felt a tinge of heat in my eyes, and the mark on Maddox's body glowed like a coal ember. Maddox groaned in pain, his right hand reaching for the mark before falling to the ground.

"We were only making sure you weren't—"

I stared into Faustus' eyes, stopping him mid-sentence. My eyes narrowed, and Faustus' voice caught in his throat.

"You made me into what I am, but I will not let you bark orders at me," I said as the mist let go of Eleanor's neck, and I stopped my hold over Faustus.

I opened my right hand in the same position as before, and the mist made its way back into the palm of my hand. I turned around and faced Maddox.

"*Gefrecht, min vulkos,*" I said as the mist dissipated into my body. *Fight, my wolf.* I walked over to Maddox and placed my right hand on the mark.

Maddox screamed in agony.

The power of the mate bond was siphoned out of him like tearing away of someone's soul. It was damage hitting straight into the very core of his body. Maddox's body was strained, veins threatening to pop as the spell destroyed every trace of the bond I could find.

They said rejecting your mate is an excruciating process, but forcing it out of one's soul was a different story.

Done wrong, and it could drive your target to insanity.

Maddox's body began to convulse, like a human experiencing a seizure. His body released his pain in shock waves.

I released my grip on him and watched as the pain forced him to defend himself. The body twisted and turned.

It was a forced shift.

Maddox's wolf, black as night, now lay on the ground.

"We move tomorrow," I said, as I took my eyes away from Maddox. "There's no time to waste here," I added as I stand up.

Faustus nodded, and Eleanor rubbed her throat.

"You... because... me..." I heard Eleanor mutter under her breath as I passed her. I paused and glared at her.

"Care to repeat that?" I commanded.

"You are what you are because of *me*!" Eleanor shouted, and I narrowed my eyes at her. I closed my eyes and sighed.

"You have my gratitude," I said before I placed my right hand on her shoulder. Her eyes turned pitch black for a moment before her body became completely still. "Now, be good and go upstairs. When you get to your office, lock yourself in until you're summoned to leave."

I let go of her and watched as she walked past me and up the steps. I turned around and faced Faustus, who gave me an amused grin. He placed a hand on my waist as he guided me upstairs.

"Shall we meet the rest?" Faustus asked.

"You act as if I have a choice," I said.

"You're the first success. The rest of us have been awaiting your awakening since the moment you crossed paths with your mate," Faustus said as we reached the corridor.

"Then let's not keep them waiting," I said.

# Chapter Thirty Four

We made our way into the meeting room, a large rectangular room with high ceilings. It was ancient and resembled a large library. Other than the illumination of the moon, we have a fireplace that cast a yellow light over the people waiting inside. There were a set of seven chairs in a circle, but at the very head was a taller one. Each seat was a carefully carved wooden piece with plush seating. At the center of the room was a large inscription laid in marble stone and silver on the ground. It glimmered below the moonlight shone on it constantly by the large round skylight roof.

"Elair Richelieu, in the flesh indeed!" a man greeted with a wild smile. His eyes were large, and he was dressed in a black outfit like all of us. Everyone here was wearing some sort of leather coat other than Faustus and myself.

"Marko," I greeted back, and he nodded enthusiastically in his seat. He was a fat old man with a face that always reminded me of a deranged clown without makeup. He was the one that drove people insane, his tactics being more than gruesome.

Faustus took a seat to the right of the center, leaving only one more seat for me to take. I made my way through the center, and my shadow cut through the light, but it wasn't a distinct silhouette of my figure. Instead, it was fuzzy like mist.

I took a seat at the center, crossing one leg over the other.

"How often is Helari in Macabre's territory?" a woman from the further end asked.

"She's been with them ever since I arrived. I suppose she will have returned there by now," I said.

"Our squadron leaders have had no problem infiltrating parts of the territory ever since your arrival. There are areas easy to access. I've sent more than a handful as lookouts," another said.

"Then we are ready," Faustus responded.

"What about the wolf?" Marko asked, and I narrowed my eyes at him.

"He is to be used to our advantage. He will not disobey. I've made sure of that," I said as I rested my head on my right hand, leaning over my knee. "There is one issue," I added, making Faustus raise his brow.

"What is that?" an older man asked.

"The dagger. It's in the pack house." I informed.

"Helari's dagger?" the woman asked, and I nodded. "Oh, dear."

"I can find it, but I'll need a distraction," I said with a smirk.

"Of course. Leave that to me," Faustus said with a curt nod.

"Of what importance is that?" Marko asked.

"It can kill my precious child," Faustus said and paused as he looked at me. "Should it fall into the wrong hands our plan would fall to shambles, and that is something we simply cannot afford... Fortunately, we have its wielder under our control," Faustus said with a smirk.

"It's wielder?" Marko asked, obviously unable to comprehend the dagger's importance.

"Cardis' only living heir," I answered. "The wolf."

Everyone's eyes glowed an icy color, revealing their interest.

"Now that it has been made clear," I said as I uncrossed my legs and leaned back against the chair. "Shall we discuss the rest of the plan?"

"Squadron four and five have been making rounds in the east and west," Marko said. "It seems to be the easiest area to sneak in."

"Cross would have sent his gamma west. It's an easy way in. I suggest going down the hills on the east. The lake will mark your location. The pack will notice your presence there a little too late." I explained.

"Helari and her servants are our top priorities. Nevertheless, send orders to kill all on sight," Faustus said. "Helari is mine to deal with."

Everyone nodded their head as we continued our discussion.

*The Betrayal*

I smirked upon reading the title of the book that I'd picked up, something I had read many times over. It told the tale of Helari and the Sentinels. In it was the story of two brothers divided by their longing for power, how one brother destroyed the lives of a peaceful family, and how that created a series of events that divided the two brothers forever.

It was a story many could not confidently read in front of Faustus.

"You know the tale already," Faustus said as he paced around my room.

"Of course," I said with a sigh. Faustus smiled before turning his back towards me and pouring himself a drink from an array of wines that were left in my room earlier.

"Are you ready?" Faustus asked as I heard him pour another glass for me.

"Of course," I said without hesitation. He turned around with a smile before offering me the wine. I took a sip, and so did Faustus.

"I expect nothing less from you," he said as he tilted my head up, his eye glowing an icy blue color.

"Of course," I muttered as I watched Faustus nod before taking his glass and walking out the door.

"I will order the assembly. Do what you must to the wolf," Faustus said before he left.

I placed the book down on my bed before exiting the room. I made my way back down to the cellars and unlocked Maddox's cell.

It was time.

A day had already passed, and the Sentinels were ready.

Maddox's wolf lay on the ground, breathing silently yet incapable of movement. I touched his head and released a mist into him. His wolf immediately got up obediently, his amber eyes replaced by pitch black orbs. I shut the door in and walked over to Maddox's wolf. I kneeled before him and stared into his eyes. I raised my right arm and pressed my thumb onto his forehead. I closed my eyes.

After a few seconds, I released him, and Maddox shifted into his human form. The mist wrapped around him like a cloak and covered him from head to toe in a black outfit. I felt a pain on my back as I stared at him. Maddox's eyes were no longer blinking and moving, only a deep void in his dull eyes stared at me.

He was ready.

I walked out of the cell, and he followed closely beside me as we headed upstairs.

Faustus grinned at the sight of Maddox before he pulled back a set of curtains and revealed the squadrons we were bringing. Unlike Maddox's pack, there were no words said to raise morale. Each squadron member bowed their head as I walked past them. The six high-ranking members stood at the end of each row, and each one wore a proud and mischievous smile.

"*Hes ti opiere. Hes ti andet,*" I said aloud. *Go with power. Go with purpose.*

Every single squadron member began to chant the words as darkness enveloped all of us.

The forest appeared before me, and the cold breeze blew against my back. My feet came in contact with freshly fallen leaves, and the woods were once again surrounding me and Maddox who was right behind me.

"I trust you will do your part," Faustus said from my side. I nodded my head as I walked forward.

Feeling Faustus leave my side, Maddox and I made our way towards the pack house. Like a puppet on strings, Maddox followed every move that I made in absolute silence. I heard the muffled noises of growls from my right, knowing full well that the attacks had begun.

I was aware of Mikhail and Scar's movements. It was hard not to when they were constantly trying to find me.

The pack house was frantic, and with a simple cloaking spell, I managed to get inside with Maddox by my side. I closed the door to our room and opened the closet, sighing in relief as I spotted the dagger.

I took it in my hands and turned around to face Maddox. I took the blade and aimed it at my chest. I plunged the dagger into my chest, but it was repelled out of my hand and onto the ground. It was worth a shot, though.

I stood up and picked the dagger of the floor. With it, I sliced my right wrist, my blood pooling and the blade burning my flesh.

*I am doing the right thing,* I thought to myself as I bit my bottom lip to fight the intense urge to scream. By the time it was done, the silver blade had turned crimson red, and the burned flesh on my wrist slowly faded, healing at an inhuman speed. The large white crystal on its hilt glowed an intense white.

I watched as the light faded, and so did the crimson color of the blade. Placing my left hand over Maddox's temple, I released a white light that seeped into his body. I handed Maddox the blade before giving him an intense look.

*Eovre andet, Elair*, I told myself before walking out of the room.

Maddox grunted before following behind me. The pack house looked empty, but I knew better. Everyone would have been hiding by now, the same way they hid the night Faustus had attacked us.

We made our way into the forest in silence, and Maddox, unable to speak to me through the mind link, kept quiet.

I felt an electric spark from my right and immediately walked in that direction. It was Helari without a doubt, and as we reached the dark clearing, it became a certainty.

Standing side by side with Maddox, I watched as Helari emerged from the shadows with Scar and Mikhail by her side.

"Elair," she called out, and I tilted my head. I glanced over at Maddox and Helari's eyes followed. "What has he done?"

"Nothing that wasn't planned." Faustus appeared to my left, and I walked towards him. Faustus took hold of my left wrist, and I felt my strength being drained away from me.

"You took her as a vessel?" Helari asked, and I watched as Mikhail's eyes revealed his concern. Scar stared directly at me, and I gave him a cold stare.

"I made her powerful the way you should have made me!" Faustus roared as the blood boil under my skin. I closed my eyes and felt a burning sensation course through me. Faustus charged a large surge of energy from his body to mine, and I could feel the adrenaline from it.

I raised my right hand so that it faced towards Helari's direction and waved my hand to the right. Black mist rose from the ground and drew a line separating Faustus and me from Helari. Maddox stood stiffly behind me, and Helari raised her own hand, and a rush of dark wisps hurled its way towards Faustus.

Faustus smiled as he released me, and the surge of adrenaline coursed through me, causing me to find some sort of release. I fell to my knees, a powerful wind surrounding me, as I repelled Helari's attack. Helari walked forward, trying to cross the line, but I balled my right hand into a fist, and it intensified, making her take a step back.

Faustus smirked as he walked over to Maddox. From the corner of my eye, I saw Faustus take Maddox onto his knees.

"Destiny is a fool's belief," Faustus said with a smile on his face.

"And you're the fool," Helari said as her eyes turned a blood red color.

Helari walked forward, and I watched as a trail of blood slipped from the corner of her mouth. A drop fell onto the ground, and the mist disappeared, recoiling in various directions. Mikhail and Scar nodded at each other before taking out their daggers. Faustus grinned as Mikhail stepped forward.

Mikhail immediately hurled one dagger at Faustus' direction, and Faustus dodged it in an almost effortless fashion. I stared at Helari and placed my palms on the ground.

Releasing the strength Faustus has redirected into me, I hurled it towards Helari'. I felt the power struggle between us, the sheer amount of strength I had to use to push forward and reach her sent a burning sensation down my back.

Scar sprinted towards Faustus, and they fought hand to hand.

"You're feeding her?" Helari asked as she exerted more power.

"How else could I control her?" Faustus replied with a maniacal grin, and Helari stared at me. The blood collected in my throat, and I could taste it as it pooled in my mouth.

"You feed her too much, and you lose power," Helari said with a smile.

"There are countermeasures to that," Faustus replied and turned to face me.

"*Eovre frei,*" I said as I coughed out blood. *I grant you your freedom.* Maddox flinched beside me, and I immediately released everything Faustus had stored inside me.

My blood felt like it was threatening to burn me whole. Helari recoiled, and a mist surrounded her in a protective, almost bubble-like nature.

Upon release, a dark mist covered Maddox and me. Faustus' shadow was visible, but he could not hear us. I turned to Maddox and traced my hand against his face.

"It's time," I said as the mist disappeared, and I let go of him.

Both Mikhail and Scar managed to survive, but the burns on their faces placed them in an unconscious state. I watched as their eyes quickly began to dilate and the two of them woke up.

Faustus smiled in triumph as I stood from the ground. I turned to find Maddox safe and standing as frozen as he possibly could. Helari revealed herself from the mist, and her eyes trailed from Faustus, to me, and to Maddox.

As Faustus focused on the little show, I lifted my right hand quickly with my palm facing the sky and immediately pulled it back, balling my fist. Faustus' eyes widened as the shadows surrounded his legs and crippled him. The sound of his bones breaking mingled with his scream of agony as he fell.

I draw more of his force into me, connecting Faustus and me together, yet numbing the pain. Our souls linked, his life and mine, and our bodies remained separated, there was only one thing left to do. A thousand voices screamed in my head... a thousand dead... a thousand broken...

*Poor little pup, broken little pup...* I heard them taunt.

"Elair!" Helari screamed, but I already knew what was going on.

"You bitch," Faustus cursed. "You—" he began, but I didn't let him finish.

"I'm sorry," I said with a sad smile as I turned to face Helari. I could feel Faustus power surge through me, and I smiled. "You bound me with your soul." I looked over at Faustus who now lay on the ground.

"I will not let you end me this way," Faustus growled as I faced Maddox. "You fool! We cannot die! He is in love with you! It's a bond Helari had secured to him the moment she placed the *scal* in your damned body!"

I ignored him.

Standing in front of Maddox, I pulled the dagger out from Maddox's hand and stared at it. Helari launched a heavy mist that was pointed towards me in an attempt to take it away.

"No!" Helari screamed, and I gave her a sad smile. I placed the dagger in Maddox's hand, and the white light I placed into Maddox's soul traveled to his eyes.

## Maddox

There was darkness. Then, all of a sudden, something heavy was lifted from my back as I opened my eyes to Helari's screams and to Mikhail and Scar struggling to get up. In front of me was a blond-haired man.

A growl escaped my lips as I saw him turn and face me. His ice-blue eyes glanced to his left, and I saw Elair on the ground, screaming at me.

My ears were ringing with a loud, high-pitched noise. I was unable to hear any words, but it didn't matter.

Elair had gotten her point across.

I felt something cold in my hand, and I looked down to find the dagger.

As soon as I realized that, I grabbed Faustus in front of me and slammed his body into a tree. The surrounding sounds began to clear up slowly, turning into muffled screams.

Faustus didn't fight back, but if he thought I was going to pity him now, he was wrong. I glanced over at Elair's body on the ground. She was screaming something and crying.

This man in front of me was her owner. If I killed him now, she would be freed.

I took the dagger in my hand and, without a moment's hesitation, pushed the dagger with all of my strength into his chest. Faustus placed a hand on my shoulder and, in the strangest of actions, smiled at me.

The sounds in my ears immediately cleared up, and I heard Helari's screams much more clearly.

"Maddox, no!" she screamed in horror, and I turned around.

I narrowed my eyes at her.

*Faustus is dead. Why would she act like this?* I thought to myself.

Mikhail and Scar turned their eyes away from me.

I searched the ground for Elair and found Faustus' body lying there instead... facing the sky, a dark red stain spreading from the center of his chest.

"You fucking fool," he hissed.

"That really fucking hurt," I heard Elair's voice and turned around. My eyes widened as I saw her against the tree, impaled by the very blade I used. I immediately sprinted towards her.

"No, no, no, no, no... Elair!" I frantically said, and she looked at me with a sad smile. I touched the blade.

"Don't! You'll only worsen the blood loss," Helari screamed as she made her way by my side.

"Y-you can fix her, right?" I asked, and Helari shook her head.

"She heals me... and he heals. As l-long as the..." Elair whispered.

"Stop," I said, hearing the pain in her voice. I touched her face and wiped her tears.

"I-I don't h-have long..." Elair said. Helari looked away with a devastated look in her eyes. "S-sorry about that... b-but at l-least... you don't f-feel my pain now. You won't f-feel my passing as bad as you sh-should've," she said as she began to cough. I felt the tears well up in my eyes as I stared into the blue of her eyes.

"What did you—"

"H-hey... stop that," she said, and I watched as tears well up in her eyes as well. Helari raised her hands and placed it above the wound.

"I can stop the bleeding for a while," Helari told me, and I nodded as I swallowed the lump in my throat.

"You..." Faustus began, but Scar and Mikhail immediately came forward.

"Shut up," Scar said with a cold look in his eyes as he took a dagger and plunged it into Faustus' right hand. Faustus screamed, but Elair only managed to smirk. I was about to stop him, but Helari held me.

"She won't feel it. She only feels the dagger, but if Faustus loses his life..."

I nodded my head, stopping Helari from saying anything more.

I stared at Elair, and she lifted her right hand. I took it, placing it on my face. I held her closer to me and placed my hand on the dagger.

"How long will she have?" I asked Helari.

"A few seconds... a minute at best," Helari said.

"She c-can't die like this," I said to myself and pulled the dagger out.

Helari's eyes were aglow as I lifted Elair's body off the tree and kneeled down.

"I'm not going to let you go," I said as I pushed Elair's body against my own, and she nodded her head softly. "Hey, don't you dare leave me," I told her.

"I'll try," she said as I took her hand and placed it on my face.

"The spells have worn off. Macabre has pushed most of them out," Mikhail said as he kneeled down before Elair. "You did well." He pulled out a tiny glass bottle with a clear white liquid.

"Mikhail—"

"What are you—"

Faustus and Helari began, but Mikhail looked at me.

"If I may?" Mikhail asked, and I watched as he poured the contents of the flask onto Elair's lips. "Sleep, Elair."

"What was that?" I asked, and Mikhail shook his head.

"You shall see," Mikhail said before taking the dagger from me.

Elair fell limp in my arms, but I felt a wave of calm wash over me.

Helari kneeled beside me. "Scar," she called out, and Scar took Elair's body from me.

"Maddox, your pack needs you," Helari said as she stood up. "We will not let her leave us. Trust Mikhail."

I looked at him and watched as Mikhail took the blade.

"You fool! How could you have wasted our family's gift on a—" Faustus screamed, but it was ended abruptly by the dagger piercing straight into Faustus' heart. I should have had the urge to stop him. It should have killed Elair, but I didn't.

"Do you trust me?" Mikhail asked, and I nodded. I couldn't utter a single word. I didn't even want to feel anything.

"Then go," Mikhail said.

I turned to head towards the south border. As I did so, my gaze landed on Elair, whose head was laid on Scar's arms... limp and lifeless.

Knowing full well what thinking about her death would do to me and not knowing whatever it was that Mikhail and Helari were going to do, I tried to numb myself from the overwhelming pain surging within me.

It would cost me my control.

So I turned my back and left everything else to the one thing that led me to her in the first place.

Fate.

# Chapter Thirty Five

**Maddox**

"Where were they?" I asked Jasper as we made our way out to the training grounds.

"We had a few more people search for them near Blood Moon. Ender's a great alpha to work with. We located a camp in Nebraska. Ender sent a few of Blood Moon in with our own people." Jasper reported. He stopped, and I followed his gaze.

I found him staring at Winter, whose white hair had grown out. She carried a little boy in her arms. He was two months old today.

"Go," I told Jasper, and he gave me a pat on my shoulder.

"Thanks," he said before walking over to his mate. Winter smiled at me and waved hello. I nodded in her direction before walking into the training grounds.

"Trevor!" I yelled, and I watched as he ran up to me immediately. Trevor and Ian were now in charge of most of the grounds.

Carson, my gamma, was almost ready to give his position to Trevor.

"Yeah?" he asked.

"A couple of teenagers rented out the old lake house. Make sure the area's safe. It's only half a mile away from the border. We don't want any trouble over there," I ordered.

"Alright. I'll bring Mason and his sister along, too," he said.

"Good," I said before turning around and heading back inside.

I made my way upstairs into my bedroom and walked over to my office. Sitting down, I quickly opened the top drawer on my desk and pulled out a piece of cloth.

It was military green... the same patch of cloth I held that night I first saw her.

"That is really fucking disgusting, you know that?" a familiar female voice said, making me freeze in place.

I looked up.

"What?" she asked me, and I watched as she smirked at me.

Her wavy blonde hair was longer, and her eyes were paler, but it was... *her*. I stood up from my seat, staring at her intently.

"When..."

"Months ago, but I couldn't come back yet. I could barely even fucking walk. Do you know what it's like to even..." she trailed off.

I walked towards her, not believing what I was seeing. She was here... finally here.

"Okay, I know I got raised from the dead and everything, but could you maybe... not stare at me like that? You're giving me the creeps," she said, as I cupped her face in my hands.

I let out a small laugh, and she touched my cheek.

"You need to shave," she said as she kissed the left side of my jaw, an electric sensation filling my entire being. I didn't say anything as she kissed the bare skin on my cheeks. "I've missed you." She placed a soft kiss on my lips.

I smiled before laughing into the kiss and pulling away to run my hands through her hair.

"You're here," I said, and she smiled as I initiated another kiss.

"I'm here," she giggled, wrapping her arms around my neck.

"Elair... you're really here," I repeated as I wrapped my arms around her. I released her and placed my hands on her hips before hoisting her over my shoulder.

"Hey, whoa there!" Elair said, and I shook my head as I plopped her onto the bed. She smiled and stared into my eyes. "You know how I took the mate bond away?" she asked, and I took her hand into mine, pressing it into my chest.

"*Tornaren*," she uttered, and I felt a certain warmth from my neck. I looked at Elair's neck. On it grew the mark I had given her, the scar that marked the first night we had together.

"I'm afraid that's the last itty-bitty spell this girl can do," a voice to my right said, and I immediately smiled.

"I don't care," I said, and Helari grinned.

"Welcome back, Elair," she greeted.

"Glad to be back," Elair replied cheerfully. "Tell Mikhail I owe him one."

"Oh, I'll name a son after him if I have to," I added, and Helari laughed. "How did he do it? What did he even do?" I said, asking the one question that's been on my mind for months.

"I'll tell you later. Right now, I think it's best for the two of you to spend time together," Helari said and turned to leave.

"Sounds good to me," I said, and I wrapped my arms around Elair.

"No more weird magic?" I asked, and Elair rolled her eyes.

"No more weird magic. I'm proud to say that my wolf has happily returned and has no intentions of leaving. What do you think I marked you for?" She asked, and I smiled as I placed a kiss on her lips. She pulled away with a smirk. "But seriously, get rid of that ripped piece of my shirt from your drawer. That shit should have gotten molds by now." I laughed before kissing her once more.

"As long as I get another one."

"No, no, no, no..." Elair began, but I tore her shirt up, and she stared at me with an unamused look on her face. "I... I don't even know what the fuck I'm supposed to say right now," she said, and I laughed before taking off my own shirt.

**Elair**

"Eleanor would have been the next person in charge, but Marko and Verno weren't exactly her biggest fans. The power struggles inside the Sentinels would make them unstable." I explained.

We were now in the conference room along with the central members of the pack.

"Are those the only two?" Jasper asked, and I shook my head.

"Faustus had a following, Squadron one, the squadron I led before. It contains his best fighters. One of them isn't a werewolf, and I wouldn't be surprised if Marko tried to make him their leader," I said. "Verno is an old man, though. He would have another lined up, but I have no idea who it would be."

"Then we have to locate those two," Mikhail said as he entered the room. I bowed my head in respect and earned a smile from him.

"No need to be so formal," he said.

"Yeah, because entrusting me with the family heirloom that saved my life is totally nothing," I replied, and Maddox chuckled as Mikhail nodded his head.

"It had more use now than it ever had in the last hundred years. Welcome back," he said.

"So... who are we looking for?" Rina asked.

"It'd be easier to find them if we had a seer," I said with a sigh.

"Leave the finding to us," Helari said as she looks at Scar. "I think it's time for this pack to relax a bit. Maddox, you've done more than enough during Elair's recuperation. She'll have to come to us for a check-up every now and then, though. Elair must maintain the *scal* or we'll experience abnormalities."

"I think we can live with that," Maddox said with a shrug.

*You reek of Alpha,* Lorraine mind linked, and I rolled my eyes.

*I know,* I replied with a wink. Lorraine struggled to stop her laughter.

"Are we done?" Trevor asked, and Maddox raised an eyebrow.

"In a hurry?" Maddox asked.

"Well, you know how you said I should check out that cabin? Something's got me real excited. And I think it's because—"

"Your mate is coming," Helari said with a knowing smirk.

"Oh, yeah. Finally! Jasper, Maddox, Rina and Lorraine already found theirs. Now it's my turn." Trevor exclaimed.

"Trevor," I said as Maddox wrapped his arms around my waist.

"Oh, shit. Yeah, sorry. I'm excited. Do I wait? Do I go now?"

"They don't arrive until seven tonight. I suspect some sort of teenaged party, so be cautious."

"I'll wait then! I'll be off Macabre by six. Tell the guys to just follow," Trevor said as Rina rolled her eyes and dragged him out of the room. "Wait, where are we…"

"Training. Now," Rina said with a smile as she waved goodbye. Lorraine did the same, and I laughed as Maddox kissed my neck.

"What exactly do I have to maintain?" Maddox asked me, and I rolled my eyes.

"This thing," I said as I turned around and lift my hair up. Instead of some large protrusion on my neck or some weird scar, there were two white gems embedded at the nape of my neck.

"Huh, that looks pretty."

"It looks like I had piercings done on my back except I can't pull them out."

"They're fine," Maddox said, and I turned around.

"Of course, they are. I'm back because of whatever they sealed inside. One of our problems is gone for good," I said as I pulled Maddox towards me.

"We have others," he said, and I rolled my eyes.

"Yeah. Well, we're wolves. We always have other problems," I said with a smirk. "I think I want a different type of problem, though." I placed a deep lingering kiss on his lips. I stared into his amber eyes, smiling as I took his hand and placed it on my stomach.

"You don't mean…" he said, and I smiled.

"I'm willing to try…" I said before sneaking out of his hands. "If you can catch me." I grinned mischievously, and Maddox laughed as I ran out of the pack house and shifted instantly.

*You're going to regret telling me that,* he mind linked.

*Maybe. We'll find out, Alpha,* I replied as I sprinted off.

We had our peace.

We'll just have to learn to keep it.

**THE END**

# Helari's Language Dictionary

En+'word' – do not/not

Farvel – farewell, forget

Hu petaris – Come to me

Wiviadere – Listen/Obey

Fenian – stop

Lyger/lygre – Little girl/boy

Eovre – You/We/I have

Frei – freed

Relesereo – release

Eistras – Traces

Vedel hæl – bad omen

Mín – my

Silder- child

Rememorari – Remember

Andet – purpose

Urserre – Of course

Nuntiare – renounce

Satren – string/connection

Tevra - love

Skeiva – he knows

Sileio/a – He/she

Warie - Who

Erchsa- speak

Inuage – language

Siouvran – but/however

En-gairun – use (different from purpose almost like useless)

Asvretum/asvrei – Die/kill

Hes – Go

Ti – with

Vre(n) – possessive (hers his yours)

Irvon – friends

Aitien – patience

Dun – thin

Opiere –power

Sefreo – freeze

Lothrían – fly, float

Echarie – Speak

Erhistor – History

Renare- strength/strong

hevaete – why

Necran – break/broke

Vulkos – wolf

vae – because

gefrecht – fight

minatre- me

leostra – leave

aieinra – incinerate/burn/fire/flames

tornaren – return

Netru – now

Rezanai – stand

einre – eat

reih – here

serthre – shut up

morie- memory

lae – all

Remera/ – I remember

Aigstra/stre – mistress, master

Velian – welcome

Krau – Calm down

neie - mean

herian – danger/harm

Can't get enough of Elair and Maddox?
Make sure you sign up for the author's blog
to find out more about them!

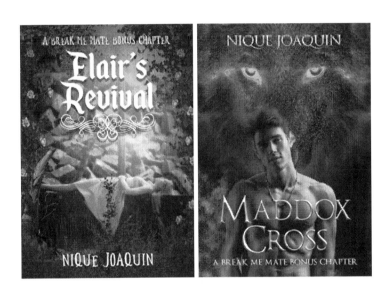

Get these two bonus chapters and
more freebies when you sign up at
nique-joaquin.awesomeauthors.org!

Here is a sample from another story you may enjoy:

AN IRREVOCABLE DESTINY.
A FATE YET TO BE DETERMINED.

# UNIQUE
# DIFFERENT
# FOUND

## VIOLET SAMUELS

# 1

**CELINA**

Have you ever felt like you can never escape? Have you ever felt like there is no one there for you? Have you ever felt like the whole world is against you and you just want to get away and be free? Have you ever felt that you can never be loved or cherished?

That's my life.

I feel all of these things. You can't change what fate has in store for you. But sometimes, I wish I could just be free and live my own life. I haven't been able to do that for a total of nine years.

My mother and father died when I was seven. I was abandoned and left with my godforsaken pack. I had no regrets when my mother and father died. I spent every second of every day with them, and they never argued. We didn't have any major fights and we all loved each other so much. I didn't think my parents had any regrets either. I think they made the mistake of leaving me alone, though.

You're probably wondering why I'm blaming it on them, aren't you? Well, I don't. I blame my pack for being worthless, unfair, stupid and plain right mean. Childish I know, but true, down to the last detail. Every beating, every bruise, every broken bone and every possible evidence of them abusing me supports that horrid theory.

Ever since my parents died, I've been like a slave to the people I call my pack. I cook, wash, clean, organize and pretty much do everything for them. They throw away money like it's no big deal, and they don't spare a second glance to anyone who's 'lower' than them.

Someone like me.

All the wolves in my pack are gorgeous with either brown or blonde fur and have a mix of either blue, green, brown, or almost black eyes. Having plain blue or green eyes is rare. They have slim or muscular bodies and have the perfect height just to be much taller than humans. Unfortunately, that beauty is tainted by their bitter egos and cold hearts.

My parents were like the pack looks wise, but not personality wise. My parents were kind and thoughtful, always putting others before themselves. They never should've been in this pack in the first place.

The funny thing is, I look nothing like my parents or anyone in the pack for that matter.

Instead of blonde or brown hair, mine is pitch black, pin straight and comes down to just below my shoulders. My eyes are a shining gold that lost its shine many years ago, so now it looks like a light shade of mud. My lips are almost red and, strangely, my skin is pale. I'm not sure why... Most Werewolves have beautifully tanned skin. I'm also a bit shorter than everyone else, but I still have that slim body that anyone would die for. In my parents' opinion, being different is what makes you special. What makes you special, is what makes you unique.

I never believed it, though. All it has ever done was got me teased, and pushed around for being 'different' and 'unique'. It has always been like that. Even with my parents, they always said the pack was just jealous of my obvious beauty, one that I am oblivious to.

Another thing. When I turned sixteen, I made sure I was far away from the pack house, almost on the borders of our territory. The reason? I was shifting. I didn't want to give everyone the satisfaction of seeing my pain, and watching my every bone break after the other. I can honestly say that it is the most painful thing you will ever experience in your life.

When I shifted, I discovered that my wolf was snow white. Not one trace of colour other than white covered me. I was astounded. I had never seen a white wolf. Even my mother's and my father's wolves were brown and blonde, respectively. They told me that when I shifted, never to show to anyone my wolf unless they have my full trust. Nobody has.

I don't know what it means to have a pure white wolf, but I know that I'm different yet again. This time, in a way, I thought I could somehow fit into my pack. I thought wrong. When I came back, I got a beating because I was gone for most of the day, and everyone missed lunch and breakfast. That night, I had to make a three-course meal instead of the usual one, and I had to clean the house until it was spotless. Let's just say I stayed up way past midnight...

I haven't been for a run since. That was three weeks ago. My wolf has been howling in my head, and it feels like she's scratching my insides apart. I badly want to let her out, but I'm too scared. I don't want to get beaten up again.

My wolf has told me multiple times to get away, and I've been considering it for months now. Tonight's the night. I'm leaving. I'm ditching this stupid place and leaving for good. When I told my wolf, she was practically jumping with joy.

I'm making the dinner right now. Although this pack has treated me like nothing, I'm gonna give them something to remember me by, and if that means food, then so be it.

I decide to make one of my favourite courses. For entree, bruschetta with mini prawn cocktails. For main, lasagna with garlic bread. Then for dessert, my personal favourite, chocolate mud cake with whipped cream, ice cream and chocolate covered strawberries on top. If it were me, I would just skip the entree and main and go straight for the dessert.

I set the table for the pack, and as soon as I finish placing the last of the entrees on the table, they walk in through the door. As soon as they get a whiff, they come barging into the dining room, taking a seat and digging in. No 'thank you' or 'this is nice', just like the usual.

I always keep a spare bit of dessert for myself after I finish cooking, so while the rest of the pack eats, I tuck into my mud cake. At least, they let me eat, I guess.

When I hear the bell, I walk back out and collect the empty plates, taking them back to the kitchen. To let them digest a bit, I wash it all up and place it on the drying rack.

I come back out with the last of the mains and am about to walk out when Tina, the pack slut, calls my name.

"Celina!"

I slowly turn around, keeping my hands behind my back, and my head bowed. I'm wearing the correct uniform for serving dinner, and my hair is neatly pulled back into a high ponytail, so I'm not sure what she wants. Whenever someone in the pack calls my name, it's usually because I'm in trouble.

"Why the whole 'fancy-fancy' food? Is it a special occasion? Let me guess... Is it for Damon's birthday? A little present from you?" She snickers at me. I feel all eyes turn to me, but I obediently keep my head down. Damon is the soon to be the alpha of our pack and is turning eighteen in about four days. It's a big thing, and I'm supposed to cook for it...

"I guess you could consider it that. If the alpha is kind enough to accept my gift, of course," I answer in a small voice. I was told from the beginning to address Damon as alpha and nothing else, unlike the rest of the pack.

The room falls silent as every eye turns to Damon, who's sitting at the head of the very large dining table. I look through my long, black lashes to see his face. I'm met with a considering expression.

He nods his head once. "I accept your gift. I will expect a grander and more appropriate gift on my actual birthday, though. Do you understand?" His tone's filled with power and authority.

"Yes, Alpha, I understand," I say, returning to my former position with my head down.

"Good. Now, off you go." He shoos me off, and as soon as I enter the kitchen, I hear their laughs and snickers. I tried not to cry. I've shed too many tears over these heartless people.

They soon finish their meals, and it's time for dessert. I've finished mine by now, so I place theirs on the table with a blank face. They eat up and by the time everyone has finished and has stayed around talking, I've cleared the large table and washed up.

I enter back into the dining room and wait in my usual spot by the door of the kitchen. Every night before I go to bed, I either get hit or nothing for the meals I've cooked. It's the same with breakfast, lunch, and any other meals they eat. As each one walks out of the room, I either get shoved or ignored, which means they liked my cooking. Tina, on the other hand, slaps me across the face. You probably think that's harsh, but that's equivalent to someone else's shove. So just imagine what someone else's slap is to her. It's not a pretty sight.

Damon is the last to leave, and he stops in front of me. I cautiously lift my head and stare into his beautiful blue-green eyes. He has a blank face, as do I. We stare at each other for a moment before he walks out and leaves me alone in the dining room to fix up.

Damon has been my crush since I was about ten, even though he treats me like the worthless thing I am. His brown hair and blue-green eyes are the main aspects that draw me and many other female wolves in. He hasn't found his mate yet either, which means he's available. He wouldn't go for me, though. Not in a million years. I'm too different.

I head to bed in the early hours of the night. The pack no longer requires me after about 7:30 pm, so I am ordered to bed, which I quickly oblige, so as not to get beaten. I still have bruises from the worst ones.

The sad thing is, I believe everything my pack had said since my parents died. That I'm not beautiful, but ugly. That I'm not unique, but different. That I'm not a part of their family, but their slave.

I sigh as I enter my makeshift room. It's bare, except for a large window that lets the moonlight from the full moon flood into my room. My bed is pretty much a sheet on the hard, splintered, wooden floor, and my pillow is a pillow cover stuffed with newspaper.

I won't be sleeping there tonight, though. Not anymore. Not ever again.

I pack what little belongings I have inside a sack – A pair of worn out jeans, an oversized shirt with holes in it, a skirt, one other shirt that appears to be clean, and a pair of socks. I don't own any shoes.

I grab the only piece of jewellery I have, my mother's silver necklace with her and my father's names engraved into the heart-shaped pendant. The pendant has a yin and yang symbol in it, but it's made with little black and white crystals. I slip it into my shirt and proceed to the window.

I open it wide, and without a glance back, or second thought, I jump. I jump to my freedom and my new life.

I shift into my snow white wolf and take off with my sack in my mouth. I don't know where I'm going. I don't know if I can survive. I am only a newly shifted wolf at the age of sixteen.

What do I know? I'll never have to see my 'pack' again. That is enough to make me smile slightly in my wolf form. As I cross the border of the territory, my wolf lets out a howl, filled with happiness and joy.

We're free. I'm free.

Never again will we have to face the Moonlight pack.

If you enjoyed this sample then look for **Unique, Different, Found.**

## Other books you might enjoy:

Kaden

Synne Jakobsen

# Available on Amazon!

**Other books you might enjoy:**

Purr, Kitten
Kristel Juurik

# Available on Amazon!

# Introducing the Characters Magazine App

Download the app to get the free issues of interviews from famous fiction characters and find your next favorite book!

iTunes: bit.ly/CharactersApple
Google Play: bit.ly/CharactersAndroid

## Acknowledgements

I would like to acknowledge my mom and dad for different reasons. Mom for being the strong female figure that I grew up to know and dad for being the best storyteller in my life. Both of you guys are my biggest inspirations in writing, and I couldn't have pushed through in pursuing writing without you (I mean, I also wouldn't exist without you guys so… you know). I also want to acknowledge my best friend Christina Kim, because you continued to encourage me to write this and read it for me even though you really didn't have to. I love you all so much, thank you for inspiring me and helping me out even if you didn't know that you helped inspire my stories.

# Author's Note

Hey there!

Thank you so much for reading Break Me, Mate! I can't express how grateful I am for reading something that was once just a thought inside my head.

I'd love to hear from you! Please feel free to email me at nique_joaquin@awesomeauthors.org and sign up at nique-joaquin.awesomeauthors.org for freebies!

One last thing: I'd love to hear your thoughts on the book. Please leave a review on Amazon or Goodreads because I just love reading your comments and getting to know YOU!

Whether that review is good or bad, I'd still love to hear it!


Can't wait to hear from you!


Nique Joaquin

# About the Author

Nique Joaquin is a student writer currently studying in New York University Abu Dhabi. Born in the Philippines and schooled in an international school, she is a lover of literature, music, and movies. Her writing inspiration arises from a variety of sources, be it dreams, daydreams, or movies.

37698482R00214

Printed in Poland
by Amazon Fulfillment
Poland Sp. z o.o., Wrocław